Charles L[illegible] s, over
fifty shor[illegible] gies,
of which [illegible] dows
series has r[illegible] Award. Grant has
also been [illegible] honoured with the Nebula Award,
given by the Science Fiction Writers of America.
He lives in New Jersey.

Also by Charles L. Grant from Futura:

THE PET

CHARLES L. GRANT

Tales from the Nightside

With a Foreword by Stephen King
and Drawings by Andrew Smith

Futura

A Futura Book

First published in the United States of America in 1981
by Arkham House Publishers, Inc., Wisconsin

First published in Great Britain in 1988
by Futura Publications, a Division of
Macdonald & Co (Publishers) Ltd
London & Sydney

ISBN 0 7088 3713 1

Printed and bound in Great Britain by
Collins, Glasgow

Futura Publications
A Division of
Macdonald & Co (Publishers) Ltd
Greater London House
Hampstead Road
London NW1 7QX

A Pergamon Press plc company

CONTENTS

TALES FROM HAWTHORNE STREET

TALES FROM THE NIGHTSIDE

FOREWORD

There is something mildly surreal about writing this introduction for Charles Grant's *Tales from the Nightside,* or so it has seemed to me in the last few days as I thought about what I might say and how I might say it. I think I finally pinned down the cause of that surreal feeling about ten minutes ago, as I changed the ribbon on the typewriter I am using to write this, the hands doing their own work, the mind tracking free. The oldest cliché in the book suddenly popped into my head as an opening line (give me credit, folks: I didn't use it). That line was: "Here is a man who needs no introduction."

Following the thought, I realized that there was more truth than whimsy in it, at least as applies to the Arkham edition of the fine collection that follows. Arkham House has specialized in exceptional volumes of fantasy, horror, and weird tales for more years than either Charlie Grant or I have lived; in its history of just over forty years it has published books by Ray Bradbury, Carl Jacobi, Ramsey Campbell, Clark Ashton Smith, Robert Bloch, and, of course, H. P. Lovecraft. All the same, they are not books you are apt to find at your local B. Dalton or Waldenbooks, and the reason is simple: Arkham House has always catered to the intelligent reader of fantasy and strange tales, the literate fan of the genre, the man or woman who has progressed beyond *The Tomb of Dracula*, *Swamp-Thing*, and the works of such writers as John Saul and Frank De Felitta. In its nearly half-century of publishing, Arkham House has, in short, served those whose imaginations crave something more than shopworn pulp and gore; it has published for those whose sense of wonder does not begin with worm-eaten corpses and end with a stake through the heart.

In this context, Grant's work really doesn't need an introduction; for me to be standing here (sitting, actually, with a can of beer close at hand, thank you very much), taking up your time introducing Charles Grant is like any of the following:

Jon Landau giving the assembled multitudes at Woodstock a lecture on the meaning of rock and roll.

An Irish priest explaining to his parish how to make a good confession.

Judith Crist telling a group of film buffs who Paul Newman is.

Sammy Davis Jr. explaining to a group of Roxbury high school students what the black experience is all about.

Me telling my grammy how to suck eggs.

The stunning (at least to me it seems stunning) fact of the matter is this: if you are holding the Arkham House edition of Charlie Grant's book in your hot little paws, the chances are very, very good that you have met the man either in person (he travels tirelessly to science fiction and fantasy conventions across the United States, spreading not the gospel of Charles Grant but the gospel of fantasy as an honorable and uplifting form of literature and storytelling) or through his work . . . which has been fairly prolific, a fact for which all fans of the imaginative story can give thanks. He won the Nebula Award for the best short sf story of the year in 1977 and for the best sf novelette in 1979, and has been nominated for that award five times. He has been nominated for the World Fantasy Award eight times—a staggering number when one considers the fact that such awards have been given for less than ten years and also when one reflects on the great number of talented writers in the fantasy field; he has also won the WFA while wearing his anthologist's hat for the original *Shadows* collection.

To suggest that Charlie Grant is a household name would be to suggest the ridiculous (we reserve that dubious honor for corrupt politicians, TV stars with big breasts, insane international leaders and international terrorists, cute dogs such as Benji, and inane comedians who make megamillions saying such things as "Mork calling Orson" and "Ex-cuuuse *ME!*"). But in the fairly circumscribed world of the fantasy fan, Charles Grant is known well enough so that I feel no compunction at all to enumerate either his bona fides or his cards of identity. I could tell you that he is one of the premier fantasists of his generation, but most of you will know that already and those of you who don't will discover that fact in the stories that follow—stories that are by turns amusing, grotesque, terrifying, dramatic, and, above all, engrossing. Some are tales that you finish and that hit you suddenly, an hour or a day later, like a blow around the heart. Some may cause you to flinch; others may leave you with a sense of thoughtful sadness . . . a sense that seems to pervade the best of Grant's work. He is an autumnal writer, and in the best of his fiction, the reader goes away with something rather more complex than a simple scare; there is a loneliness in these tales that is also civilized and, in the best sense, sensual. They are good stories, but you don't need me to tell you that when you can read the stories themselves.

The things I *don't* know about Charlie Grant would fill a book. I don't know what kind of shaving cream he uses, what kind of chair he sits in when he writes, what his bookcases look like, what sort of pictures hang in the room where he sleeps. Because we've corresponded, I know that he has an IBM electric typewriter, but I don't know if he types two-finger (as I do, using the Biblical Typing Method—"seek and ye shall find") or ten-finger touch. I don't know if he has pets, a favorite fast-food restaurant, a favorite barber shop.

I know that he is a bit taller than average, that his face is narrow in a way that seems scholarly, that his eyes are wide-set enough in that narrow face to be arresting even behind his spectacles. He speaks rapidly and can be wildly funny . . . but never in an angry or cruel way. I suspect that he may be the only man of my acquaintance who could wear red pants, a white belt, and white shoes . . . and get away with them.

And none of that matters at all to the person holding this book at this moment. The one thing that does (and I suppose the stories also say this, but it is worth pointing out) can be summed up in five words of one syllable, none of them longer than three letters. It doesn't take long to write or to say, but from where I sit, those five words say about everything that needs to be said: *The man is a pro.*

Charlie Grant works at it. Not all of these stories came easy; he probably had physical headaches over some and mental headaches over plenty. His stomach was probably upset as he wrote some of them, he probably smoked too much over some of them, lay awake over some of them. He probably wrote some of them thinking in the back of his mind that it would be a hell of a nice day to go to the beach and wrote others thinking it would be a hell of a nice day to find some long field bordered with blazing autumn trees and ramble it to its far end. If he's like most writers, I imagine his back ached and his kidneys felt crunched during more than one stint at the typewriter, and I imagine that more than once his brain itself felt crunched, dismal, and as devoid of inspiration as a sleety afternoon in late December.

But the opposite holds, the sunny side to this art/business that balances off the writer's sometime (often!) malaise, and his almost constant sense of loneliness as he voyages at his typewriter alone (writing a story is like having a pee—you can't get anyone else to do it for you): the days when your head feels like it's busting with the need to tell the story, the days when the story simply spills out all at once, and you are reduced to chasing it with a silly, slap-happy grin on your face, the days when you feel you got, in one story or on one page or in one phrase, *exactly what you meant.* There are days when you finish, and put a paper clip on the manuscript, and put the manuscript in an envelope, and mail it off somewhere, and you think, "I sent off a good one. Boy, did I ever."

One of the crucial differences between the pro and the amateur is that the pro is able to place both of these sets of feelings—the good and the bad—within a fairly narrow range; unlike the students of many college creative-writing courses, who may consider themselves Prousts one day and feel like killing themselves the next, the pro is able simply to push on, determined to do the best he can possibly do, to grow as much as he can grow, and to perform, each day, one almost incredible feat of intellectual and imaginative strength: to look at the ream of blank paper beside the typewriter without quailing, to see not so much hostile and inimical white-space but invisible words that need only be brought up and out.

Charlie Grant is this sort of writer, and, so far as I know, always has been. If you don't thank God for it, I'll thank Him for both of us. In a world that is usually far too grim and much too grey, the writer who can produce consistently good fiction is a rare and wonderful resource.

Listen here, sir or madam: these stories break out. Let me tell you what I mean by that by using an example. In the first of C. S. Lewis's Narnia novels, the girl Lucy reaches the land of Narnia by stepping through a wardrobe into which she has gone to hide herself during a game of what our British cousins call "seek-and-find." There is darkness, a stuffy smell of wool and mothballs . . . and a sense of space. Lucy advances into the wardrobe, marveling to herself at its size. She feels a particular coldness around her ankles, bends down, and scoops up snow. She has entered Narnia.

It is a breakout moment, a fancy so right and yet so breathtaking that we are transfixed with the wonder of it: the magical and the commonplace are juxtaposed with the courage and the imagination of a Magritte painting, the kicker of a good *Twilight Zone* episode, or the instrumental break in a Chuck Berry top-tenner. We may be horrified or transfixed with the strangeness of the situation, but we are also simply delighted. When a story breaks out in this fashion, it enhances our lives.

In the first of these stories, "Coin of the Realm," the toll takers in Charles Grant's half-magical little town of Oxrun Station begin to receive strange coins from the drivers shooting through—in size and shape they could almost pass for quarters, but when the toll takers look at them closely, they find a stylized pyramid on one side, and various designs they can't understand on the other. The story progresses from there, of course, moving toward a denouement that is both bizarre and believable, but that is almost secondary to the point I'm trying to make; the fact of those coins themselves, so strange and out of place in a situation we can all visualize, is the breakout—Charlie Grant has managed to shunt us off the major tracks of everyday reality and onto his own weird and compelling spur line . . . and all without even breathing hard.

The rest of the tales here are as equally compelling and as equally well told. You'll meet the inhabitants of Oxrun Station, of Hawthorne Street, and of half a dozen other locations. I could summarize the tales, but as Richard Nixon so memorably said, "that would be wrong." Charlie can tell you this set of tales better than I could; he can draw the line between the living and the dead indelibly in your mind. You'll meet a man who keeps toys on his lawn and a sandbox in his backyard in what may be one of the three finest horror stories I have ever read (the other two would be Ramsey Campbell's "The Companion" and "The Yellow Wallpaper" by Charlotte Perkins Gilman). You'll meet a Montagnard boy with a pony . . . a carnival pitchman with a particularly sinister grab-bag concession . . . a baker's dozen more.

None of them takes place on distant planets, none of them takes place in any environment more exotic than suburban England. Most of them could have happened two streets over and one block down from where you yourself live—this is your world and my world, but Charlie Grant's world has some vital differences. Deadly differences, you might say.

But in each case (yes, I'm going now, I'm going, dammit, be patient a minute longer and I'll be out of your hair), watch for that wonderful moment when the story breaks out, when—to make a phrase—the quarter with the stylized pyramid on one side and the curious indecipherable designs on the other is slapped into your unwary hand. Only here you don't have to stand in the gate while the car passing through takes off for some strange and unknown place; Charles Grant is inviting you along for the ride. Because he's a pro, the ride is going to be a good one. Because he cares about stories and the people who walk through his stories, it may be something more than just good; it may be memorable.

This is what Charles Grant does to earn his living, and because he does it well, I don't think there's any need for me to ramble on any longer, telling you how good he is or how lucky you are. Both are true, but enough is enough, already.

We're headed over to the nightside now, so grab on, people. Get ready to break out.

In a hellish sort of way, I think you're going to enjoy yourself.

STEPHEN KING

Bangor, Maine

TALES FROM OXRUN STATION

COIN OF THE REALM

It was the wrong time of year and the wrong hour of the day. In sunlight, in spring, the tollbooths that stretched eight across the highway bounced back the clean sharp air of April as though they had just been painted. Green, and gold, with red lights, green lights, guiding into the lanes beyond the cars that jerked, that halted, that separated once through and vanished down the road.

In autumn, in the afternoon, the paint on the booths mellowed in tune with the trees that flanked the tarmac, and the air was brisk and brittle and filled with the cries of Canadian geese.

But it was November, past midnight, and Wes rubbed at his heavy arms encased in khaki as he waited for the next automobile to break from the darkness and feed him its toll.

The air was damp, the stars gone, birds gone, and there seemed nothing left alive on the road except him.

He'd taken the job, though hating the night shift, when the electronics firm he'd managed folded in the dead wake of a dying space industry, and his engineering skills abruptly cheapened to less than a dime a dozen. For months he'd driven; from California to Florida to Houston and finally to a small apartment in Oxrun Station. For months he had filled with his precise small handwriting all the blanks and the boxes and the circles on applications, answered questions about his ambitions, and shook soft tanned hands that bade him wait by the telephone for that miraculous call. That never came.

"Wes?" It was a woman's voice, and he looked up and across the narrow space to the booth opposite. Terry was there, beckoning, and he shrugged.

"Can't," he said ruefully. "Pete's not out here yet."

"Oh, come on! There's no one coming. We'll get him out of the office, okay?"

She was dark, less than half his weight, an Oxrun native and mother of six who needed the money as badly as he and worked the nights because the pay was twice as high. Normally she grinned constantly even when she was silent; but now her face, too much aged, was folded into a concerned frown that bothered him. She called him again, impatiently, and he nodded, pushed open the gate that penned him in, and lumbered down the single step to the gap between them. He glanced back up the road with an uncertain shudder, saw nothing, and hurried out of the November dark into the garish fluorescent glare of the highway-authority office building squatting green and gold between four large pines.

There were generally four on duty throughout the graveyard shift: two in the booths, to keep each other awake, and two inside who spelled the others several times an hour . . . to keep them all awake.

Pete Hawkins, Wes's relief, pushed past him through the door, a punch to his arm and a smile and a nod. Wes didn't speak to him. There was nothing to say. Hawkins had known him for less than a week, and since they'd never shared coffee, they never shared dreams.

Terry was already sitting at a long and low table, a paper cup in front of her, steaming grey.

Wes sat, rubbing gratefully at his stomach, scratching at his thick neck. He remembered a time when he was reasonably thin, but with money tight only starches and the like were easy to come by.

"Wes, I've been had again."

"Again?" He couldn't believe Terry would allow herself to be cheated more than once a month. But twice? Twice in the past two days some jokers had driven through her lane and had given her fake coins in place of the real. And they weren't even imitations of quarters, but only the same size and texture. On their front a small stylized pyramid, on their backs various designs he hadn't understood.

"Wes, what am I going to do, huh? I can't keep putting in my own money this way. I need every penny I can get. You know that. Four dollars' worth in the last two weeks. You know how much I can do with four dollars and six kids?"

Wes nodded, and a strand of black hair dropped to his forehead. He pushed at it, waited with one hand poised until he was satisfied it would stay. "They must know when you're on, Ter," he said finally. "They must think you're a sucker—"

"I am, obviously."

"—so they'll keep at it until you tumble at the wrong time. Wrong time for them, I mean. Don't you ever look at the money first?"

She laughed and shook her head. "You like people too much, Wes, and you trust them too far. Someone could hand you a boiler plate and you wouldn't know it until they were in Canada. Of course I look at them, but they're silvery and they weigh the same. Only when I got time to count and stack, then I notice. Damn, Wes, what am I going to do?"

You're going to get fired, he thought, when Pete finds out and tells the right people—for him—what's happening. And she must have sensed it because immediately her eyes filled with watery light.

"If Lou were still here, or Jess—"

"Or Mac or Dave," he finished. "But they're not, Terry. They're gone."

Over the past four weeks, as many workers had walked off their jobs. Wes, who had been on the booths for just over three months, had gaped in astonishment each time it happened. It was, invariably, in the middle of the shift, somewhere near three when the road was at its most still, its most invisible. The lights from the gas station a mile east were out, the goosenecked lamps overhanging the broad toll plaza had been reduced to one on either side, and all the toll lights were red save one green facing in either direction. One by one, then, the men had climbed out of their booths and into their cars. Backed them up, went through the lanes like ordinary commuter travelers or tourists, and vanished beyond the edge of the light.

Not a word to anyone, not a letter once they had gone.

And each one had passed to Terry one of the bogus coins.

"Listen, Terry," he said when the silence began to unnerve him, "tell you what I'll do. I'll switch booths with you, all right? And when one of them jerks tries anything on me, I'll . . ."

"Break their arms?"

"Sit on them," he said, and spread his arms to display his bulk.

She pushed at her hair, shaking her head but smiling in spite of herself, and Wes relaxed. It would have been a hell of a long night if he and Terry hadn't been able to call to each other from their respective stations. Jokes. Stories. About her kids, his jobs, complaints about traffic and the lack of it . . . anything at all to keep from turning on the portable radio. Radios were death in the middle of the night. The music was loud enough to keep him awake, but the jockeys kept telling him the time he didn't want to know until the sun broke over the horizon.

He supposed, he *knew*, it would have been cheaper just to keep the exact-change lane open, but there was always some idiot with a five-dollar bill . . . at four in the morning with a five-dollar bill. His eyes would be stinging by then, because instead of sleeping when the sun came up he would write his résumés and make calls and once in a while take a sick day to drive out to an interview. He had done that yesterday, in fact, and finally there was a chance that he could kiss nickels and quarters and dimes good-bye forever. He had not mentioned it to Terry, though, because he didn't want to jinx it.

He waited, instead.

And walked with her back to the road.

A yellow van was waiting in his lane, honking his horn and shouting for attention. At first Wes thought the driver might be in trouble, but when he hurried to the island and tightroped to the gate, the booth was empty.

The driver was mad.

Wes apologized for the delay, received a curse for a tip, and the quarter was thrown against his chest as the van sped away.

"Terry," he called, "do you see Pete anywhere?"

Silence. Then, "No," her voice thin in the damp air.

It wasn't the best damned job in the world, he thought as he strode angrily toward the parking lot behind the authority building, but damnit, whoever's doing it ought to do it right, for God's sake.

He heard Terry calling him, ignored her and rounded the back corner, and stopped. The lot was empty except for her station wagon and his sedan. Both of them were old, and both of them were alone.

Good God, he thought, walked back to the plaza and stared east, then west, shaking his head.

The following night there were two new takers, and one, a young blond man with a wisp for a mustache, appealed to Wes instantly. During one break, then, instead of going inside with Terry, he leaned against the booth and they talked, trading lies and histories until Wes learned that Joseph was a student looking to make ends and tuitions meet somewhere, it was hoped in the direction of a bank account.

"You're crazy, you know that?" Wes said with a grin. "How you going to study and do your papers out here, huh? You'll be dead for your classes, you know. You won't be able to stay awake."

Joseph grinned, gap-toothed and pleasant. "I'll work it out, Wes, don't worry. As long as I don't get fired for being cheated—"

"Terry told you?"

"Yeah. As a matter of fact, I got one of them things just a few minutes ago, while you were getting coffee."

He held out his palm and Wes picked at the coin clumsily, finally grabbing it and holding it close to his face. There was the pyramid, and on the opposite face . . . an odd representation of what looked to be some kind of bird. A hawk, he thought, or maybe an eagle.

"Osiris," Joseph said.

"What?"

"That's Osiris there, I think. The head, I mean."

"You're kidding," Wes said. "You mean, folks are dumping Egyptian coins on us?"

He couldn't wait to tell Terry. Not that it would do her much good . . . but he shrugged and had turned to step down from the ledge when a station wagon pulled up and a hand stuck out. He couldn't move. It was Terry. He saw her through the windshield and she was . . . not exactly crying, not exactly happy. Her lips fought to give him a smile, but as soon as Joseph had taken her toll, her hand snapped back to the steering wheel and he had to press tight against the booth to keep from being knocked off the island when she floored the accelerator and raced west toward the hills.

"Goddamn," Joseph said. "She stuck me! Do you believe it? Terry . . ." He held out his hand. The coin was there.

In the glove compartment, Wes remembered suddenly; when they had arrived simultaneously at the parking lot and he'd hurried over to greet her and help her from the wagon, she'd been fumbling in the glove compartment, had snatched back her hand as though it had been burned. She'd slid out quickly, grabbing his arm, but not before he saw the silver glitter lying on top of a folded worn map.

"Joe, cover for me," he said quickly, and without waiting for an answer, raced for his car, put it in gear, and spewed gravel and dust in his haste to get on the highway.

West of the toll plaza the road ran straight for nearly two miles, then began a sinuous curve that climbed up the sides of two consecutive mountains. At the end of the level stretch was an exit, closed now for repairs and barricaded heavily, the shoulders flush against massive boulders that would prevent a car of any size from squeezing around it. Because of the land and the trees, then, he knew there wouldn't be any way for Terry to leave the road for the next twenty-two miles. Foolish, he thought, as the speedometer climbed from fifty to sixty, sixty-five to seventy. What the hell is she running away from?

His headlights punched weak holes in the blackness, and it seemed less like he was driving, more like he was floating through air that thickened the faster he went.

He glanced down at the odometer and frowned when he realized it wasn't registering the miles he was traveling. Damn, he thought; another expense.

He looked up, suddenly wrenched at the wheel and slammed on the brakes, the car skewing to one side, the smell of burning rubber already sharp in his nostrils. When he stopped, he was shaking and he laid his forehead against the cool plastic of the wheel until his stomach calmed and his arms stopped trembling.

Then he slid out of the car.

Directly ahead of him was a soft wavering light that stretched across the road from forest to forest. It wasn't the sun, he was facing west, and it wasn't a fire because he could smell nothing but the rubber, felt no heat as he approached it. It was . . . just a light, that illuminated nothing.

He wiped his hands nervously against his shirt, telling himself he was too tired to think straight, too anxious about the possible new job to think anything through. But he walked cautiously forward until, with a step, he was in the light. In it, not beyond it. And stretched for what seemed like miles in every direction were lines of automobiles. Abandoned. Rusting. He reached out to touch one, pulled his hand back when his legs began to feel weak.

Tired, that's all.

The land was sloped down and away from him, and in the middle distance was a broad blue-white river. He could see on the near bank a small group of people straggling onto a rivercraft whose bow and stern were arched high and bent down toward the center of the deck; like a double-sting scorpion, he thought. In the middle of the deck was a tiny cabin. The people, their faces dimmed by the suffusion of the light, bent and entered until they were all inside. Then, from a shadow on the bank came a tall man who stepped up the gangway, pulled it to after him, and reached out for a pole attached to a rudder. As he did so he looked up . . . and Wes blinked, turned abruptly, and ran.

The man's head was not human. It was black. It was a dog.

Suddenly the light was behind him and he was in his car, racing the engine and skidding into a U-turn. A cloud of deep black fear settled over him until, with a check in his rearview mirror, he realized that the light was gone. There was nothing behind him but the road. And it wasn't until he had stopped his sedan in the parking lot that he realized the car he'd almost touched on that congregated slope had been a station wagon, had been Terry's.

* * *

"So," Joe said near the end of the shift, "he would finish wrapping up the dead, see, and take them to something like a courthouse where they'd be judged for whatever they did when they were alive. But Wes, I don't understand what all this has to do with Terry."

Wes smiled weakly, said nothing, and as soon as the morning shift began filing out of the office, he waved a brusque good-bye and headed for his car. He drove for several hours, aimlessly, though keeping to the back roads to minimize contact with other cars. Then, when he could no longer see without squinting, he returned to his apartment and threw himself onto the couch, one arm over his eyes.

He slept.

Did not dream.

Woke only once: when the telephone rang and a man, his voice officiously contrite, said, *I'm sorry, Wes, but that's the way it goes. Good luck.*

It was nearly nine when he roused himself again, showered the sleep and fog from his mind, and dressed in the near-military uniform of khaki and green he was required to wear. Then he made himself a dinner of steak and potatoes, carrots and lima beans—the steak he had been saving for the celebration of freedom. He tasted almost nothing, spent most of the time chewing absently and staring at the wall clock over the counter by the sink.

I am an engineer, he told himself; I do not believe in what I saw last night.

But he could see how others might, and that's what frightened him. Times were bad—not for everyone, but for enough—and when this town becomes intolerable you look toward the next one. The same with worlds. When life is lousy, like butting against a wall that doesn't even show the marks, you look for the afterlife; it has to be better there, right? It sure as hell can't get worse. And with organized religions falling apart under the weight of secular advancement and no scientific proof, it didn't take him long to see that somewhere, someone decided that maybe the good old days might hold the answer—and in this case, those "good old days" were numbered in the thousands of years. Someone who was steeped in Egyptology. Someone who deluded himself into thinking that if this life wasn't fair, maybe the gods would be.

After all, gods don't die; they simply go into retirement until someone believes again.

And if enough people believe, if enough people are miserable . . .

"Nonsense," he snapped at his knife and fork. "Damned utter nonsense."

But, something told him, you can't deny the coins and you can't deny the light, and you can't deny the fact that Terry has gone.

He raced into the living room and scrambled for the phone book, found Terry's number and called it.

"I'm sorry," a man's voice said, "but there's no one here by that name."

"Are you sure?"

"I'm sure, believe me. I've lived here for six years."

He tried Peter Hawkins, who had lived with two friends.

"Hawkins? I'm sorry, there's no one here by that name."

He tried Dave Sparker, who lived with his parents.

"Is this a joke? We ain't never had any kids, Mac."

I'm sorry, Wes, but that's the way it goes.

He closed his eyes to imagine Terry as he'd last seen her: hands clutching the wheel, eyes determinedly straight ahead; but the look she had given him before she drove off . . . relief. Sad, but relieved.

He shook his head and left for work, found Joe already seated at the table in the break room, and slid in beside him with a cup of coffee. "I'm cracking up, kid," he said, and explained.

Joe listened attentively, tracing designs on the table's plastic top until Wes had done. "Interesting," he said. "But for crying out loud, Wes, you know it can't be true."

"I know what I saw."

The young man grinned. "You know what you think you saw, right? Look, Wes, just for the sake of argument let's assume that what you're saying is true. Then why are there still ghettos and rundown slums and unemployment and stuff like that? I mean, if life is so rotten, why haven't all those people taken this way out? It doesn't make sense. Terry just decided it was time to get out before she cracked, that's all. She was doing something for herself for a change."

"But the kids!"

"Did you ever see them?"

Wes frowned. Shook his head. "But," he said, "our whole society is based on the reach of the automobile, right? How many really poor folks have one? The car gets you out, see. You wake up one day and your fare is in the glove compartment and off you go. A little sad, maybe, because you're leaving your friends and what all, but you know it's going to be better, so you go."

Joe shook his head, grinning. "Wes, you should have been a writer or something. For an engineer, you got a hell of an imagination. But," he added quickly, a hand up to quiet him, "assuming one more time that this is all so, what do you and I have to worry about? We're not starving, are we? I'm getting good grades all the time, and you're getting more and more interviews so that you're bound to hit one sooner or later. You're too good. It's just a matter of time."

He clapped Wes on the shoulder, pointed at the clock on the wall, and reached up for the fur-lined jackets they would be wearing that night. He helped Wes into his, Wes returned the favor, and they trudged out to the tollbooths to begin the shift.

He's right, Wes thought, as he nodded to the man leaving his booth; I'm letting myself panic, that's all. I'm losing faith in myself, and I can't let that happen.

At the first break, neither of them had been handed the silver pyramid coins.

At the second, Joe had had one.

Wes decided to do some figuring and, for the next few nights, kept a record of the fake coins as they flowed into the booths. Joe was getting worried, but like Terry he replaced the fares with money of his own. So did Wes. And by the end of the month, he noted with curious calm that there was an increase in the number of cars that passed along the road between the hours of twelve and three, so much so that the authority was toying with the idea of putting on two extra men. And as the cars increased, so did the coins. There was no geometric progression, only one or two more each night, but in no case was he able to catch a glimpse of the driver after he'd realized what he'd been handed.

"If this keeps up," he said to Joe one January night, "we're both going to be broke."

"Not me," Joe said, grinning. "You'll be happy to know, sir, that this toll taker is giving his notice."

"What?"

"That's right, Wes. I just got word there's a scholarship waiting for me on the West Coast, and I'm taking the first flight to San Francisco I can get." He slapped at the table and laughed. "Done, pal. This boy is done taking quarters for the rest of his life."

"I'll kill him," the supervisor said when Joe left an hour early, laughing, shrieking his delight that his nights would now be his own. "I'll get that punk if it's the last thing I do. He can't leave me short like this, damnit! He can't!"

Wes tsked and shook his head. "Revenge is not charity," he said, unable to keep back a grin.

He slept well that day, rose just after six, and made himself breakfast. Then he checked his mail, opened one rather thick envelope, and threw the rest into the air. It had come. In Iowa, a firm was looking for an electronics man with just his qualifications; and more importantly, it had the funds to offer him a salary not much less than he'd been making with his own company. Unashamedly he stood in front of the bathroom mirror, shaving, crying, shaking his head and wishing Joe had waited one more day to hear his own fine news. And Terry; he rinsed the razor under the faucet and wondered if he would have had the nerve to ask her to marry him. It would have meant instant family, of course, but it would have . . . might have stopped her from . . .

He scowled and threw the razor into the sink, stalked into the bedroom and pulled on his clothes, so viciously that he tore two shirts at the shoulder before calming enough to get one on properly.

"Knock it off, pal," he muttered to himself as he hurried downstairs to the parking lot and his car. "You got the wrong number, and she took off someplace else. Someplace real, pal, someplace real."

Hawkins.

Sparker.

His mood grew heavy, grey, like a storm grumbling on the horizon. He snarled at everyone at the office, including his supervisor, and it was well past midnight before he was able to force himself to relax and remember the job. The job. He laughed aloud as a car pulled into the gap and a hand reached up to him. He leaned down to take the coin, still laughing until he saw Joe's face in the dim dashboard light.

The young man was unshaven, pale, perspiration running down his face as though it were the middle of summer. His jaw trembled, his lips quivered, and before his hand slapped back to the wheel as if magnetized, he gasped one word: "Supervisor."

Wes yelled as the car shot out of the gap and vanished down the black road, the taillights glaring at him redly until, abruptly, they vanished.

He had no intention of looking at his palm.

He knew what would be there.

For several minutes he stood there numbly, unthinking, then snapping back to the day Joe had quit and the supervisor had ranted for the rest of the night.

Wes groaned and threw the coin away.

Joe *believed.* Joe *knew.*

That Wes's intellectual game-playing was not playing at all, that he was right about the depression that had fallen on people, the need to escape, the need for comfort. But he was also wrong about one vital matter: those gods, all of them shunted aside in the glare of science's advance, were not calmly returning to embrace their people again.

They were angry.

They hated.

Wes bolted from the booth and ran for his car. As he rounded the corner of the building, the supervisor slammed open the rear door and began shouting at him, cursing, then running to the exit and grabbing for the open-windowed door as Wes slowed for the narrow gate.

"Where the hell do you think you're going?"

"Iowa," Wes said, punching at the hand until it fell away.

"Fine! Then take this, and don't expect to be paid!"

SMITH

Something flew from the supervisor's hand into Wes's lap, but he ignored it until he'd pulled onto the highway and was heading rapidly west. Then he freed a hand from the wheel and picked it up. It was his time card. He laughed, made to toss it out the window, then decided to hang on to it as a souvenir of his tenure in the booths. As his headlights turned the air grey in front of him, he leaned over and dropped the glove compartment lid, took his eyes from the road long enough to shove the card in . . . and saw the silvered coin.

"But I don't believe it!" he screamed to the steering wheel that refused to release him.

"I don't," he insisted when the light engulfed him and the car stalled and the slope to the river pulled him gently.

"Please," he whispered to the dogheaded man, "I don't believe in you."

"That," said the man with the head of a jackal, "is no longer *my* problem."

OLD FRIENDS

David told himself there was nothing to be afraid of, nothing at all. It was, of course, only the delicious sense of anticipation he was feeling and not the fear that he could be mistaken. No. After all these years, all that pain, all that twisting of what he thought he knew . . . mistaken. No. No, it wasn't that at all. He was not afraid. He knew he wasn't. And yet, in spite of what he knew, he vacillated between the very real danger of disobeying his mother and running inside, now, away from the sun.

Crazy, he thought. God, if I'm wrong, I'm crazy.

But are you really crazy if you think you're crazy?

He grinned broadly, almost laughing aloud, realizing that he sounded like any one of a hundred different characters on a hundred different channels at two o'clock in the morning.

Am I really nuts, Doc? I can take it. Let me have it straight.

This time he did laugh, shaking his head slowly at his own dark whimsy.

Nevertheless, the thought remained.

And he sighed at the unfairness of it all.

Of a life fully nineteen years long that not once moved from a place called Oxrun Station; of a search that could have ended years before if only he had had the wit, the brains, the pure and simple imagination to pursue it; of a girl like all girls and unlike any other he would have to leave behind.

If, that is, he was not crazy.

Vagrant spears of melancholy light pierced the heavy November overcast and repulsed him, convinced him completely that he was physically agonized. Obsidian eyes squinted, fighting the dim glow that seemed determined to sear from what remained of his soul the memories of shadow—delightful shadow, enticing shadow, shadow that writhed away from the sun, silently screaming. He glared at the sky and despised the way that sun, in behind a grey veil, disregarded his pale, almost ivory skin, reddening it, puckering it, sloughing it off like a leprous serpent and twisting it into a mocking dark brown. He shrank from the light as often as he could, as best he could.

But there were his instructions.

And to get what he wanted—after all these years, all this pain—to get what he wanted now, he had to endure.

Another glance heavenward, and he decided to be grateful for the clouds, whispering a brief and undirected prayer for the added comfort of a light and steady rain. That, however, was icing on the cake. He had his instructions, and he was determined to obey them. And to wait. The time had come. He believed it now; he knew it. The time had come indeed, and there would be no more thwarting the reunion with his friends.

Stoically resigned then, he covered as much of himself, of his very long and very thin frame, as he could, and huddled by the door on the front porch. He shaded his eyes with a palm when there were no shadows to protect him, and grimaced at the occasional brightness of that Saturday afternoon. While he waited he told himself repeatedly—in a liturgical monotone very much like a chant—that it was, and it would be worth the small pains, the pricks, the tiny slashes. His mother had been in a remarkably fine mood for some days now, and he did not want her to lose it just when he was drawing so tantalizingly near.

"I won't be very long, dear," she had told him that morning

before driving away. "I'm only going down to Centre Street to do a little shopping. You just be a good boy and keep an eye on the house while I'm gone. All right, dear?" She had smiled her beautiful snake smile then, and added, "It's been quite a while, hasn't it, Davey?"

He knew that. She did not have to make such a poisonous point of reminding him. But he was pleased that she had because it meant he would probably be able to get it down that night.

Or, though he dared not think about it, sooner.

She had kissed his forehead, patted his cheek, and he had squirmed with impatience to see her leave so she might return. She had laughed then, like a jackal, and he had pretended to grin.

And if she knew he was hating her, she never said a word.

So he waited on the porch that faced Chancellor Avenue and allowed himself to daydream a little, plan a little, until he finally relaxed and let the day die around him. He did not mind the damp wooden flooring that was so long unpainted the neighbors were whispering (and a few of them outright complaining), nor the splinters that now and then found their way through his black trousers into his calves and thighs. The small jabs, the momentary stings, were nothing, nothing at all . . . and he concentrated on looking, and listening, and once in a while smiling a death's-head grin.

Ah, Mother, he thought, I can't wait for you to meet all my old friends.

He stifled a short laugh with his fingers, blinked, squinted, and decided that today it was beautiful in the place they called the Station. There was autumn grass slowly browning under brightly dying leaves; the brittle cold air that seemed to make the pavement crisp under the feet of the passersby who were hurrying to the college's stadium where the high school games were played; the languid haze of burning piles of leaves; a ragged cloud of starlings that swooped silently toward the scent of popcorn and candy; the clouds.

David half smiled and answered the waves from the cars that sped past with bicolored pompons swinging in time to riders' cheers and the off-the-beat blasts of horns and whistles. He found the nerve, the quiet and timid nerve, to nod when the principal walked by with his young pudgy wife; and he grinned when a covey of girls giggled loudly as they closed ranks against the swaggering pride of boys who followed. A few of them called to him, and he called back, and they disappeared around his neighbor's hedge without stopping.

He was not disappointed.

They never stopped.

In school it was because of the load of books he carried; downtown it was because of the way he kept close to the buildings; and today it was football. He could smell it, taste it, feel it in the dull yellow leaf he crushed absently in his hand.

And regret.

It was the season's last game, and he had to watch the house. The one cloudy Saturday afternoon of the entire season, practically of the entire year, and his mother had told him he had better watch the house. But as soon as bile rose angrily to his throat, he swallowed it with a stern reminder that it had been his choice, after all. He could have easily drifted off to the game with the rest of them and, after a fashion, perhaps even enjoyed himself. It would have been nice. The last game. But in the light—he grinned—of his mother's unspoken promise, and the gathering at last of the nerve and the knowledge, the regret became an unimportant thing. A little thing. Inconsequential. He soon ignored it, and soon it passed.

Hate was much better; and the distant scent of power.

He shifted, feeling the onset of a cramp in his left foot. He knew he was growing anxious. The afternoon's voice had faded into the restless rustling of the few last leaves. The shadow of the old house—that might have been called a Victorian had it held a sense of history—the shadow stretched to merge with the trees and the shrubs. The temperature fell. He shivered then, and decided to take a short walk, to kill the time moving now in a slow-motion race toward a grey and bleak sunset. He stretched carefully to relieve the stiffness that had settled in his arms and legs, bent at the waist to loosen his back. Then he vaulted the railing, wishing Claire had walked by to see him sailing. The ground was damp and pillow-soft; he leaned over to see if it were really as black as he imagined.

It was. He smiled.

He moved deliberately, with small measured steps, staring up at each window, envisioning each room huddling beyond, all of them unchanged and most of them unused for as long as he could remember. A late-leaving sparrow was playing in a rusted, canted gutter, knocking frail twigs and clumps of dirt over the side. David ducked away from one of the harmless bombs and laughed.

Little bird, he thought, would you come with me if you knew?

Probably not. Birds don't have emotions; and especially, they don't hate.

Halfway to the back he stopped involuntarily at one window heavily curtained and streaked with an accumulation of dust-turned-grime. The top half was covered by a screen that was torn and laced with debris the wind had thrown. It was his father's study. He closed his eyes for a moment to search for a reminder of the time when the family was three; but nothing came to him, not even a voice. He shrugged the effort away. It wasn't important enough to worry about. For all he knew, the man was little more than a bedtime myth. Or he might be dead. Or he might have run away when he had gotten to know his wife. Or he might be locked in a padded room. Or he might be dead. Might be . . . David shrugged again.

Somewhere down the street a telephone shrilled and a woman shouted shrilly.

In the backyard he spotted the dull green throw rug from his mother's sitting room draped limply over the clothesline. It made him think of spring, of grass, of trees . . . of the sun. He stepped up to it and reached out timidly to stroke the worn tasseled fringe. "Hello, Mother," he whispered. The rug hung there until a sudden gust of rain-promising wind shoved it firmly against him. He stumbled back with one arm upraised. "Hey, Mother," he said, less softly. Then he turned away quickly before the rug could move again, and as he passed the plants in the garden he was not allowed to touch, he muttered, "Wait, Mother. Wait."

And he thought about the plan, and was cheered.

Thought about his old friends, and smiled.

Twice, then, and three times he circled the house; twice and three times he huddled on the porch, taking all the comfort he could from the shadows, trying to crouch away from the rising wind's rush as it hummed through the railing and dragged dark clouds closer.

Up again, and this time he stopped in front of the slanting, double cellar doors with the rusted combination lock forced through the latch. His hands were bunched in his pockets, his shoulders stooped.

Playmate, he thought, come out and play with me.

His hair fell blackly against his face and scattered, alternately blinding him and freeing his vision while he worked at a game:

a little boy inside there, down there in the dark, pale and raven-haired, breaking a fruit juice glass, spilling his ration of milk over a shabby kitchen tablecloth. Often. Too often. A flurry of cloths from the scratched and stained porcelain sink, or an artificial sponge from the cabinet beneath. A storm of yelling, shrieking, commandments to be damned, and his mother who said she loved him would grab his shoulders with strong lovely hands that gripped like talons and squeezed for blood . . . strong lovely hands that would lead him and push him and shove him and guide him to the stairs that led into the empty coal bin, barren woodpile, grumbling furnace, damp concrete cellar floor. He would stumble down the steps through his I'm-sorry-I'm-sorry tears, and her words, and the door, would slam shut and lock solidly behind him.

always.

for as long as he could remember.

for as long as memory would allow him to go back.

home late from his first real date alone with a girl and the smear of lipstick on his chin.

the shrieking and the commandments and the cellar door locked solidly behind him.

always; for as long as he could remember.

longer.

little Davey would scream . . . while darkness would entrap him in a thick barless cage and blind him;

Davey would whimper . . . while the darkness would blacken to blot out the thin crack of kitchen-light that escaped to outline the door and hide the rickety rotting stairs and the coal bin and the woodpile and the shovels and the brooms and the empty preserve jars and the musty cartons and the cyclopean glow of the grumbling furnace fire;

David would weep in frustration and rage . . . and the darkness would blacken . . .

. . . and everywhere he went there would be light so bright it would shame the summer sun.

"Imagine that," he whispered to the double doors, with a memory smile as wide as his face. "Imagine me acting like that."

"Acting like what?"

He spun around, terrified, excuses tumbling over themselves to his lips until he collided with the girl who had crept up behind him. She stood with her arms folded loosely over her chest, her face partially hidden in a billowing golden fur collar. He laughed easily, relievedly, and shook his head slowly. "Just remembering some times I had when I was a kid, Claire. That's all. It really wasn't very important."

"When you were a kid, huh?" she said, grinning. "You that close to retiring, old man?"

They stared at each other without awkwardness, without shifting their feet, without clearing their throats. Then they walked to the front without speaking. As they did, David watched her from the corner of his eye—and the hint of soft rose at her high cheeks, the growing pink at the tip of her stubby nose, made him doubt for the first time the wish behind the plan. He stood silently, facing the sidewalk, while she sat on the bottom porch step and hugged her knees, watching him measure the crawl of the hedge's shadow into the deserted street.

There was the scent of rain in the air.

Would it be the same, he wondered; would Claire be the same if she . . . would she be the same?

When he had been fourteen and she was living across the street in the English Tudor with the leaded bow window, he had trusted her so much that he'd confided in her what he now understood was an extraordinarily abnormal fear of the dark. He gave her none of the reasons; he just told her it was the dark. She had listened intently, and she had laughed—not at him, however, and that was why he had permitted himself to love her.

"My father," she had said, "used to tell me—nuts, he still does—but he told me that I had to study and understand and then be kind of like a friend to whatever it was I was afraid of. You know, like snakes and spiders and big dogs and things like that. If you know what they are and how they work and what they can do, you can get rid of . . . well, whatever it was that made you afraid in the first

SMITH

place. Except I still hate spiders." She had shuddered, then frowned. "Did that make any sense, Davey?"

He had laughed, too, but he had not forgotten.

He spent a long time thinking about what she had said, and about the cellar doors and what lay down there, and the next night he deliberately smashed a plate while washing the supper dishes—and it was bad in the dark, so bad he used Claire's name as the worst obscenity he knew.

Two nights later, while his mother was watching him from her place at the table, smiling her smile and filing her nails, he broke another—again it was bad, but the screaming was gone.

He hefted a rock, waited, and tossed it through the living-room window—the crying dried to sobs.

The fourth time—a jam jar, grape, whose stains were still on the floor—was an accident—but now he understood, and now he knew his friends.

Claire, he had discovered, only knew part of the answer.

"Davey?"

Thank you, Claire, he had said each time he greeted the cellar and its masque.

She called him Ghost because of his skin; he called her Spot because of her freckles.

"Davey!"

But would it be the same?

"Well, damnit, if you're not going to talk to me, David Sinclair Hancock, maybe I'll just go on home and wait for Eddie Price to call. At least he has a civil tongue."

She had moved to stand directly in front of him, was glaring into his unseeing eyes. He blinked when he saw her, and shrugged an apology. "Daydreaming again," he muttered, and slid an arm around her waist. She tensed—just to show him that she could not be bought—but let him pull her close enough for him to kiss her forehead.

"When'll you pick me up?"

"Seven-thirty," he answered without thinking. "I probably can get the car tonight. I don't know for sure. Probably."

"Well, I'll be damned and this ain't hell," she said, slapping his shoulder. "The man gets his prize for being so persistent. A girl does get tired of walking all the time, you know. And don't you think I'm so terribly delicate? Don't you think so, Davey? Don't you think I'm ever so delicate?"

She pressed into his embrace, and he forced his laugh to merge with hers. The sun was almost down, and he was growing nervous. When she poked his ribs, hard, he laughed again and squeezed.

"You know," she said then, slowly, as if she were not at all sure she should be speaking, "I'm really surprised your mother's letting you out like this. It's weird sometimes, Davey. The way she keeps hold of you . . ." She shook her head. "You ever take that Psych course with Bromley? You should, you know. I'll bet he'd be able to—"

The explosive roar of a racing engine broke them apart, but not, he knew, before his mother had seen them. She slid gracefully out from behind the wheel, a large bag of groceries cradled in one arm. She was tall and blonde and warmly lovely, and David's eyes hardened when he saw her smile. Snakelike. Luring. Claire muttered something under her breath and was already across the lawn and on the sidewalk before his mother reached the porch.

"Interesting," she purred as she waited for him to hurry ahead and open the door. "You must come inside and tell me all about it, dear." She was dressed in black, David's favorite color. "You will tell me about her, won't you, Davey?"

He did.

Sitting at the kitchen table, his hands moist and pulling nervously at the bottom of his sweater, he recited a detailed account of his passing of the afternoon. He said nothing about missing the last game of the season, however, and nothing about the rug. He tried to keep sight of her eyes, to read them, to anticipate them, but she only smiled and murmured "how nice" every few minutes. Only once did she frown—when he mentioned the temptation to leave the house and wander toward the football stadium. But the moment passed, and all he could do now was wait.

They dined, and the sun went down. In the corners of the room warmed by the oven the shadows hovered and shrank away from the light. The clouds shredded and vanished. The stars rose on the train of the moon. The refrigerator hummed, slightly out of tune. The clouds returned. The rain returned. A single bulb hung unshaded over the table, and the shadows were warm and loving on David's stiff back.

Finally, when he thought he was going to have to beg her like a child, his mother rose and stood by the cellar door, a large iron key resting in her palm. He licked at his lips in spite of himself and gripped the edge of the table as tightly as he could to prevent himself from lunging.

Rain pelted the windows.

He did not hear it.

Claire, he thought, would you come if you knew?

"Well, now, Davey." The voice was soft, sleek, deceptively gentle. "Well, do you think you've done well enough these past few days to deserve it, dear?" He felt himself nodding as though in a trance. "I wonder," she said then, "if we might truthfully call this an addiction. You know, dear, like drugs and things." She pursed her lips, considered, rejected with a toss of her hair. "Oh, well, no matter. Come on, Davey, do you deserve it?"

He swallowed. "Yes, Mother." His voice was years away, to the first time she had discovered he liked the darkness, preferred it. Her laugh, then, and the snake's glint in her eyes.

There was a silence. Only the rain.

Finally she nodded her agreement and opened the door.

"Davey?"

He rose, and for a long moment dared not release the table. When he did he moved quickly, brushing past her and taking the first step down, waiting in terror for her to summon him back the way she did when he appeared too anxious, eager, desperate, laughing at him with her eyes closed and the key catching the light and warning him that he would never escape her as the dream-father had done.

He glanced up at her and was delighted to see her look startled when he grinned suddenly, broadly, completely without mirth.

"Good-bye, Mother," he said calmly, and he yanked the door from her hand and slammed it shut.

The furnace was out.

Below him there was . . . nothing.

He made his way down and stood in the center of the floor, perspiration gathering in ice-runs along his spine, his sides, the inner sweep of his thighs.

For so very long he had waited, prayed, planned, and dreamed—and now, suddenly, he wondered.

Crazy.

If I'm wrong, I'm crazy.

And if I'm right . . .

. . . no more football or sleigh rides or holding hands; no more gropings on the porch or the urgings of his loins; no more Oxrun; no more tests to fail because he would rather talk to the dark than read a book; no more sunlight; no more . . .

Crazy.

Unless . . .

Slowly, not quite fearfully, he stripped off his clothes and shivered in the clammy sheath that rose through him from the soles of his feet.

No more teachers who yelled . . .

He swallowed. He listened. And when he finally understood that he wasn't crazy after all, that he knew he really knew and it wasn't so bad not to be crazy . . . when he understood it and believed it, he lifted his arms wide to feel the warming black air, smiling, loosening every muscle and nerve and cell and thought and dream and prayer and sight and scream; he believed; and he believed; and felt himself drifting, sailing, floating . . . felt himself grow and shrink and lift and swirl.

No . . . more . . . Mother.

And in time, in a very long time that was no time at all, he learned at last how the shadows in attics and cellars and dark empty closets were born and survived. He studied his clothes lying in a pile on the damp concrete floor. He learned the difference between a nightmare and a wish, a death and a dying, November grey and December black.

He learned that his old friends were true friends indeed.

He learned that Claire, despite her teaching, was no friend at all.

So . . . he waited.

And in time, in a very long time that was no time at all, the door at the top of the stairs opened. The light still burned in the kitchen, and he saw from every dark angle the dark figure at the threshold.

"Davey?" A snake-word.

He felt himself smiling, and wondered if he could.

"Davey, that little girl is here to see you." The voice was clear, was light, was diamond hard and serpent hissing. "She *says* you were supposed to pick her up this evening." A breath. "You didn't tell me about that, Davey." A sigh. "You'll have to come out now, dear." She waited. "Come out, David, you have a visitor."

Claire, he thought then, it'll only take a minute.

"David!"

His mother hesitated a moment longer before following her elongated shadow down the stairs, paused before leaving the path of dim light and hurrying toward the furnace at the far side of the room. Her heels struck the floor like the burr of a rattler.

"Hey, Davey," Claire whispered from the kitchen.

"David, you can come out now, dear," his mother said sweetly. "We've had quite enough of your games, your little friend and I."

No friend at all.

The silence. Not even the rain.

"Hello . . . Mother."

She spun around just in time to see the darkness gather to blacken the light and bury the stairs.

"David?"

To swallow the coal bin, the woodpile, the furnace, the door.

"David?"

"Good-bye . . . Mother."

Her scream was cut off before it reached her blackening lips; her eyes were closed before she dissolved.

A pause.

A . . . breathing.

"Davey?" Claire called from the head of the stairs. "Davey, it's spooky down there. Mrs. Hancock? Davey? Come up here, please, Davey? Please?"

She knew, he thought, and there was always the chance that she might remember.

The darkness moved, and the kitchen light died.

A whisper: "Davey?"

A smile: "Hello, Claire."

HOME

The fight, if that's what it was, had been vicious, swift, and punctuated with such high shrieking yelps and truncated dying howls that Art wondered if anyone in the neighborhood had gotten back to sleep—or even wanted to sleep while agony clung to the dark long after the sounds had faded.

He had been yanked out of a softdream, so rare these days, in which he and Felicity were once again enjoying a candlelight dinner on one of the slow-moving *bateaux mouche* that caressed the Seine after the sun had gone down. He had been leaning over the table to kiss her when the fight began, shattering candles to sparks and Felicity to nightmare. And by the time he was fully awake, it was over.

"What the . . . ?" He started to rise, staring at the bedroom window.

"Dogs," Felicity muttered sleepily beside him. "It was dogs."

"Jesus!" He wiped a hand over his face, trying to reconcile what he had heard with what he had been seeing.

"Go back to sleep, love," she said, her voice muffled against the pillow. "You'll find out in the morning."

He had not argued, but neither had he been able to recapture sleep, not to mention the boat and the dinner and the light in his wife's eyes; and he'd spent the rest of the dark hours alternately dozing and waiting for the window to lighten . . . and praying that the screams would not be repeated.

Now he stood on the sidewalk in front of their small Cape Cod and stared up Western Road. There was a small crowd, mostly women, standing near the intersection at Chancellor Avenue two blocks up. A patrol car was angled in toward the curb, behind it a van from the ASPCA in Harley. He moved no closer; he could see through the jeans and skirts and one or two bathrobes infrequent glints of bright, damp red. Saw one of the animal shelter attendants grimace distastefully as he lifted a bundle from the pavement and placed it gingerly in the van.

"Great way to start the day," Felicity said from the doorway, arms folded loosely over her chest.

"From what I can tell it was Kenner's setter," Art told her with a nod toward the people now slowly dispersing. "Looks like he ran into a big one this time, the dope."

"Y'know, that's right in front of Calvin's house, Art. Why don't you go up and see if he knows what happened?"

He shook his head without bothering to consider it, and Felicity shrugged before blowing him a kiss and vanishing inside. He stared a few moments longer—until the patrol car drove away—then slipped his hands into his pockets and headed for the bus stop three blocks distant. Later, he thought; maybe I'll see him later.

Probably not.

It wasn't that he didn't like Cal Schiller—they really didn't know each other well enough for feelings one way or the other—but the old man was part of a mystery Art did not think he could handle this early in the morning. Just as Felicity found the engine of their station wagon something akin to an alchemist's child, he could not help but puzzle over the territory Schiller had apparently claimed for himself.

Not that there was anything unusually special about the mock English Tudor on the corner lot. It was like more than one other home in Oxrun Station, yet unlike any others. Its lawn was a carefully tended green, pocked with bee-luring clover in the spring, browning toward the end of September, and shaded by red maples and willows when the sun and rain worked properly. And, like every other lawn on Western Road, it was mowed by one of the high school students who worked the street for spending money during the summer.

By the broad front stoop, however, was a gleaming blue tricycle, and beside that a silver skateboard elegantly designed for maximum speed. A large striped beach ball was generally set in the middle of the lawn, and down the side by the back corner was a sandbox nearly four by four that was always, as far as he could tell, covered with a bright red square of wet-shining canvas. A swing-and-slide set in the backyard, chrome and polished.

Nothing at all out of place for Western Road in Oxrun Station in the middle of the summer.

But Schiller, so far as Art understood, had never been married, had no nieces or nephews who descended on him for the weekend, nor went out of his way to lure the neighborhood children past the redwood picket fence. Yet every morning, as Art walked toward his bus stop, he could see the old man setting out the toys one by one, muttering to himself and smiling. Never looking up. Never waving a greeting.

For no reason at all it spooked him. And for no reason at all, in the year since Schiller had moved in, he had not once found the courage to ask him straight out what he was doing. No reason at all.

"I can't stand it," he told Felicity one evening in late August. It was a week after the Kenners' setter had been killed, two days after the boy who mowed Art's lawn was reported missing by his parents.

"You can't stand what," she said, leaning back against the sink and putting her hands on her hips.

"Calvin, that's what."

"What, again?" She shook her head at his folly and pushed off to the stove where she was making enough iced tea to last them several days. As she sliced the lemons and squeezed the juice into a bowl already filled with sugar, orange rinds, and wedges of fresh plums, he sighed and left the table, stood beside her with an arm loosely around her waist.

"All right," he said, "so it's crazy."

"No. You are; it isn't."

"Thanks a lot."

She licked lemon juice off her fingers and shuddered. "I'm not the one who's nuts about an old man who just happens to like kids, you know. Would you like him better if he were something like a W. C. Fields? You want him, would it make you feel better if he chased the brats with a cane or something?"

Art had his hand slapped for swiping a plum. He bit into it and wiped his mouth with a sleeve. "I'm not nuts about it, Fel, I'm just curious, that's all. I mean, he does it every day the minute the weather gets warm or it doesn't look like it's going to rain. Every day, like he was some kind of robot. And I never once—never once, I tell you—have seen one single kid playing there with those things."

"Wrong," she said with a grin, pouring the congealed mixture into a four-gallon pot of hot dark tea. "You're wrong, Art." She stirred the steaming liquid with a wooden spoon. "There've been some."

"All right—some," he conceded. "But is it enough to—"

"Oh, come on, drop it, Art," she said wearily, pushing him away from the stove. "Just drop it, all right? It's too hot and I'm too tired and whatever Cal Schiller wants to do with his own spare time is his own business. Right?"

Well . . . maybe, he thought sourly, and spent the rest of the evening in front of the television, watching a ball game that didn't interest him, drinking the iced tea without tasting it, and wondering what in hell had happened to his life that it should be so boring, so empty, that he was forced into uncovering mysteries whose solutions were so obvious he didn't want to know them. Hell. A hundred years ago, when he was single, he would have challenged the heat and the summer and the month and the world. Now he only sat and pouted and didn't give a damn at all that the man who just slid into third base was so safe the umpire should have been lynched on the spot. Hell. And it wasn't until nearly midnight that Felicity finally teased him out of his sulking and into their bed.

That night, shortly before dawn, old Ellie Nedsworth's Siamese tom died; her daughter found its left hind paw in the gutter, gouts of bloodstained tan fur scattered all over the street.

Almost without realizing it, Art found himself emerging as the neighborhood's leader. He organized a block search for signs of a dog pack, spurred by reports—though vague and unsubstantiated—that one was in fact roaming through the village. There had been incidents of children being bitten after sunset, and at least two young runaways were thought privately to have been killed by the night-marauding animals. And though they were given every cooperation by Chief Stockton and the police, Art and his neighbors finally decided that Western Road, at least, was not being terrorized by something out of a B-movie's nightmare.

There were, however, no alternatives given.

"Great White Hunter," Felicity said when he finally returned home an hour past dark. "The stupid cat was hit by a car and dragged. Lord, Art, you've seen it before." She grinned and pushed a strand of hair back from her forehead. "The story really is that everyone here except Cal wants to be in Ellie's will when she dies."

He opened his mouth to protest, saw the look on her face and grinned sheepishly. She could very well be right—about the cat. The other rumors were, as rumors tend to be, convenient, especially during a summer as boring as this one had turned out to be. And now that he looked back on it, tramping through gardens and vegetable patches, poking in alleys, and beating the brush around the pond in the park seemed more foolhardy than brave, far more romantic than practical. It was, he thought, almost as though he were actually wishing there was a pack so he could prove his manhood.

Felicity took care of that, however, when she stripped off his trousers.

But when they were done, entwined and dozing, he could not help listening to the night and imagining himself fending off a horde of slavering beasts with blood on their fangs and his name in their growls.

The following day, as though in punishment for his imagination, was the first in a debilitating sequence marked by temperatures that remained well into the nineties. The bus was hot and stifling, the riders and driver cranky, and he and Felicity entered into another of their rounds of increasingly harsh bickering.

About the raise that did not come when they had expected it and had purchased the new station wagon on the basis of its place in a revised and now utterly useless budget; about their son's having to attend summer sessions in New York because of a failure in biology during his freshman year at Cornell and his refusal to take his credits at Hawksted College in the Station; about his own reluctance to acknowledge his sullen dissatisfaction with his present job, the lack of extra money definitely not included. Felicity had been after him for over a year to take any one of the several offers he had had, to stop being so pigheadedly and unrealistically loyal to a company that clearly did not appreciate his talent for figures as much as it took him smugly for granted; and, she concluded as she always did, if he was going to stay with the firm in spite of everything, then he should stop bitching about not having any money, time, respect, and the dozens of other things that made his coming home during the heat wave something to be dreaded.

"I see," he said slowly at last, on Thursday night, when the latest skirmish had ended. He reached for the kitchen's screen door. "I suppose you'd rather have me stay in town, is that it? Is that what you're trying to say?"

She did not look up from the table where her hands were clasped knuckle-white. "When you're like this, Art, day after day after . . . yes." She took a deep breath. "Yes."

He slammed the door without satisfaction and shoved his hands into his jean pockets, walked stiff-legged down the driveway to the sidewalk and turned left. He ignored the muted heavy-summer sounds of televisions and radios, stereos and faint laughter, that hung over the street like the humidity that clung to the foliage in a timid fog; he paid no heed to a convertible blaring past that screamed out-of-date acid rock like a calliope in the hands of a madman; and he prayed once, fervently, that the dog—whatever kind of dog it was—that had killed the Irish setter would take hold of Julius Delarenzo's wattled neck and squeeze until Art got himself the raise, and a goddamned new office.

Love you, too, Julius, he said to the scowling image of his boss that floated about the trees; you goddamned ape.

He walked aimlessly for several blocks, listening to his breathing and the slap of his loafers on the pavement.

He blamed his temper, and Felicity's, on the sodden blanket heat.

Just as he blamed their winter's arguments on the brittle, dry cold.

He counted himself lucky he was not drinking; he wished his son home for someone to talk to; he wanted very much, and suddenly, not to be so predictably faithful that he had to refuse to accept the none-too-subtle blandishments of Carole Neuman across the street, who seemed to be spending more time lately vamping him than she did making dinner for her husband.

Just one quick tumble, he thought, almost wistfully; get hold of those boobs and ride those hips . . . just one. Just one. And he smiled ruefully as he kicked at a stone and watched it scuttle into the gutter. Guilt. There would be too much guilt. And though his affection for his wife might not always recall those earlier Hollywood-romantic days of drifting gently on the Seine, there was still something . . . something he could not quite name, though he would never call it love.

Another car, and he blinked, rubbed the heels of his hands against his eyes, and saw himself standing in front of Schiller's house. Then, glancing down, he shuddered when he realized the darkness beneath his feet just might be the bloodstains left from the setter. The thought propelled him without thinking through the unlatched gate and up to the door, had him knocking before he knew what he was doing. And before he could turn around, Cal was peering through the screen door and grinning.

He was tall, stooped as a man might be who had carried the height for a decade too long, with a head of blinding white hair that Art had once claimed had to have come from a bottle somewhere. His face, despite the age it proclaimed, was full, his eyes squinting, and his pale lips worked soundlessly for a few moments as he considered.

"Art? That you, Art?" Such astonishment in anyone else would have been close to insulting.

"Me, Cal. Just . . . you know, just walking around it's so damned hot. Thought I would drop by and say hello."

Schiller opened the door without hesitating, and Art shrugged a *why the hell not?* to himself as he stepped over the threshold.

It was hot inside, but a pair of fans on the counter eased the pressure in the kitchen where they sat at a small round table gleaming wetly from a fresh cleaning. A can of Australian beer appeared in his hand. He nodded his thanks and took several full swallows to fill in the suddenly uncomfortable silence.

"It's been a while, Art," Schiller said. His voice was high, thin, a reed waiting for the wind to snap it.

"Couple of weeks, I guess, yeah." He took another drink, another, and passed the cold can over his forehead.

Calvin shrugged. "Could be worse."

Art finished the can—nearly a full quart—and there was another in front of him before he could refuse.

"What can I do for you?"

He didn't know what to say, but he said it anyway: "Cal, we're not exactly brothers under the skin and all that, and I don't want you to take offense—"

"None taken, Art. You must know me well enough for that, anyway, right?"

"—but I can't . . ." He inhaled deeply. Felicity, he knew, would kill him when she found out. His smile was weak, though it pretended to be hearty. "Look, this is silly, Cal, but . . . y'know, I can't help seeing all those toys out there every day when I go to work. Now, my wife says it's none of my business, and perhaps it isn't, but . . . ah, damnit!"

Calvin chuckled, his hands cupped loosely around a beer can and rolling it slowly. "It really isn't your business, you know," he said, not unkindly. Then his grin became mischievous. "But it is damned curious, isn't it."

Art looked at him and away, wondering if he should smile, wondering further if this cadaverous old man were mocking him behind that squint. Finally, he nodded.

"Thing is," the old man said, "they're for my little darlin's."

"Oh?"

"Yep."

"You mean, grandchildren, something like that?"

Calvin smiled again. "Grandchildren?" He leaned back in his chair and look heavenward. "Lord, no! My God, no!" He scratched at one barely shaven cheek. "No, just those little darlin's that come around now and again, off and on, you know how it is. Milk and cookies, a few hours on the slides and swings, and home again.

Sometimes they come back, sometimes they don't. Ellie Nedsworth down the street there, she sends over her grandnieces and such when they come up from Jersey. Can't stand them around the house, she says. I keep 'em out of her hair. Mrs. Heidleman—the one what lost her daughter last winter?—she has seven grandchildren and hates every last one of them. She should, believe me. And especially this time of year. You know how it is—the heat makes them restless. Sometimes you can't control them."

Art thought of his son at that age and nodded.

"'Course, what with them stupid animals having to up and die right in my front yard almost . . ." The old man shook his head. "Poor old Ellie, she wanted me to rake the sandbox to look for the rest of that fool cat's body. Can you imagine it? Poor old soul. Crazy as a loon."

Art blinked. "A . . . babysitter." He felt incredibly foolish when Calvin nodded. "You know, Cal, if you knew how I feel right now—"

"No need," Calvin said, waving a generous hand. "No need at all. Look at it this way—if I hadn't those things out there, you wouldn't have come by, we wouldn't talked. I don't have kids here at night, of course. They're all asleep."

"Just the same, that's all pretty damned good of you, you know that, Cal."

"Oh, not at all. A man moves around as much as I have in my life, he likes to get to know the neighborhood. Best way for that is with the kids. Little ones, the way I look at it, are the best introduction."

"You've been to a lot of places, then?"

They opened another round of beer.

"A few," the old man said. "Don't like towns much, you know. A man my age, I don't like to put down roots I can't yank out when I've a mind to. Been all over, now that I think about it. But this place, the Station, I surely would hate to leave it. Best little place in the country to my way of thinking."

Art nodded his agreement, and they drank in silence while he stared unseeing through the screen door at the back. Then his hand froze as it lifted still another new can to his lips. One of the swings was moving, as if someone had just jumped off. He half rose, almost pointed, then shook his head. Probably some teenager cutting through the yard. Squirrel. The wind. He brushed a hand back through his sandy hair and spent the next hour talking about nothings from baseball to his job. And when it was done—at a signal he did not recognize—he found himself standing on the sidewalk, on the other side of the gate. He looked around the yard; the toys were gone, the sandbox still covered.

But the wind . . .

"Arthur," he told himself, his words carefully spaced after a long satisfying belch, "you have too many beers on not enough food on a night that's too damned hot. Go home, idiot, and sin no more."

His voice sounded hollow, the words inane, and his temper barely stirred when he saw thin blanket and pillow on the family-room sofa.

The next day began badly: Felicity was still in bed when he left for work; Delarenzo announced that all salaries would be frozen for at least ten months because of the recession; his secretary announced she was quitting at the end of the month to get married; and his son called from New York to say he did not like college anymore, was considering dropping out, and did his father have any contacts in the city so he could get himself a job.

Felicity saved him from murdering the next living creature who walked into the room; she called just before closing and apologized. He apologized. And before she started crying he hung up. Ignored the bus and took a cab from Harley to his front door. Made her dress and took her to dinner at the Chancellor Inn.

Afterward, they made love, with the fan in the bedroom window drowning out the noises of the car racers in the street.

Saturday he returned to the office and finished everything he had filed on his desk. He didn't think Delarenzo would notice, but you never knew, he told himself—miracles sometimes do happen. That night Felicity went off to visit her sister on the other side of the village, and after an hour's prowling through the empty house and finding nothing but unpleasant shadows, he left and headed straight for Calvin's.

The old man was surprised.

"Didn't expect you here for another two, maybe three weeks, Art."

Art accepted the gibe with good grace and a shrug, stared out the back door while Calvin fetched the beers; the swings, their chains winking in the light spilling from the house, were still.

The heat shifted in a desultory breeze that died as though the effort was too much to make.

He drank excessively while the old man reminisced, kept looking to the swings, kept frowning . . . kept drinking. And by the time midnight had come and gone he knew he was going to have a difficult time maneuvering home. Calvin did not seem to notice. Instead, he laughed heartily at Art's wobbling and guided him to the front.

"Take care now," he called from the stoop. "Don't let them monsters get you, hear?" His laugh was a cackling.

Art waved and laughed back, then leaned quickly against the picket fence, swallowing convulsively to keep his stomach from heaving. He spat to rid his mouth of an acrid metallic taste . . . and saw the sandbox. A hundred years, by God, he thought; it's been a hundred years. He hiccoughed. Belched. Spat again and glanced furtively toward the front door. All the lights were out as far as he could tell, and there was nothing on the road that he could see. Hushing himself, and grinning, he climbed awkwardly over the fence and dropped into a wavering crouch, ran to the house and pressed his back against it. Stupid, he thought; this is really stupid.

He belched.

A few more steps, and he knelt gingerly on the dew-damp grass. The shining red cover was off and folded neatly on the ground. He poked a finger at the grey sand. It was cool. He laid a palm to it. Cool. He plunged his hand under the surface—damp. He piled a handful in the center and jabbed at it, cocked his head and jabbed again. Smoothed. Piled. Angled and smoothed. One last jab, and he hiccoughed. The sound frightened him, and he looked up quickly toward the dark windows overhead, toward the swing set in the backyard.

The plastic seats were moving. All of them. All of them in time.

There was no wind.

He had heard no footsteps.

Moving. In time. Chains creaking faintly.

As steadily as he could, he pushed himself to his feet and hurried to the fence, climbed, swore loudly when a point snagged at his crotch. He shambled off toward home, hoping he would not throw up before he reached the bathroom.

He made it—barely.

Was in bed and pretending deep sleep when Felicity returned.

The next morning she sat with pillows pounded behind her and filled the room with disgust for her sister. When she finally noticed his inattention, however, she glared.

"You look like hell."

He smiled wanly. "I was over at Cal's last night. Damned old man could drink a horse under the table."

"You, I take it, are not a horse."

He fired a finger-and-thumb gun at her.

She sighed. "Do I get the paper, or you?"

He closed his eyes briefly, opened them quickly. "I'd better," he said with a martyr's groan, "or I won't get out until next year."

She kissed him, and he smiled. Five minutes later he was dressed and walking slowly through the early morning haze to the Centre Street luncheonette where the Sunday newspapers were hawked. As he passed Schiller's house he saw Cal kneeling by the sandbox, a small rake in his hand. He called out a greeting, faltered when he saw the dark scowl on the old man's face.

"Trouble?" he asked.

Calvin jabbed angrily at the sand. "This . . . this is for my little darlin's, Art. They don't like it when someone else plays with their stuff."

He could say nothing. His face tried a series of weak apologies, but there were no words. First there was a rush of shame that he had been seen, then a surge of irrational anger that he had been spied upon. But he decided quickly that neither contrition nor argument was worth the effort—the heat was still simmering, and those so-called little darlin's weren't the only things in town the temperature made restless.

He waved again and moved on.

At the luncheonette he picked up the local paper and the *New York Times*, and stood patiently in line at the counter while the air conditioning helped to sponge clear his mood and his head. Then Ellie Nedsworth waddled past him with a box of chocolates in her hand, saw him and grinned broadly.

"Art!"

"Lovely day, Ellie."

"Crap," she said. "It's too damned hot." She hefted the five-pound box and looked at it sourly. "Tell you the truth, Art, I wish I had a sister or something in Alaska. I'd walk there on my knees just to feel the cool."

"No kidding," he said, distracted by a headline. "Where does she live, then?"

"Nowhere. Don't have one," she told him, fishing in her purse for the price of the candy. "Just the one fool daughter, and she ain't got the brains to come in out of the rain."

He nodded again dutifully, paid for the newspapers, and froze as his hand was still out for his change. "What?" he said, nearly shouting as he turned toward the door. "What?" But Ellie was gone.

"You what?" Felicity said, her eyes wide and disbelieving.

"You heard me. Ellie Nedsworth has no sister and her daughter isn't married, that's what."

She shook her head and slumped into a chair. "I don't believe you actually asked him about that, Art. I really don't believe it."

"What difference does it make, Fel? I mean, the man lied to me. More than once, as a matter of fact." He ignored the sudden stare. "On the way back I checked around a little. Mrs. Heidleman's grandchildren are all grown and live out of state. No one that I talked to has ever sent their kids to play in Schiller's yard. He lied, Fel. The man lied to me."

After a moment's thought she shrugged. "Okay, so he lied. So what?"

He sat opposite her and took her hands in his. Mysteries. Mysteries and . . . boredom. "Listen for a minute, Fel. I've been doing some thinking."

"It's the heat," she muttered, but said nothing more when she saw the expression on his face.

"Now bear with me for a minute, all right?" He waited for her to nod. "Okay. Now—the setter, the cat, I think there was a sheepdog, too. Those runaways—two of them, at least, not a sign of them. Schiller told me himself, Fel—he *told* me—that he hasn't lived in any one place for more than a couple of years at a time. That's right. And do you know why? I'll tell you. Because—"

"No!" she said sharply, pulling her hands back, rubbing them lightly against her jeans. "Now that's just plain idiotic, Art."

Art pressed. "Fel, the man is senile. Crazy. I don't know. But you should have seen him when he found out what I'd done to his precious sandbox." He thought for a moment, one hand pulling at the side of his jaw. "Yeah. Right. The sandbox. You know, it's an awfully damned big sandbox, Fel."

She rose with a slap to the table. "This is . . . *he's* crazy? No," she said when he opened his mouth to protest. "No, Art. You just sit there and think about what you just said to me. Think about it, and then . . ." She lifted her hands helplessly. "I don't know. Just don't mention it again."

When she walked out of the room there were tears in her eyes.

They said little to each other for the rest of the day. And he did not blame her. Cal Schiller of the tricycle and Australian beer a sadistic mass murderer? He may be a little strange here and there, he thought, but . . . but . . . it *was* an awfully damned big sandbox.

He couldn't sleep, and he knew he wouldn't be able to.

He called himself an idiot, a man desperate for adventure, or attention, when he slipped out of the bed; an idiot when he stood in front of the redwood picket fence; and a goddamned idiot when he climbed over and crept to the side of the house.

The red cover was gone.

The grey sand was smooth, was cool, and when he finally lost his nerve—what had she called him? the Great White Hunter?—and could not bring himself to do any digging, he looked up and saw the shadows on the swings . . . and the swings were moving.

Jesus, he thought; Schiller's little darlin's.

"Damned fool."

He did not move when the voice spoke behind him. He could not take his eyes off the shadows, off the harsh glints of red, of amber, that could only be their eyes.

"Playing in the sand like some fool baby."

The swinging . . . slowed.

"I told you, son, you shouldn't have touched what just wasn't yours. They don't like that, you know. They get the scent, they just don't like it."

I know, I know, he thought, his legs bunching to run as he rose from his crouch; the heat makes them restless.

Schiller brushed past him, knelt and plunged a hand into the sand, flung a palmful to one side and dug again. Again. Again. The sand like heavy rain on the grass. Art finally looked down, slowly, reluctant to take his eyes from those shadows, those eyes; he looked down and realized there was far too much sand being dumped on the ground for the size of the box that squatted before him.

Schiller sighed, clucked, spat dryly. "Damned fool, you know that, don't you. Hell. It happens every time. Every time. I find the right place they can get out and breathe a little, stretch their muscles, get themselves something to eat, and some damned fool comes along and tries to spoil it for them. Poor little darlin's."

There was too much sand.

Schiller glanced up at him, grunted, and bent his head again.

"What . . ." Art put a hand to his throat; it felt as though he were choking. "What are you doing?"

"Got to make room," Schiller said, jerking a thumb in the direction of the swings. "They're too lazy to do their own work in heat like this. Damn!"

Art backed off a pace, but the up-and-out blurred motion of the old man's hands mesmerized him. He kept his gaze on the hands, on the sand . . . on the hands . . . on the sand . . .

"You tell your wife, Art?"

He nodded before he could catch himself.

"Oh, well, no harm done," the old man said. He paused to scratch at his chin. "I'll call her, I guess. Tell her you fell down. Drank too much. She'll come get you." He looked back over his shoulder and grinned.

The hole was deep. Reaching far below the level of the grass.

"Felicity?" Art said.

There was a chittering behind him. Bark against bark; nails drawn over glass.

He looked up—the swings were still, the shadows gone.

"Well, I tell you one thing, boy, I ain't moving again," Schiller said. The sand piled high; the hole blackened. "Too much . . . trouble." He grunted. "I like this place, y'know. It's home now. And the little ones get plenty to eat when they need it."

The chittering. Teeth against teeth.

Art turned around quickly . . . and saw them. Red, amber, chittering . . . massing.

He choked back a scream.

The old man scowled, and tossed aside a bone. "Tell me something, son," he said, "how tall are you?"

And kept on digging.

IF DAMON COMES

Fog, nightbreath of the river, luring without whispering in the thick crown of an elm, huddling without creaking around the base of a chimney; it drifted past porch lights, and in passing blurred them, dropped over the street lights, and in dropping greyed them. It crept in with midnight to stay until dawn, and there was no wind to bring the light out of hiding.

Frank shivered and drew his raincoat's collar closer around his neck, held it closed with one hand while the other wiped at the pricks of moisture that clung to his cheeks, his short dark hair. He whistled once, loudly, but in listening heard nothing, not even an echo. He stamped his feet against the November cold and moved to the nearest corner, squinted and saw nothing. He knew the cat was gone, had known it from the moment he had seen the saucer still brimming with milk on the back porch. Damon had been sitting beside it, hands folded, knees pressed tightly together, elbows tucked into his sides. He was cold, but refused to acknowledge it, and Frank had only tousled his son's softly brown hair, squeezed his shoulder once, and went inside to say good-bye to his wife.

And now . . . now he walked, through the streets of Oxrun

Station, looking for an animal he had seen only once—a half-breed Siamese with a milk-white face—whistling like a fool afraid of the dark, searching for the note that would bring the animal running.

And in walking, he was unpleasantly reminded of a night the year before, when he had had one drink too many at someone's party, made one amorous boast too many in someone's ear, and had ended up on a street corner with a woman he knew only vaguely. They had kissed once and long, and once broken, he had turned around to see Damon staring up at him. The boy had turned, had fled, and Frank had stayed away most of the night, not knowing what Susan had heard, fearing more what Damon had thought.

It had been worse than horrid facing the boy again, but Damon had acted as though nothing had happened; and the guilt passed as the months passed, and the wondering why his son had been out in the first place.

He whistled. Crouched and snapped his fingers at the dark of some shrubbery. Then he straightened and blew out a deeply held breath. There was no cat, there were no cars, and he finally gave in to his aching feet and sore back and headed for home. Quickly. Watching the fog tease the road before him, cut it sharply off behind.

It wasn't fair, he thought, his hands shoved in his pockets, his shoulders hunched as though expecting a blow. Damon, in his short eight years, had lost two dogs already to speeders, a canary to some disease he couldn't even pronounce, and two brothers stillborn—it was getting to be a problem. *He* was getting to be a problem, fighting each day that he had to go to school, whining and weeping whenever vacations came around and trips were planned.

He'd asked Doc Simpson about it when Damon turned seven. Dependency, he was told; clinging to the only three things left in his life—his short, short life—that he still believed to be constant: his home, his mother . . . and Frank.

And Frank had kissed a woman on a corner and Damon had seen him.

Frank shuddered and shook his head quickly, remembering how the boy had come to the office at least once a day for the next three weeks, saying nothing, just standing on the sidewalk looking in through the window. Just for a moment. Long enough to be sure that his father was still there.

Once home, then, Frank shed his coat and hung it on the rack by the front door. A call, a muffled reply, and he took the stairs two at a time and trotted down the hall to Damon's room set over the kitchen.

"Sorry, old pal," he said with a shrug as he made himself a place on the edge of the mattress. "I guess he went home."

Damon, small beneath the flowered quilt, innocent from behind long curling lashes, shook his head sharply. "No," he said. "This is his home. It is, Dad, it really is."

Frank scratched at the back of his neck. "Well, I guess he didn't think of it quite that way."

"Maybe he got lost, huh? It's awfully spooky out there. Maybe he's afraid to come out of where he's hiding."

"A cat's never—" He stopped as soon as he saw the expression on the boy's thin face. Then he nodded and broke out a rueful smile. "Well, maybe you're right, pal. Maybe the fog messed him up a little." Damon's hand crept into his, and he squeezed it while thinking that the boy was too thin by far; it made his head look ungainly. "In the morning," he promised. "In the morning. If he's not back by then, I'll take the day off and we'll hunt him together."

Damon nodded solemnly, withdrew the hand, and pulled the quilt up to his chin. "When's Mom coming home?"

"In a while. It's Friday, you know. She's always late on Fridays. And Saturdays." And, he thought, Wednesdays and Thursdays, too.

Damon nodded again. And, as Frank reached the door and switched off the light: "Dad, does she sing pretty?"

"Like a bird, pal," he said, grinning. "Like a bird."

The voice was small in the dark: "I love you, Dad."

Frank swallowed hard, and nodded before he realized the boy couldn't see him. "Well, pal, it seems I love you, too. Now you'd better get some rest."

"I thought you were going to get lost in the fog."

Frank stopped the move to close the door. He'd better get some rest himself, he thought; that sounded like a threat.

"Not me," he finally said. "You'd always come for me, right?"

"Right, Dad."

Frank grinned, closed the door, and wandered through the small house for nearly half an hour before finding himself in the kitchen, his hands waving at his sides for something to do. Coffee. No. He'd had too much of that today already. But the walk had chilled him, made his bones seem brittle. Warm milk, maybe, and he opened the refrigerator, stared, then took out a container and poured half its contents into a pot. He stood by the stove, every few seconds stirring a finger through the milk to check its progress. Stupid cat, he thought; there ought to be a law against doing something like that to a small boy that never hurt anyone, never had anyone to hurt.

He poured himself a glass, smiling when he didn't spill a drop, but he refused to turn around and look up at the clock; instead, he stared at the flames as he finished the second glass, wondering what it would be like to stick his finger into the fire. He read somewhere . . . he thought he'd read somewhere that the blue near the center was the hottest part and it wasn't so bad elsewhere. His hand wavered, but he changed his mind, not wanting to risk a burn on something he only thought he had read; besides, he decided as he headed into the living room, the way things were going these days, he probably had it backward.

He sat in an armchair flanking the television, took out a magazine from the rack at his side, and had just found the table of contents when he heard a car door slam in the drive. He waited, looked up and smiled when the front door swung open and Susan rushed in. She blew him a distant kiss, mouthed *I'll be back in a second,* and ran up the stairs. She was much shorter than he, her hair waist-long black and left free to fan in the wind of her own making. She'd been taking voice lessons for several years now, and when they'd moved to the Station when Damon was five, she had landed a job singing at the Chancellor Inn. Torch songs, love songs, slow songs, sinner songs; she was liked well enough to be asked to stay on after the first night, but she began so late that Damon had never heard her. And for the last six months, the two-nights-a-week became four, and Frank became adept at cooking supper.

When she returned, her makeup was gone and she was in a

shimmering green robe. She flopped on the sofa opposite him and rubbed her knees, her thighs, her upper arms. "If that creep drummer tries to pinch me again, so help me I'll castrate him."

"That is hardly the way for a lady to talk," he said, smiling. "If you're not careful, I'll have to punish you. Whips at thirty paces."

In the old days—the very old days, he thought—she would have laughed and entered a game that would last for nearly an hour. Lately, however, and tonight, she only frowned at him as though she were dealing with a dense unlettered child. He ignored it, and listened politely as she detailed her evening, the customers, the compliments, the raise she was looking for so she could buy her own car.

"You don't need a car," he said without thinking.

"But aren't you tired of walking home every night?"

He closed the magazine and dropped it on the floor. "Lawyers, my dear, are a sedentary breed. I could use the exercise."

"If you didn't work so late on those damned briefs," she said without looking at him, "and came to bed on time, I'd give you all the exercise you need."

He looked at his watch. It was going on two.

"The cat's gone."

"Oh, no," she said. "No wonder you look so tired. You go out after him?"

He nodded, and she rolled herself suddenly into a sitting position. "Not with Damon."

"No. He was in bed when I came home."

She said nothing more, only examined her nails. He watched her closely, the play of her hair falling over her face, the squint that told him her contact lenses were still on her dresser. And he knew she hadn't meant: *did you take Damon with you?* She was asking if Damon had followed him. Like the night in the fog, with the woman; like the times at the office; like the dozens of other instances when the boy just happened to show up at the courthouse, in the park while Frank was eating lunch under a tree, at a nearby friend's house late one evening, claiming to have had a nightmare and the sitter wouldn't help him.

Like a shadow.

Like a conscience.

"Are you going to replace it?" He blinked. "The cat, stupid. Are you going to get him a new cat?"

He shook his head. "We've had too much bad luck with animals. I don't think he could take it again."

She swung herself off the sofa and stood in front of him, her hands on her hips, her lips taut, her eyes narrowed. "You don't care about him, do you?"

"What?"

"He follows you around like a goddamn pet because he's afraid of losing you, and you won't even buy him a lousy puppy or something. You're something else again, Frank, you really are. I work my tail off trying to help—"

"My salary is plenty good enough," he said quickly.

"—this family and you're even trying to get me to stop that, too."

He shoved himself to his feet, his chest brushing against hers and forcing her back. "Listen," he said tightly, "I don't care if you sing your heart out a million times a week, lady, but when it starts to interfere with your duties here—"

"My *duties?*"

"—then yes, I'll do everything I can to make sure you stay home when you're supposed to."

"You're raising your voice. You'll wake Damon."

The argument was familiar, and old, and so was the rage he felt stiffening his muscles. But this time she wouldn't stop when she saw his anger. She kept on, and on, and he didn't even realize it when his hand lifted and struck her across the cheek. She stumbled back a step, whirled to run out of the room, and stopped.

Damon was standing at the foot of the stairs.

He was sucking his thumb.

He was staring at his father.

"Go to bed, son," Frank said quietly. "Everything's all right."

For the next week the tension in the house was proverbially knife-cutting thick. Damon stayed up as late as he could, sitting by his father as they watched television together or read from the boy's favorite books. Susan remained close, but not touching, humming to herself and playing with her son whenever he left—for the moment—his father's side; each time, however, her smile was more forced, her laughter more strained, and it was apparent to Frank that Damon was merely tolerating her, nothing more. That puzzled him. It was he who had struck her, not the other way around, and the boy's loyalty should have been thrown into his mother's camp. Yet it hadn't. And it was apparent that Susan was growing more resentful of the fact each day. Each hour. Each time Damon walked silently to Frank's side and slid his hand around the man's waist, or into his palm, or into his pocket.

He began showing up at the office again, until one afternoon when Susan skidded the car to a halt at the curb and ran out, grabbed the boy and practically threw him, arms and legs thrashing, into the front seat. Frank raced from his desk and out the front door, leaned over and rapped at the window until Susan lowered it.

"What the hell are you doing?" he whispered, with a glance to the boy.

"You hit me, or had you forgotten," she whispered back. "And there's my son's alienation of affection."

He almost straightened. "That's lawyer talk, Susan," he said.

"Not here," she answered. "Not in front of the boy."

He stepped back quickly as the car growled away from the curb, walked in a daze back to his desk and sat there, chin in one palm, staring out the window as the afternoon darkened and a faint drizzle began to fall. His secretary muttered something about a court case the following morning, and Frank nodded until she stared at him, gathered her purse and raincoat, and left hurriedly. He continued to nod, not knowing the movement, trying to understand what he had done, what both of them had done to bring themselves to this moment. Ambition, surely. A conflict of generations where women were housebodies and women had careers; where men tried to adjust when they couldn't have both. But he had tried, he told himself . . . or he thought he had, until the dishes began to pile up and the dust stayed on the furniture and Damon said *does she sing pretty?*

It's always the children who get hurt, he thought angrily.

Held that idea in early December when separation papers had been prepared and he stood on the front porch watching his car, his wife, and his son drive away from Oxrun Station south toward the city. Damon's face was in the rear window, nose flat, palms flat, hair pressed down over his forehead. He waved, and Frank answered.

I love you, Dad.

Frank wiped a hand under his nose and went back inside, searched the house for some liquor, and, in failing, went straight to bed where he watched the moonshadows make monsters of the curtains.

"Dad," the boy had said, "do I have to go with Mommy?"

"I'm afraid so. The judge . . . well, he knows better, believe it or not, what's best right now. Don't worry, pal. I'll see you at Christmas. It won't be forever."

"I don't like it, Dad. I'll run away."

"No! You'll do what your mother tells you, you hear me? You behave yourself and go to school every day, and I'll . . . call you whenever I can."

"The city doesn't like me, Dad. I want to stay at the Station."

Frank said nothing.

"It's because of the lady, isn't it?"

He had stared, but Susan's back was turned, bent over a suitcase that would not close once it had sprung open again by the front door.

"What are you talking about?" he'd said harshly.

"I told," Damon said as though it were nothing. "You weren't supposed to do that."

When Susan straightened, her smile was grotesque.

And when they had driven away, Damon had said *I love you, Dad.*

Frank woke early, made himself breakfast, and stood at the back door, looking out into the yard. There was a fog again, nothing unusual as the Connecticut weather fought to stabilize into winter. But as he sipped at his coffee, thinking how large the house had become, how large and how empty, he saw a movement beside the cherry tree in the middle of the yard. The fog swirled, but he was sure . . .

He yanked open the door and shouted: "Damon!"

The fog closed, and he shook his head. Easy, pal, he told himself; you're not cracking up, yet.

Days.

Nights.

He called Susan regularly, twice a week at preappointed times. But as Christmas came and Christmas went, she became more terse, and his son more sullen.

"He's getting fine grades, Frank, I'm seeing to that."

"He sounds terrible."

"He's losing a little weight, that's all. Picks up colds easily. It takes a while, Frank, to get used to the city."

"He doesn't like the city."

"It's his home. He will."

In mid-January Susan did not answer the phone, and finally, in desperation, he called the school, was told that Damon had been in the hospital for nearly a week. The nurse thought it was something like pneumonia.

When he arrived that night, the waiting room was crowded with drab bundles of scarves and overcoats, whispers and moans and a few muffled sobs. Susan was standing by the window, looking out at the lights far colder than stars. She didn't turn when she heard him, didn't answer when he demanded to know why she had not contacted him. He grabbed her shoulder and spun her around; her eyes were dull, her face pinched with red hints of cold.

"All right," she said. "All right, Frank, it's because I didn't want you to upset him."

"What in hell are you talking about?"

"He would have seen you and he would have wanted to go back to Oxrun." Her eyes narrowed. "This is his home, Frank! He's got to learn to live with it."

"I'll get a lawyer."

She smiled. "Do that. You do that, Frank."

He didn't have to. He saw Damon a few minutes later and could not stay more than a moment. The boy was in dim light and almost invisible, too thin to be real beneath the clear plastic tent and the tubes and the monitors . . . too frail, the doctor said in professional conciliation, too frail for too long, and Frank remembered the day on the porch with the saucer of milk when he had thought the same thing and had thought nothing of it.

SMITH

He returned after the funeral, all anger gone. He had accused Susan of murder, knowing at the same time how foolish it had been, but feeling better for it in his own absolution. He had apologized. Had been, for the moment, forgiven.

Had stepped off the train, had wept, had taken a deep breath and decided to live on.

Returned to the office the following day, piled folders onto his desk and hid behind them for most of the morning. He looked up only once, when his secretary tried to explain about a new client's interest, and saw around her waist the indistinct form of his son peering through the window.

"Damon," he muttered, brushed the woman to one side and ran out to the sidewalk. A fog encased the road whitely, but he could see nothing, not even a car, not even the blinking amber light at the nearest intersection.

Immediately after lunch he dialed Susan's number, stared at the receiver when there was no answer, and returned it to the cradle. Wondering.

"You look pale," his secretary said softly. She pointed with a pencil at his desk. "You've already done a full day's work. Why don't you go home and lie down? I can lock up. I don't mind."

He smiled, turned as she held his coat for him, touched her cheek . . . and froze.

Damon was in the window.

No, he told himself . . . and Damon was gone.

He rested for two days, returned to work and lost himself in a battle over a will probated by a judge he thought nothing less than senile, to be charitable. He tried calling Susan again, and again received no answer.

And Damon would not leave him alone.

When there was fog, rain, clouds, wind . . . he would be there by the window, there by the cherry tree, there in the darkest corner of the porch.

He knew it was guilt, for not fighting hard enough to keep his son with him, thinking that if he had the boy might still be alive; seeing his face everywhere and the accusations that if the boy loved him, why wasn't he loved just as much in return?

By February's end he decided it was time to make a friendly call on a fellow professional, a doctor who shared the office building with him. It wasn't so much the faces that he saw—he had grown somewhat accustomed to them and assumed they would vanish in time—but that morning there had been snow on the ground; and in the snow by the cherry tree the footprints of a small boy. When he brought the doctor out to the yard to show him, they were gone.

"You're quite right, Frank. You're feeling guilty. But not because of the boy in and of himself. The law and the leanings of most judges are quite clear—you couldn't be expected to keep him at his age. You're still worrying yourself about that woman you kissed and the fact that Damon saw you; and the fact that you think you could have saved his life somehow, even if the doctors couldn't; and lastly, the fact that you weren't able to give him things, like pets, like that cat. None of it is your fault, really. It's merely something unpleasant you'll have to face up to. Now."

Though he didn't feel all that much better, Frank appreciated the calm that swept over him when the talk was done and they parted. He worked hard for the rest of the day, for the rest of the week, but he knew that it was not guilt and it was not his imagination and it was not anything the doctor would be able to explain away when he opened his door on Saturday morning and found, lying carefully atop his newspaper, the white-faced Siamese. Dead. Its neck broken.

He stumbled back over the threshold, whirled around and raced into the downstairs bathroom where he fell onto his knees beside the bowl and lost his breakfast. The tears were acid, the sobs like blows to his lungs and stomach, and by the time he had pulled himself together, he knew what was happening.

The doctor, the secretary, even his wife . . . they were all wrong.

There was no guilt.

There was only . . . Damon.

A little boy with large brown eyes who loved his father. Who loved his father so much that he would never leave him. Who loved his father so much that he was going to make sure, absolutely sure, that he would never be alone.

You've been a bad boy, Daddy.

Frank stumbled to his feet, into the kitchen, leaned against the back door. There was a figure by the cherry tree, dark and formless; but he knew there was no use running outside. The figure would vanish.

You never did like that cat, Daddy. Or the dogs. Or Mommy.

The telephone rang. He took his time getting to it, stared at it dumbly for several moments before lifting the receiver. He could see straight down the hall and into the kitchen. He had not turned on the overhead light and, as a consequence, could see through the small panes of the back door to the yard beyond. The air outside was heavy with impending snow. Grey. Almost lifeless.

"Frank? Frank, it's Susan. Frank, I've been thinking . . . about you and me and . . . and what happened."

He kept his eyes on the door. "It's done, Sue. Done."

"Frank, I don't know what happened. Honest to God, I was trying, really I was. He was getting the best grades in school, had lots of friends . . . I even bought him a little dog, a poodle, two weeks before he . . . I don't know what happened, Frank! I woke up this morning and all of a sudden I was so damned *alone.* Frank, I'm frightened. Can . . . can I come home?"

The grey darkened. There was a shadow on the porch, much larger now than the shadow in the yard.

"No," he said.

"He thought about you all the damned time," she said, her voice rising into hysteria. "He tried to run away once, to get back to you."

The shadow filled the panes, the windows on either side, and suddenly there was static on the line and Susan's voice vanished. He dropped the receiver and turned around.

In the front.

Shadows.

He heard the furnace humming, but the house was growing cold.

The lamp in the living room flickered, died, shone brightly for a moment before the bulb shattered.

He was . . . wrong.

God, he was wrong!

Damon . . . Damon didn't love him.

Not since the night on the corner in the fog; not since the night he had not really tried to locate a cat with a milk-white face.

Damon knew.

And Damon didn't love him.

He dropped to his hands and knees and searched in the darkness for the receiver, found it and nearly threw it away when the bitterly cold plastic threatened to burn through his fingers.

"Susan!" he shouted. "Susan, damnit, can you hear me?"

A bad boy, Daddy.

There was static, but he thought he could hear her crying into the wind.

"Susan . . . Susan, this is crazy, I've no time to explain, but you've got to help me. You've got to do something for me."

Daddy.

"Susan, please . . . he'll be back, I know he will. Don't ask me how, but I know! Listen, you've got to do something for me. Susan, damnit, can you hear me?"

Daddy, I'm

"For God's sake, Susan, if Damon comes, tell him I'm sorry!"

home.

A NIGHT OF DARK INTENT

The moon was a ghost in the house of night. It rose from the ashes of a sunset in crimson—silent, stained, setting free the shadows that drifted slowly round its passing. Its breath was the darkwind, drawn from catacombs of chilled and chilling dust; its voice the parchment husking of solitary leaves on solitary boughs that clawed at the nightair for purchase of a soul. Few saw it without turning aside to a friend, few heard it without wishing they hadn't known the tune.

And it crouched above the road that bound the summit of Pointer Hill where it watched, waited, and turned the single row of pine that flanked each shoulder into posts beneath a black bannister, posts through which startling white eyes blinked against the gathering of the mist . . . white eyes that became headlights nervously probing, searching the road for a sign, or an excuse, until they swept over the low mansion once the trees had fallen back.

It was a true English Tudor, white stone crisscrossed by thick dark beams, the second story overshadowing the first with leaded arched windows. Evergreen shrubs pressed close to the walls, and a brown brittle garden marked the center of the drive. To one side was a stable converted to a garage, to the other a shed in which tools were stored. The doors of the former had been pried open by the wind; the door of the latter was padlocked and warped.

Martin parked his car behind a row of four others, sat for a moment to hear the warm metal snap into cooling. His overcoat was heavy on his shoulders, his grey gloves tossed onto the seat beside him. Though there was plenty of comfortable light from the sheer-curtained windows, no one came to the door and there were no shadows that he could see.

He had been driving for almost an hour, out of Oxrun Station and through the farmland east of the village; a hesitation before slipping into foliage still dense despite the season, and across a broad stream that whispered when it should have laughed. And now that he was here, he wished he hadn't come. He should have kept his own promise: to quit his job on the *Station Herald*, head in the other direction, and not stop until he came to Boston. It wasn't that his pay was bad, but the quiet of the Station was driving him nuts.

And now he was paying for his curiosity's hold.

He considered lighting a cigarette, changed his mind when he saw a man bending over the hood of the first car in line. He frowned, opened the door, and pushed himself out. Immediately, the wind took hold of his thin sandy hair and veiled him. The frown turned to scowling, and he pulled his collar high, brushed back the hair, and walked slowly, loudly, along the slate walk that bordered the drive. When he was close enough, he saw that the man held what looked like a huge black moth in his left hand. It fluttered, darted, rose and poised before diving again.

Martin couldn't believe it; in the middle of the night the man was dusting the car.

The man turned then, startled, his free hand jumping to his chest. He was short, thin, his face sallow, his lips grinning.

"Scared me, sir," he said, stuffing the rag into his hip pocket. "You must be Mr. Worthy. From around here, huh? with a name like that."

Martin nodded, returned the smile.

"Well, they're waiting on you, sir." The man pointed to the front door, a gleaming split panel of darkly grained oak. "Don't bother to knock. Just walk in." He wasn't wearing a cap, but his hand made the gesture of tipping it just the same. "Good of you to come, Mr. Worthy. Hope you're not disappointed."

The black moth leaped to his hand again, and he turned back to the car.

Martin watched him a moment longer, then turned up the walk, climbed the four steps to the door, and hesitated. It was all right for that one to say just walk in, but he felt uneasy. Surely they suspected he would be something more than skeptical, and it somehow just didn't seem right to enter without invitation. On the other hand, he told himself, you could stand out here all night, idiot, and catch your death.

The door opened easily, almost at a touch, and he closed it quickly behind him, to keep the nightwind from following. He was in a small foyer with oak wainscoting, coatrack, portraits on the wall. Idly, wondering how much all this would cost if it were built today, he slipped off his overcoat and hung it on the rack, smoothed a hand down the lapels of his brown suit, straightened his tie, and stepped to the middle of the bare hardwood floor.

To his right was a room with double doors solidly closed; to his left, what looked like a parlor similar in tone and style to the foyer and the outside. In the center of a faded oriental carpet was a round walnut table polished to glass, and around that four people were sitting, their hands flat on the insubstantial surface. Several lamps and a chandelier blazed brightly, and Martin thought it was hardly the proper setting for raising a spook.

He cleared his throat behind a loosely held fist.

Instantly, four heads turned to him, four pairs of lips smiled, and an elderly man rose with hand extended. He was dressed in a dark green velvet tuxedo, softly bronze and ruffled shirt, with diamond cuff links that caught the light and flared. His face was ruddy, hair white, eyes a steady and disconcerting blue.

"Mr. Worthy," he said, as though Martin had brought him the Fountain of Youth. "Come in, come in. My lord, we didn't expect you so soon." He took Martin's hand in a politely strong grip and led him to the others, all of whom had left their seats and were waiting patiently, smiling.

"I am, of course, Arthur Drummond," the man said, "and this is my wife, Dorothy."

Dorothy was blonde and slight, the age on her features proudly borne without cosmetics or surgery. Her dress was simple, a floral print pale and demanding no inspection.

"Kenneth Longwood."

Was a round head and a round stomach, a haircut that would have done justice to Oliver Cromwell, and a blue serge suit so shiny at the knees they seemed made of water.

"Zachery Child."

Was no child at all but the oldest of the lot. Once heavy and now inordinately thin, he wore his broad-lapelled evening clothes as though he were stumbling around inside them, searching for a way out.

Mrs. Drummond giggled when Martin took her soft hand, then turned to a Regency lowboard and poured him a glass of strong nutty sherry. They babbled, then, without clustering around him, their efforts to warm and comfort him making him feel as Judas must have done. But he kept his smile, nodded when he thought the time was right, listened attentively to every word that was said.

They didn't seem like nuts, he thought, believing that most people who involved themselves with mediums and crystal balls were either too desperate to know what lay beyond death to have better sense, or too delicately unbalanced to understand they were being conned. These people, however . . . they appeared perfectly normal. Their laughter was genuine, their attempts to put him at ease almost heroic. And when Child said again how delighted they were that he'd come so soon, he glanced at his watch and saw it was just gone eleven. He said nothing, however, but accepted another drink.

"I'll tell you something, Martin," Drummond said, taking him to one side, standing in front of the room's bay window, "when I sent the invitation to your editor, I half expected him to toss it out with the trash. But you're here, aren't you. Extraordinary." And he laughed. "Extraordinary how things work out, isn't it."

Martin nodded, sipped at the strong sherry, and wondered if he should tell the old man that his editor hadn't shown him the invitation at all. He had been at his desk in the office last Monday, trying to complete still another stale article on finance and survival. He hated the stuff, but it was what the Station demanded, and he'd overheard the editor laughing about something on the phone with his wife. He heard the word "séance," but not a single word more. And tonight, as he was driving around in search of the courage to leave, he had wondered what would happen if he'd just dropped in for a snoop. That they knew his name was no surprise—there were only two others on the *Herald*'s staff, and each one of them had a by-line.

And how he knew it would be tonight was something only his subconscious could tell him. Subliminal hearing was the obvious source.

No. He'd say nothing about it. The Drummonds and the others were being far too kind, and it was already difficult enough to keep his guilt from choking him.

"They think, of course," Drummond was saying, with Child nodding, "that we do nothing more than sit around waiting for some manifestation to appear to us. A long-lost relative, a wife, an aunt, something like that. Ridiculous, in point of fact. We do no such thing. There are no glass bowls to peer into, no tea leaves to read, no pretty little cards to set up in curious designs. No, nothing like that at all."

"Right," Child said, poking a boney finger toward Martin's chest. His voice was brittle, a long dead leaf refusing to fall from a long dead limb. "We see all the movies, you know. We know what the . . . what the . . ."

"Theatrics," Drummond supplied quietly.

"Right. Theatrics." He laughed suddenly, quickly. "Houdini would love us. No charlatans here, m'boy. You can count on that."

Martin tried not to look sheepish, felt the room grow perceptively warmer as if the five of them had somehow become five hundred and were sucking out all the air. He was taller than all of them and kept his head down as though listening intently, his face an encyclopedia of nuance from which they could draw their inferences without effort. His gaze moved from face to face. Hands spotted with old decades swooped and postured in front of him. His glass was refilled.

But when, he wanted to ask them, was this séance going to begin?

He had almost found the courage to ask—not at all sure why he hadn't the courage in the first place—when he realized they were probably waiting for midnight. The magical hour. The witching time. Ghosts, spirits, specters walking. He grinned and called himself four kinds of a fool, turned to the window, and the grin froze to a grimace.

The moonlight was still strong, the wind still pushing futilely at the panes.

There had been four cars in the drive when he'd pulled up; there were only four cars now, his still the last. In the shimmering cold reflection of the room behind him he could see the Drummonds, Child, and Longwood. Who had left? The man with the dustrag? It was hard to credit—the four cars he had seen were vintage and expensive; a man who spent his autumn evenings keeping them clean would hardly own one himself.

Longwood laughed at something Mrs. Drummond said and slapped a hand against the table. Martin turned quickly, inexplicably annoyed at the sound. It was too much, he thought, and set the wine glass down on the sill. The whole thing was ridiculous. He should have kept on going, north to Boston and whatever job he could find. He didn't need to humiliate himself by waiting around for spooks to knock on wood or toot rasping horns.

And that, he suddenly understood, was exactly what he was doing to himself. An act of self-abasement because the whole of his life until now had been littered with the kind of small gnawing failures he had always laughed at in others. His marriages, his abortive novels, his attempts at windmill-tilting in politics and finance. For a moment, just a moment, he supposed that he really wasn't all that great a failure, that he only tended to magnify his setbacks because his goals were so high.

But the moment passed, and he was angry again.

He looked across the large room, searching for Drummond, had a hand lifted to summon him for the parting when a narrow door set in the far corner opened, and a woman entered.

The others fell muttering into a respectful silence.

At last, Martin thought; the medium arrives.

She was a full head taller than he, her parted-in-the-center hair the black of a winter's crisp night—it settled in more waves than seemed possible onto her shoulders, spilled down her back and chest in shadowed cascades. She wore a simple long-sleeved white blouse that hovered close to grey, a matching skirt that reached just below the knee. Deep blue slippers on her feet. A blue satin scarf tied loosely around her throat.

Drummond seemed to be blushing as he approached her, taking her hand and bringing it to his lips.

It was almost, Martin thought, as if the man expected to be scolded.

Then Dorothy fluttered a gesture toward Martin. "Look who's here, Elizabeth! It's Mr. Worthy!"

Elizabeth circled the table with long assured strides, and smiled at him. "Mr. Worthy," she said, a slight nodding as she accepted his hand. "I hope my friends haven't been talking your ear off. They have a tendency to do that once in a while." Though the tone was light, the rebuke was there, and he saw Child scowling as he headed for the sideboard. "But there's no harm done, is there. At least I hope not. I tell you what, Martin—may I call you Martin?—why don't we leave these people for a few minutes and you can ask all the questions you want. I'm sure they won't mind."

Martin didn't care if they minded or not. The eyes that locked to his as she settled her hand on his arm were deeply green, large, and blatant invitations to accept her confidence. He smiled weakly at the others and allowed himself to be led from the room, turning left in the foyer and down a narrow corridor that crouched beside the staircase. Here there was no light; here was the faint tang of must, luxuriant age, the type of acquiescence to age he imagined was instilled in the great houses of Europe.

Their footsteps were soft on the uncovered flooring.

Elizabeth's breathing the only sound he cared to hear.

He could feel her hand through his jacket, a pressure that wound him around a corner, through a smaller and darker room, to a pair of open French doors and onto a marble veranda.

The wind was gone, the moon less swollen, and the trees at the back of the sprawling tended yard had merged into a serrated silhouette pricked only by the stars.

"They really are dears," Elizabeth said, leaning lightly against him as they watched the night deepening. "But they really do tend to be overenthusiastic sometimes. In a way . . . well, I suppose it's something like fear. Nobody likes to think about the end, isn't that right? Some people exercise until they keel over, thinking they can become immortal if they take the right vitamins. Others, like Kenneth and Zachery, turn so hard to religion that their knees get scars, if you know what I mean." She sniffed, as though testing the air, then put her left hand to her cheek and laughed quietly. "Listen to me, Martin. Honestly, you'd think I had some kind of degree from Harvard or something."

She looked down at him, smiling, and he felt himself leaning closer. A kiss, he thought. Good God, just one lousy kiss.

"But you want to know about the séance, don't you."

No, he tried to tell her with his eyes; I don't give a damn about séances. Just tell me how much you've taken from these people, and how much of it you'll let me share.

The thought didn't shock him. He had met women before who had auras of power and auras of lust—it was the magnetism of self-confidence he usually found easy to divert. But Elizabeth was different. He almost frowned in the attempt to find the words to suit the feeling, and all he could come up with was . . . the woman was different.

She turned to him suddenly and placed a hand on his shoulder. "Tell me something," she said, "are you disappointed that I'm not dressed like a gypsy?" She laughed, dropped her hand, and looked up at the moon. "A lot of them are, you know. And in the beginning we thought it would be fun to give them what they wanted. You know what I mean—the unlighted room, the howling wind, large earrings and odd-looking jewelry . . . everything we could think of. The problem was, they still thought it was all a fake.

"And it isn't, Martin. Not a bit of it is fake. You can poke and snoop all you want, and you won't find a single secret passage, no electronics, no assistants hiding in cupboards."

She clapped her hands suddenly, and he started, realizing how he'd allowed himself to feel the mesmerizing pull of that soft and low voice. He felt silly. He felt she thought him silly. He wished again that he'd skipped over the impulse and left the Station as he'd planned.

"The séance," she said then. "I imagine you expected us to sit around the table and hold hands. Then I would fall into a trance and wait for my contact with the spirit world to get in touch. After that, a few questions about the stock market, the dear departed, some startling revelations about your own life, Martin, that you were sure no one knew but you. Is that what you expected?"

In spite of the fear he would anger her, he nodded.

Instead, she smiled, leaned down and kissed his cheek.

"You're wrong," she said softly. "Oh, not about the table-sitting. That part's right. But everything else isn't, not at all what you were thinking. Can you guess, Martin?" She kissed him again. "Go ahead. Guess."

The tone; it was different. Gone was the soothing texture of silk, the underlying urging to suspend his belief and join in the fun. There was mockery now, a daring, a challenge. He stepped back a pace to see her more clearly, puzzled and unsure how he should respond.

"Oh, Martin," she said in exaggerated sorrow.

All right, he thought angrily, it's time to stop playing games.

He shuddered once, as though shaking off the stuporous effects of the sherry, the drive, the self-pity and weariness he'd allowed to infect and slow him. He allowed himself to think. Of the little man brushing the dust from the cars, of the four people at the table, of their knowing his name; of Elizabeth and the way she looked at him now, a stalking without moving, a wariness born of instinct and caution. He suspected she was trying to decide if she'd pushed him too far, that the so-called séance should have begun before he'd had the chance to question. Now it was too late. The directionless irritation he'd been nurturing all evening found focus, and nothing she or her cohorts could show him would blind him to the fakery he would expose and see in print.

"Oh, Martin." Her voice lower, and deeper.

He snapped his fingers to give himself sound, then brushed past her and made his way quickly through the dark toward the front. It would be easy enough to check through the Station, to find out how many others had come up here to be bilked. It had to be quite a few, or a carefully chosen handful who had money to squander.

He reached the corridor and marched toward the front door.

Stopped at the parlor with a hand stroking his chin.

All five of them, of course, would be in on the sham. All five of them complete with utterly convincing tales of how Elizabeth and her powers had brought them release, or fulfillment, or a lasting peace of mind. It would be for money, most likely, though he imagined Arthur Drummond was trapped also by sex.

His hand moved to scratch at the back of his neck. Excitement made him lick at his lips, made him feel as if he were just about floating. He turned toward the parlor. He wondered how it would be if he called their bluff and accused them to their faces. The reactions would be interesting, and there wasn't a one of them he feared if violence erupted.

Then he frowned, was unsure.

The light in the room was dimmer. The Drummonds, Child, and Longwood were standing by the table, behind the chairs they were in when he'd first entered the house. He had to squint to see them clearly, and took a step closer when he saw what he thought was dust on the table.

Dust on the table . . . dust on the cars.

"Oh, Martin." Deeper, and growling.

Part of the trickery, he told himself quickly. The sherry had been mildly drugged, and Elizabeth had taken him away so they could spread dust on the table, on the carpet, on the walls. So they could change their clothes that in the room's twilight were more now like tatters not even dared to be called rags.

They all smiled, and Longwood beckoned, and the tips of his fingers were not flesh but yellowed bone.

The light brightened for a moment—they had no eyes—then faded to dark—they had no *eyes*—and he whirled around just as Elizabeth reached toward him—skin taut and tearing, lips smiling and shredding, blouse rustling and rotting. He threw himself backward, felt a knob punch at his hip. He grabbed it, turned it, and flung the door open. Leaped off the stoop and ran down the walk, not bothering to stop at the fourth car in the line, not bothering to scream at the black moth still dusting.

Later, he promised himself as he ran down the hill, he would find out how they did it. For now, however, he had to admit that what they had done was effective—they had lulled him, and frightened him, then driven him from the house because they knew he would expose them.

But it was a good idea, he thought as he neared the trees. It was obvious the séance had been over long before he'd arrived, and they wanted him to think it was *he* they had summoned, not the ghost of a friend, or an aunt, or a sorely missed spouse.

Because he was still alive, and they were . . . not quite dead.

Elizabeth had given him the clue if he'd been thinking—nobody likes to think about the end.

So somehow he was supposed to believe they would use him in some horrid way to keep themselves . . . not dying.

He tripped over a shadow and sprawled in the road, and the burning in his palms felt curiously reassuring.

He stood, swayed, and started running again. The cold air a brace that held rigid his fear, a fear he couldn't shake in spite of his reason.

Tomorrow, of course, it would be different in the sun; and he would come back for his car and search the house if he could. Because Elizabeth had lied when she told him "no electronics," and he wanted to have pictures of whatever gimmicks they'd used.

He slowed.

Tomorrow . . . in the sun.

He stopped.

He put his hands hard to his hips and bent over slightly, waiting for the air to return to his lungs. He felt stupid and was glad he hadn't brought anyone with him. Foolish because the con he'd been seeking had worked only too well. He looked over his shoulder, and the mansion was dark, the cars in the drive deeper shadows against the night.

There was no sound at all but the rasp of his breathing.

He spat dryly and shook his head, wishing for the first time in months that he hadn't quit smoking. Then, annoyed with himself because he was still playing the mark, he decided there was no reason at all why he shouldn't drive home.

He turned around and scowled.

And the moon was a ghost in the house of night—silent, stained, setting free the shadow that rose in his path, setting free the first sound he'd uttered since his coming.

He screamed.

"Oh . . . Martin."

TALES FROM HAWTHORNE STREET

THE GENTLE PASSING OF A HAND

There must have been a hundred kids in Ellie DePaul's backyard, back then on her birthday; everybody from Hawthorne Street it seemed like, and the rest from places I hadn't even heard of. While I was getting dressed that morning I heard Aunt Helen saying to Uncle Steve it was a waste of good money, but I just thought it was plain and simple silly. Ellie had just turned ten, but you'd think she was the stupid Queen of England the way people were fussing over her. It was making me sick to my stomach. I was only ten then, too, but you didn't see people acting that way around me.

Of course, that was then—before I learned about my hand.

The way Ellie's mother set it up, we had to sit on those little wooden chairs that fold up when you're done with them, and I had to sit on the end in the back row because of my leg that I had to keep straight sort of. I could have adjusted the brace, I guess, but I didn't feel like it. Ellie was prancing around in a pink dress and a pink ribbon in her hair, and I almost couldn't stand it she was acting so bad. So I kept the brace tight and kept my leg out, hoping all the time she would prance by and trip over me so her mother would scold her and I could pretend how bad it hurt.

She didn't, though, so I had to be good, even though I would've rather have been back in my room, thinking about . . . things.

Actually, I didn't mind sitting in the back. I could see pretty good, because the yard bunched up into a little hill there before it sloped down to the river, and all the big kids had to sit on the ground in front so the little kids didn't have to stand up. And way down there at the bottom was the Great And Astounding Albert, doing his tricks in a black suit that made him look like he was going to a wedding.

"Nothing up this sleeve," he said, his handlebar mustache making him look like a gorilla, "and nothing up this sleeve." And the next thing you know he had a little bird in his hand or a blown-up balloon or flowers or miles and miles and miles of pretty ribbons and streamers.

Mrs. DePaul and my aunt were sitting on the ground right behind me, and after a while I could hear Ellie's mother whisper, "Oh, dear, do you think he's having a good time?"

And my aunt said, "Sure he is. Why do you say that, Alice?"

"Well, he seems so . . . so solemn, I guess. Damn, you don't think anybody was teasing him, do you? About, well, you know."

"No, dear, he hasn't been teased, believe me." And she sighed like she does when Uncle Steve tickles her in the hall. "He's just studying, that's all."

I didn't turn around, but my aunt was right. Right then, right there in the backyard with the hundred kids and the million trees and all the cake and ice cream in the whole world sitting there on the card table, I decided I wanted to be a magician when I grew up. I couldn't play ball or anything like that because of my leg, and my mother always told me that the best person you could be was the person who was nice to other people all the time. Well, the Great And Astounding Albert must have been a nice person, because he was making us all laugh and clap, and he was giving out pretty things and winking at the girls, so I spent the whole time trying to see how he did it.

Nothing up this sleeve, and nothing up this sleeve.

Jay, I told myself then, you could really do that if you tried, you really could.

So the minute Aunt Helen took me home and supper was over, I went into my room and I practiced. I stood in front of the mirror and tried to figure out how the Great And Astounding Albert got all those birds and ribbons and things from his sleeve. It had to be a trick, though, because there's no such thing as magic, and when I couldn't do it I almost cried. I almost gave up. But I didn't. When you have a leg like mine and you can't be like other people, you don't give up just because you want to cry. You try and try again, just like my mother told me. Try and try again.

So I did.

I took spoons from the kitchen and sticks from the yard, and I put them up my sleeve and tried to make them drop into my hand just like the magic man did. It never worked. And by the time two weeks was gone I was moping around the house and not eating and just making myself miserable. That was silly, I know, and I should have gone to Uncle Steve right away, but I wasn't real used to him yet.

See, it was raining one night, and my mother and father and my three sisters and me, we were coming home from the restaurant where we always go when something good happens at my father's store. Then all of a sudden there was this tree and a lot of light that hurt my eyes and a lot of darkness that hurt me, too. And the next thing I knew I was in this funny-smelling bed in this funny-smelling room, and lots of people in white were standing around, and Helen and Steve were there in the corner.

Helen was crying. Steve wasn't smiling.

They told me mother and father and Marlene and Deirdre and Ginny had passed away in the accident. That means they were dead. I knew that, and it hurt for a long time. It still does, at night, when my covers need tucking in and Aunt Helen tries to do it but she doesn't do it the way my mother used to do it and . . . well, it just isn't the same. I know that because I heard Uncle Steve say that one night when I was supposed to be asleep instead of going to the bathroom.

"Damnit, Helen, I feel sorry for the boy, you know I do, and Frank was my brother, for God's sake, so I have an obligation. But that still doesn't change the fact that you and I hadn't planned on children, and suddenly we've got one ten years old, and a cripple at that. I mean, it just isn't fair."

He really isn't mean, but he doesn't understand, sometimes.

So it was a while before I told him what I wanted to do, and after he looked at me funny for a minute he grabbed me up from the floor and took me out to the car. We went right downtown to this gigantic bookstore, and Steve picked out four or five magic books he thought I'd understand.

On the way home he said, "It's funny, Jay, but there was a time when I wanted to be a magician, too."

"So why didn't you?"

He shrugged a little. "I guess I didn't want it badly enough. See, when you grow up and you have to decide what it is you want to do with your life, you really have to want it badly enough or it isn't going to work. If you want to be a doctor, you have to realize there's an awful lot of school to go through—"

"Boy, I sure wouldn't want that."

"—and money and things like that. Or if you want to be a teacher you have different things to learn. Or a writer or a—"

"Magic man," I said, grinning.

"Right," he said. "A magic man." Then he reached over and touched me on the leg. "Now you listen to me, pal—this magic stuff is hard work. It takes a long time to get right, and I don't want you to give up."

"Oh, I won't," I promised. "I'm going to be the best magic man in the whole world when I grow up."

He didn't say anything for a while. Then: "Why, Jay? Why magic?"

"I don't know," I said. "Because it's nice."

And it was work. Boy, it was hard work. Some things I couldn't do because my fingers were too short or I didn't have the right hidden things and I couldn't make them or buy them because I hadn't saved enough. But I got pretty good with cards and the shell trick and the coin trick and things like that. And every night I would show Helen and Steve a new trick, and they would applaud and ask me how I did it. I never told. I never told them once. You never tell a trick or it isn't magic anymore.

But I still couldn't get anything to come out of my sleeve.

Then it was May, and I was sitting out in back, wishing our house was on the river like Ellie's. I was wearing shorts because it felt good on my leg—though I still couldn't look at it all pink and shrively like that—and I was trying to get a pebble out of my sleeve without lowering my arm. The kitchen window was right over my head, and it was a while before I realized they were arguing in there.

"Well, I don't care," she said, like she was about to start crying. "I just don't care."

"Helen, please be reasonable." And I could see without seeing him that he was standing with one hand on his hip and the other shoved in his hair, with this look on his face like nobody ever listens to anything he says. "Helen, this is the chance we've been waiting for, and we simply cannot take Jay with us."

"But why not?"

"Damnit, Helen, use your head! Kuwait isn't London, y'know. It may have tons of money, but it isn't the kind of place I'd want the boy to grow up in. It'll be at least a year, and he's barely hanging in school as it is. God, doesn't he have enough problems?"

"We could get tutors."

"Helen."

"We . . ."

I couldn't hear anymore for a while, but it didn't matter. The sun went cold, and the trees seemed like they were covered in ice. I snapped my brace back on and walked out to the street. Ellie and a few others were playing hopscotch on the sidewalk across the way, but when they called to me I didn't answer. I didn't feel like it. They only played with me because their mothers told them to. Not all of them; some of them. And it was hard to tell from one day to another which ones it was.

So I walked for a couple of blocks until I was in front of the luncheonette, looking at the pictures of the sundaes and sodas that were all white from the sun. Then this man walked out, and before I knew I grabbed his arm to stop him. It was the Great And Astounding Albert, only he didn't look so great or astounding without his wedding suit or his mustache.

"Mr. Albert," I said, and then I saw what I was doing, so I tried a smile that felt real silly and backed away from him.

He stared down at me from about a mile up, frowning like he thought he should know me but he didn't. We stood there for a couple of seconds before I told him where I was from and where I saw him, and he smiled and nodded as if he'd guessed it all along. And when I told him I was going to be a magic man when I grew up, he put a hand on my shoulder and took me inside where he lifted me onto a red counter stool, and we each had a double ice-cream soda while he told me all the places he'd been and the famous people he'd known, and how all the other magic men used to come see him but now they don't anymore.

It was the first time I noticed how old he was.

"It's hard, Jay," he said, suddenly sad and looking tired. "I've lost the knack, it seems, to make the grown-ups believe."

"But it's all tricks, isn't it?"

"Sure it is. But the real trick is to make it look like it isn't a trick, but magic."

I thought about that for a moment, not really understanding. Then we talked some more, and he reached out and pulled a dollar bill from behind my ear. I brushed a hand through my hair and laughed, and before I knew it I was telling him how I couldn't pull anything out of my sleeve because every time I let my arm down the things would fall out. Well, he looked really serious at me for a while, and I was afraid I'd said something to get him mad. There were other people coming in and out and buying the papers and smiling at me like they knew me, but I didn't pay them any attention because just then the Great And Astounding Albert held up his arm and pulled down the cuff of his jacket and said, "What do you see up there, boy?"

I kind of leaned forward and squinted. "Air."

He snapped his arm straight out and I ducked, frowned, looked up the sleeve again and said, "Still air."

Then he made a pass in front of me, slow and gentle, like a snake charming a robin. Slow and gentle before he cupped his hand like there was something in it. I waited, and one by one his fingers opened. "Now what do you see?"

I didn't know what to say. "Air."

"And that's all there ever is, son. Air. Everything else comes from someplace else, and there's nothing up my sleeve but air." He closed his fingers again, blew on them, opened them and said, "What's there now?"

It was getting awfully silly. "Air."

"See? Now you try it."

Well, I thought he was kind of crazy being so old, but he told me again so I rubbed my hands together, made the same moves he did as best I could, and pulled air from my sleeve, making the kind of trumpet sound with my lips like they do on television when the elephant disappears. Then Albert laughed and I laughed, and before I knew it I'd made the slow pass in front of the waitress's face and tucked the air back in my sleeve. She giggled and started to cough, but I was excited because I suddenly knew what Albert was saying about tricks and magic, and I thanked him politely because my mother always told me to be polite, then I slid off the stool and hurried home as fast as I could.

Ellie and the others were still playing hopscotch, and when they saw me run-hobbling like that they thought something was wrong so they ran across the street. I told them not to worry, though, and before I could stop myself I had shown them my trick.

"Hey, that's not magic," she said, twisting up her face like she'd eaten something terrible.

"That's what you think," I told her, then ran-hobbled inside and went straight to my room. I practiced. I practiced hard. And after dinner that night I told Helen and Steve I was going to put on a big show for them.

"Jay, I'm really not in the mood," Steve said. "I've had a bad day."

"Oh, Steve," Helen said. Her eyes weren't normal; they were all red and swollen, and I knew it was because of the things I'd heard.

"Hey," I said, "it's all right, don't worry. I'm going to be such a great magic man that Uncle Steve can stay home and he can tell his boss to—" And I snapped my fingers in the air.

I thought they would laugh.

They didn't.

Steve only got a funny red in his face, and Helen started to cry again. Then Steve put his hands around my waist and pulled me close and said, "Jay, there's no better boy in the whole world than you. And I swear, if I ever regretted having you with us I take it all back." I think he was going to cry, too, but he swallowed hard and didn't. "But son, this is the most important part of my career right now. If I make this move and do a good job, I'm going to be the most important man in the office. And when your aunt and I—"

The telephone rang. Helen went to answer it, but Steve kept on talking. I didn't hear him, though. There was a noise in my head, like the ocean makes when you listen at a seashell. I was trying with all my might to know what he was saying to me, but all I got was that I was going to stay at a place called Greenbriar until they came back from the Arabs—and that was going to be a very long time. I didn't like that, and I tried to tell him my magic trick was all we ever needed, but just then Helen came back.

"What is it, love?" Steve said, pushing me back a little and getting up.

"That was Alice." She looked at me and I looked back and all of a sudden she was on her knees and hugging me, telling me it was going to be all right, dear, and it happened sometimes, and it sure was a long time before I figured out that Ellie had gone to where my parents and my sisters had gone, that night in the rain.

Helen thought I was going to feel bad, but I didn't. Ellie wasn't a family person. She was the little girl who lived on the other side of Hawthorne Street, and there are lots of little girls like that around here, so I was sorry for Ellie's mother instead. But I wasn't all that sad about it. I just said that if they didn't want to see my new trick because of Ellie's mother then that was all right, and Helen said would I mind waiting a day or so, so I said no, that was okay.

The next day in school the teacher had us all say a prayer to God for Ellie and Jenny and Eddie and Sissy and Kristy, and then the nurse came in and looked at our tongues and felt our necks and foreheads, and a couple of the kids were sent home to their doctors. I was glad I didn't have to go home, because it was hard for me in school some days since I missed a lot whenever I had to go into the hospital for the operations to fix the bones and muscles in my leg.

I did all my work the best way I knew how, got a gold star for my spelling and a silver one for arithmetic, and brought the papers home to show Helen and Steve.

But there was no one in the kitchen, and no one in the backyard, so I decided to go upstairs and practice my new magic. I was almost

SMITH

in my room when I heard the noise down the hall. It sounded like laughing, but the kind of laughing you get because something hurts but not bad enough to cry. I was scared. I didn't want anyone to be sick, or go where mother and father went, so I ran down there and opened the door.

Steve and Helen were in the bed. Steve was on top of my aunt, and he was naked. And she was shaking her head all over the pillow and making those laughing-hurt noises, and I didn't know what to do so I just stood there until Helen opened her eyes and made a kind of squeak, like a mouse. Steve rolled off her and pulled the sheet up to his stomach.

"What the hell do you think you're doing?" He was mad, real mad. "Explain yourself, Jay. Why were you watching us?"

I tried to think as fast as I could, and the only thing I could think of was the magic. So I started to talk, so fast I couldn't understand what I was saying. And while I talked I went over to the bed and winked at Aunt Helen and made a slow and gentle pass in front of Steve, and tucked the air up my sleeve.

"What," he said, "the hell was that supposed to be?"

I blinked. "Magic."

He looked at Helen, but she only shrugged and tried to smile.

When he looked back to me, though, he wasn't smiling at all. "Jay, I don't know what to say to you. What you've done . . ." He swallowed, and I thought he was going to cry again. He coughed and punched his chest. "You've got to learn . . . you've got . . ." He frowned, then reached out and pushed me away. I fell back against the wall he pushed me so hard, but I didn't cry because the next thing I knew he was lying on the floor, his legs all tangled in the sheets and his face so blue it was almost purple.

Aunt Helen screamed.

So I screamed, too. But when I went over so she could hold me and tell me what was wrong, she crawled away like I was some kind of snake or something, screaming and shrieking and making my head ache. I ran away. I should have stayed there and taken care of her, but I couldn't stand all the screaming because I had heard the screaming before, at night, in the rain, while the fire came in the car and took my parents away.

I heard footsteps on the stairs a few minutes later. A lot of people running in and out. A doctor came in and checked me over, and it wasn't until I slipped off the bed and went into the hall that I heard someone say Uncle Steve was dead. I don't know what the word was, but it means you don't have any air left in your lungs.

I looked down at my hand. I looked up and saw Aunt Helen in her pink bathrobe watching me. Alice was standing beside her, and she was watching me, too.

"I don't want Uncle Steve dead," I said, feeling the tears and the bump inside my chest.

A policeman came by, and another doctor, and they all started talking. And I started thinking. It wasn't very hard, though, to know what the Great And Astounding Albert had taught me, and I felt so bad that I could barely see through all the crying. I started to walk down the hall, down to Steve's bedroom, and no one paid any attention to me. Helen was making little sounds, and the policeman and the doctor were talking very quietly, and Mrs. DePaul was somewhere there, so no one saw me when I went into the room.

There was a stretcher on the floor. And two doctors were kneeling by Uncle Steve's body, looking like they were getting ready to put him on this green plastic stuff that looked like a garbage bag. I didn't want Steve in a garbage bag. I didn't want him dead. So when the men turned around I went over there and knelt beside him and took his hand and put it next to my cheek, and I promised him I would never do magic again. Then I took the air from the sleeve and made a slow and gentle pass in front of his face. The doctors yelled at me, Helen screamed again, and suddenly everyone was jumping around and pushing me away and Steve was sitting up with a nothing look in his face.

A nothing look. Nothing behind his eyes, and spit coming out of his mouth, and he wet himself like a baby while Helen fell to the floor.

And there was no one left to take care of me.

They took Aunt Helen and Uncle Steve away in an ambulance. Then a nice woman in a green dress said she was from the town and would see that I wouldn't be alone anymore.

And that's how I came to Greenbriar.

A lot of brick buildings and kids like me who have something wrong with their legs or their arms or they can't get out of bed; teachers and classrooms and lots of television and special ways to play ball. Every Saturday afternoon they show movies in the little theater. Every Saturday night and on holidays someone comes to do a show, like cowboy singers and clowns and people with animals . . . and a whole lot of magicians.

On Sundays there's visitors.

But no one for me. Uncle Steve is in a place like mine, only I don't think it's as much fun, and no one will tell me what happened to Aunt Helen. The kids from my old school don't come at all, and I'll bet that's because their mothers won't let them.

And maybe it's wrong, but I don't care. I have my own little room and I practice every night. And as soon as I know I'm good enough, I'll go away. I know exactly where I'm going and what I'm going to do. See, it isn't any fun to be the best magic man in the world if nobody wants to see you. So I'm going to this place way down on the other side of the park on Hawthorne Street. I'm going to do slow and gentle passes. Then Marlene and Deirdre and Ginny and father will come home with me, just like always.

And mother, of course, because she was always my friend.

Like Uncle Steve said—if you want it bad enough, you can do it. And I want this very badly. After all, who's going to stop me?

With nothing up this sleeve, and nothing up this sleeve . . . but lots and lots of air.

WHEN ALL THE CHILDREN CALL MY NAME

Poe asked the question: *Is all that we see or seem but a dream within a dream?*

No. But I wish it was.

And in the meantime, in the waiting . . . another drink, another cigarette—one follows the other like sip and swallow as I look out over the porch to the fence, and the gate. In darkness.

In memories.

It used to be, this time of year, a season of excitement for me, when my skin tingled and my blood sped its youth—when you knew how much better it felt to go from cold to warm than hot to cool. Fireplaces and hearths and a warm soothing brandy meant something then, and mufflers and blankets fresh from the attic trunk and the soft easy comfort of a grumbling furnace. It all meant something then, just as it all means something now; but the difference between something and something is a years-long crossing, and if I could only find a detour I might have missed, maybe then I could go to bed.

I retired from the force nearly five years ago, long before the age when my uniform and waistline would label me dinosaur. I wanted to travel, to experience, to obey the cliché of doing that which I had never done before it was too late, and remember it with fondness. So I did, and I did, and when I returned to the village nothing had changed that I could see, and there were no deaths that surprised me.

Last spring it was, then, when I was offered a part-time job as a guard/confessor/patcher-of-wounds in a small playground on the far side of town.

It was a dastardly move old Greshton made. He knew I'd be chafing as soon as I grew tired of bending over the roses that thorned and the apple trees that bore fruit despite my clumsiness and the delusion that I knew what I was doing.

"Kit," he said not two weeks after I'd returned, "I'll be honest with you. Nobody wants to do it for the money we're offering."

"Well, I wouldn't either, Marve," I said, "except that I might run against you next fall, and I'll need your vote."

He laughed, a single explosion of sound that threatened to clear his desk of its clutter. Then he tugged at an earlobe, pushed a hand through the wisps of hair clinging defiantly to the memory of their fullness. He'll make that gesture when he finally loses it all, I thought, and every time he does he'll look surprised when his fingers don't find anything.

I reached over to pluck a cigar from his humidor and stuck it into my jacket pocket. "But I'll take it, Marve, as long as I don't have to wear a uniform."

"Well, I don't know about that," he hedged. "There are regulations, you know. And even if you are an old friend, we can't go making exceptions. The younger ones might not understand. Why, the Park Commissioner—"

"Hell," I said, "you're the Park Commissioner, and the Sanitation Commissioner, and the—"

"All right, all right," he said. "But carry something with you, okay?"

I frowned, puzzled. "What do you mean, something? What do you think's going to happen out there, a riot because the swings break down, for crying out loud?"

Marve pulled off his glasses and rubbed them vigorously against his shirt. "Big kids," he said, blinking through his myopia as if he resented my independence of artificial lenses. "They like to come around and bother the little ones. You know what they're like, Kit. Carry something in your pocket, just in case."

I would have argued, but the morning was fading and I had an appointment. I agreed to find something menacing, and harmless, and we shook hands as we always did, in silence. But as I left the office, a trick of shadows that had no business being where they were halved his age to an ambitious thirty. It was a disturbing moment because I seldom remembered how old we were, always overlooked the added fold beneath the eye, the turkey-wrinkle under the chin. Not that Marve and I kidded ourselves—with his sixty and my fifty-five—but neither did we spend our evenings in regretful lament. He was too busy being mayor and all the rest of it in a town just the right size for people like us, too busy watching his grandchildren grow and leave and return in the pages of hastily written letters.

And me, I was too busy planning my campaign.

Why is it, I wondered as I hurried outside, that men always seem to look at women as objects of a military campaign? As if they were instinctively the enemy, and we the brash young majors who would storm them into submission.

Ridiculous posturing, I thought as I stepped into the Franklin Inn. And yet I paused to allow my eyes adjustment as they scanned the faces of the luncheon customers: a throwback reaction to the days of my beat when I was the Wichita marshal seeking trouble and danger in the local saloon.

Immediately I realized what I was doing, however, I grinned and shook my head, moved hurriedly to the back-wall booth where Catherine was waiting.

Though she was the first one I'd called after my return three weeks before, I hadn't had the nerve to see her until now. Slender, dark-haired still, aware that an inch of pancake no matter how artfully applied to a fifty-year-old face was always an inch of pancake. I'd been gone for nearly two years, and the measure of my fear of finding things changed sent my glance instantly to her left hand. Ringless. To her faintly red lip. Smiling. She half rose and I gallantly waved her down, snapped my fingers for a waitress, and ordered our drinks without consultation.

"Is that the way they do it in France?" she said. She took a cigarette from her purse, screwed it into an amber filter, and waited for me to light it. Not impatient. Bemused, because she knew it annoyed me when her match flared before mine.

"France, Belgium, Italia—they're all the same to me," I said in mock boredom.

"And the women," she said.

"Scrawny, busty, no hips, and no sense of humor."

She pouted her sympathy. "Oh, poor Kit, he couldn't pick one up, could he? You mean to say they weren't impressed by your policeman's record? Your exploits in the colonies?"

"More by the size of my traveler's checks," I said. "And I suppose you were similarly besieged? Dansworth pounding on your door, Falkner chasing you around your desk, Greshton cheating on his wife and holding secret trysts in a luxury motel?"

She nodded, and blew smoke into my face. "Take that, dirty old man."

"Dirty, yes," I said, and left the other unspoken. A finger reached out and traced a cross on the back of my hand. The waitress set down our order and, with a smile of recognition when I spoke to her by name, hurried off to leave us wrapped in the dim light, the dark wood, the quiet conversations that drifted without touching us. We were silent, and said much; we ate as though there could be no further intimacy. Wine, then, and we toasted.

"And how are things at the paper?" I asked. "The weekly scandals keeping you busy?"

She shrugged. Being secretary and jack-of-all-trades to the editor of a small-town newssheet, she once told me, wasn't nearly as glamorous as being a hooker, but definitely more promising than hushing kids in a library.

"Well, I myself have a new job," I said when she couldn't offer me gossip. "I just saw Marve and he thought I'd make a great Chief of Police."

"You're kidding."

"Yeah," I said, and grinned. "Actually, he wants me to babysit a playground."

"You don't mean the one on Hawthorne Street?"

"That's right! How'd you know that was the one?"

She fussed with the ashes of her cigarette, took a nervous puff and sent the smoke toward her lap. "Well, a lucky guess. It's the only one I know of not watched by a school guard." She faked a smile and brushed a strand of hair back behind one ear. "Aren't you superstitious?"

"About what, a playground?"

"For God's sake, Kit, haven't you talked to anyone since you got back? Didn't Marve tell you?"

I blinked stupidly and shook my head.

"Just around the time you came back," she said, "one of the kids was murdered there."

"Here? Murder?" My voice rose and I coughed to cover my embarrassment. Our community wasn't pristine, but murder was something usually relegated to old maids' nightmares.

"A young boy, fifteen. He was found by his mother."

"Jesus," I whispered. "How?"

"I don't know. Nobody's talked. Chief Dansworth had the mother and the body out of there before anyone knew what had happened. All he gave the paper was a statement."

My first reaction was suspicious disbelief. In all the time I'd worked for him, Danny had never held anything back from anyone with a vested interest in police work. That he was refusing cooperation with Falkner's admittedly minor newspaper seemed not only out of character, it was just plain wrong. But he did it, and was doing it, and Falkner was apparently willing to wait. It must have been a particularly brutal slaying, however, because not even the coroner was willing to discuss the condition of the body.

"Dumb," I said finally. "Danny knows better than to act that way. Maybe if I went—"

Catherine smiled tolerant encouragement, like a pat on the head. "It's over," she said. "The family's moved to New England, and as far as I can tell, your former cellmates are only going through the motions, praying for a miracle. You, on the other hand, are going back on the front lines, and you'd better get in shape." She stared pointedly at my stomach, which, while not quite barreled yet, was at last hinting in that direction.

"No problem," I said, slapping my chest and flexing my biceps.

"I can still handle any kid who wants to test my reputation. But now I know why Marve wants me to carry something."

"Something?" she said. "What's that mean?"

"For Marve, it could mean anything from a tank to a derringer."

I could see she wanted to second the motion, but I forestalled her by rising and holding her coat while she slipped into it. We walked, then, until it was time for her to return to the office, and at our parting she made me promise to call her that night. And every night, though she wouldn't say it.

Nice girl, I thought as I headed for home; and I must have been smiling because people kept giving me the oddest looks as they passed me.

I wasn't supposed to start work until the weekend was over, but a light Sunday rain turned the hours into years and I fled the house before I began screaming. I walked, to renew my acquaintance with the neighborhood, my old beat, the stores downtown. And though I didn't know precisely what to expect, I was rather disappointed that nothing drastic had altered. A few new houses here and there, two shops replaced by two others—but otherwise I could have just slept for two weeks for all that the traveling did to make things different.

Disappointed, then, but oddly pleased that I had no more culture shocks to absorb as I slipped back into my living.

And not surprisingly, I ended up on Hawthorne Street.

The playground was small, a couple of acres on a corner, surrounded by a twelve-foot cyclone fence, bordered by woodland on the two sides not touched by streets. In its center were a half-dozen oaks so rich in their foliage the green looked like cloud, and their shadows midnight. At the base of the trees the earth had been undisturbed except to admit a concrete bench, but the rest of the area had been paved over with a blacktop supposedly softer to land on; somehow, though, a skinned knee tinged with dirt was more natural than a torn elbow with bits of black clinging to it. Progress, I thought, and turned my attention to the far-rear corner and the swings and slides, jungle gyms and seesaws; they had been painted recently and mocked the sun in their gaiety, and seemed rather pathetic without children clambering all over them. The remainder of the area was open. For baseball, I supposed, and touch and those screaming games of tag that jar your nerves and make you want to join rather than leave them.

Then I stepped closer to the fence.

There was a lone sliding board beyond the swings, one of many, but the only one that faced directly into the corner. Mats of some kind had been fastened to the fence, battered now by the weather and the kids who charged down the metal slope and slammed into their protection. Some mother's idea, no doubt, to keep her fragile son from jamming his head between the links. I grinned, turned for home, and saw four children walking quickly toward me.

Now, two years is a millennium when children are growing, but I didn't need help recognizing these; and they knew me right away. The eldest was Darlene the redhead, followed like an entourage by Miffy the brunette, Tim the freckled, and finally, lagging as usual and vociferous about it, Stevie—who spent more time biting people's legs than his meals. They were glad to see me, and I them—they'd been regular features on my beat since the day each had been born. We grew up together, so to speak, and they were laughing when they ran up to hug me.

Now, damnit, I thought as I crouched to receive them, leaned back against the fence to consider the smiles and the grins and the giggles they gave me—now, damnit, I'm home!

"How do you like our place?" Darlene said. As scrawny as the others, if it hadn't been for her Celtic green eyes I would have sworn she was a boy.

"Your place?" I said. "That's funny, but I thought everyone could use it."

"Anyone can," Tim said from behind his freckles. "If we let them."

"Oh, now that's really big of you," I said, poking at Steve, who was eyeing my thigh. "And I suppose you charge a fee, right? Come on, now, I know you better. You make the little kids give you pennies, right?"

"Not me," Steve said.

"You they wouldn't dare touch or you'd eat them for lunch," I laughed, and he darted behind Miffy's back, peered around her and grinned with his thumb in his mouth.

"How come you're here?" said Darlene.

"Who, me? Well, I like the swings."

"You're too big," Miffy said, and pushed at my arm.

"Well, maybe. Actually, I'm going to be working here starting tomorrow."

"You can't work here," said Tim. "There's nothing to do."

"Sure there is. I'm going to beat you guys up when you get into trouble."

"Are you going to be a cop again?" Miffy asked, wide-eyed and tugging at Darlene's elbow. "Are you going to arrest people?"

"Only if they try to steal from you," I said. "Nope, just keep an eye on things is all. Like I used to."

"But Mr. Craig, how—"

A faint shouting distracted us. I rose, stiffly, and looked through the oak stand to a group of boys no older than seventeen scaling the fence. The first one to reach the ground began tossing a football into the air, laughing and waving at his friends. Dressed as I was in civilian clothes, I didn't think any orders of mine to vacate the place would be appreciated, much less obeyed, so I only watched until I knew I'd recognize them again if I saw them on the street.

On the street.

Come on, Christopher, I scolded myself; you're no more a policeman now than the sun is the moon.

It was a bad feeling. Like looking over your shoulder and finding a fine-edged knife protruding from your spine.

I hunched my shoulders and turned to leave, stopped when I saw Darlene and the others leaning against the fence. If looks could kill, I thought.

"You kids interested in some ice cream or something?"

They declined without looking up. I shrugged and tried to console them by explaining that things like this invasion wouldn't happen again while I was on the job. "They have their own places to mess with, don't worry. When they see I'm back they won't bother you, okay?"

They said nothing.

"Okay?"

"Okay," said Darlene, took Stevie by the hand and led them all away. I waited as they rounded the corner, keeping close to the fence, then vanished beyond the trees. I stayed for a few minutes longer to watch the game, feeling my muscles tense and relax as passes were caught, end runs were made, touchdowns sent them into screaming hysterics. Their language wasn't the language I remembered using at their age, but then nothing is the same when you outgrow a playground.

Finally, stomach growling, I left for the roast I had simmering in the oven. Something about the group disturbed me, but I didn't realize what it was until I had cleaned up after eating. There had been five of the boys, and for some inexplicable and unpleasant reason, I knew without proof that they were incomplete. I wish I'd known why then, but one of the boys was missing.

And when I mentioned it, laughingly, to Marve a few days later, he nodded thoughtfully. And not without some guilt.

"Gary George," he said. "He was part of that long-haired mob."

"Was?"

"I thought you knew already. He was killed a few weeks ago, right there in the playground."

I kicked myself for forgetting what Catherine had told me, but when I pressed him for more details he was evasive and told me it was over and done. One of those small-town tragedies that never seem to be solved.

"But how is the job?" he said. "Not too difficult for your feet, I hope."

"If you're subtly and cleverly asking me if I'm still in shape to keep standing all day, then don't worry. I'm doing just fine. Besides, I use the bench a lot. Read, and it's right where I can see everything that's going on."

"No problems?"

"Come on, Marve, what the hell kind of problems could I have? Look, this whole job is featherbedding and you know it. There are more mothers there than kids. More carriages than I've seen in my whole life. Listen, those women can outscream the whole damned police department when it comes to spotting a kid even thinking about doing something wrong."

"All right, all right," he said. "Don't get excited."

I wasn't, and I told him so, and we finished our dinner, had a few drinks, and went back to his house to get drunk on the sofa.

Just like the old days.

When one of us was young.

So passed July and August and the first three weeks of September.

Catherine and I saw each other several times a week, usually for dinner and a drive to the movies. It was a drifting game we were playing, and a purposeful one—the widow and the widower still clinging to their prime. Sooner or later we'd steady the current and stop at Marve's office so he could say the words. Sooner or later. In the meantime, however, we drifted and gossiped and remembered with lessening pain the way it had been with spouses long gone.

That playground, on the other hand, was becoming a trial.

Not because of the sullen summer heat that defied even the shade, slowed tag to a walk, made slides and swings unbearable to touch.

And not because of the others who shattered the humidity with shrill warning shrieks.

The kids, led by Darlene and Tim, accepted me rapidly, and once in a while I joined in their sport. They were often, as kids have a habit of being, cruel to each other and laughing friends five minutes later. Unbrainwashed by the adult scheme of things, they played in what I'd often thought to be the real world, as opposed to those playlets we acted in each day. But they were never cruel to me, not even unintentionally. They brought me cones when that ice-cream man jangled his infernal bells twice a day; they told me stories of their playmates and their birthdays and their visiting aunts; and once Miffy brought wrapped in a napkin a piece of a cake her mother had made.

We did fine.

It was the teenagers who consistently threw rocks into our pond.

Greshton's Law, tacit but enforced, warned the older kids to keep to the schoolyards, which were always opened from midmorning to past dark. But the friends of the late Gary George refused to acknowledge the mayor's warnings, my threats, even the occasional passing of a mobile patrol. They persisted in swaggering through the gates each morning, confronting me with muttered taunts, and generally hanging on just long enough for my stomach to cry out for antacids before taking a swipe at Miffy or Steve and racing off.

When El Daniels ran away from home the group became four; and worse: belligerent. And one September Saturday they bowled over at least a dozen of my little people before running out of reach.

The following week, however, I saw them sneaking over the fence by the slide's corner. One had caught his jeans on a jagged shard of metal, and I ran over to grab his leg and yank him down. The others raced back into the woods, but this one I had and I wouldn't let go.

"All right, Davey," I said, holding his arm and walking him back to my bench. "Let's have a seat and a talk."

"Ain't nothing to talk about."

"Davey," I said, trying and failing to make his eyes meet mine, "when I was a cop and your house was along my patrol, you were a pretty good kid. You never gave anyone trouble, ever. So what in hell is going on around here? You know the rules. Why are you wasting your time hassling a bunch of kids just out of diapers?"

Despite Marve's description, Davey didn't have long hair. It was tightly curled and nearly covered his ears, but it stayed clear of his shoulders and gleamed with constant washing. He was a slight boy, fighting to grow a mustache and losing, determined that the tighter his shirts the more attractive he would be to the opposite sex. He was proud, but I had never known him to be arrogant.

"You know about Gary, right?"

Only it took him several minutes to speak to me. First he stared at the children gathered around the corner slide; then he worked at his hands for a while before brushing nervously at his hair. I knew it wasn't me. Black going grey, pudgy after a summer's good eating, dressed in comfortable old clothes that fit me loosely; imposing I wasn't, so I knew it wasn't me.

"You know about Gary, right?"

I nodded.

"You heard about El, too?"

"Sure I did, but what do they—"

He jerked his head toward the children. Playing jacks. Catch. On the swings. No one used that corner slide, but I had become accustomed to that. I think it was because of the mats—it took all the fun out of getting hurt.

"They did it."

"Davey, damnit—"

"Well, they did, Mr. Craig, honest! I wouldn't lie to you."

"Oh, sure they did." Already he was beginning to annoy me. "And after they murdered poor Gary, they kidnapped El and took him to their hideout in the hills, right? Come off it, Davey!"

He stood, his face lifted to catch the leaves' fragmentary shadows. "They don't like us, Mr. Craig, and—"

"Well, I don't blame them. After what you guys do to them, what do you want, an invitation to a party?"

"You don't understand."

"Oh, get the hell out of here," I said, waving him away in disgust. "You're as bad as they are. And stay away from here, you understand?" I called after him. "Stay where you belong and don't bother us anymore."

He ran, not looking back, and when I glanced over to the children they were laughing, and applauding. I grinned, rose in a half-bow, and went back to my book I kept under the bench. But I wasn't able to concentrate. Davey, no matter how he'd changed since I had last seen him, was not the kind of boy who delighted in tormenting children. I had no answer, but I didn't like it.

The following morning, then, I was the first to arrive, and after unlocking the gates and propping them open, I toured the inside perimeter searching for lost shoes, socks, buttons, whatever the children and the mothers had left behind. When I reached the slide, however, I stopped and grabbed at the railing that bordered the rusted steps. At the foot of the curved metal slope was Eliot Daniels. His head was resting against the slide's lip, and as I walked slowly around to kneel before him, I saw that his eyes were opened. And staring. And his mouth was agape in a silent, terrified scream. I was no medical expert, but I knew without checking that the young boy was dead; and I knew, just knew, that this was the way they had discovered Gary George.

Footsteps snapped my head up.

Darlene was approaching me timidly, a puzzled smile on her baby-fat face. I rose quickly, nearly ran to her side, and turned her around with a hand at her waist. "We're going to open late today, dear," I said. "Do me a favor and tell the others, will you? Tell them . . . well, just tell them we'll be opening late."

I didn't stay to watch where she ran after she left me; I hurried immediately to the nearest call box and phoned in the report. Mechanically. As if I'd never left the force and I was still wearing the blue. No one questioned me after I'd identified myself; it was enough for someone to recognize my voice. Five minutes later, a patrol car and ambulance had screeched through the gates, and I told Dansworth all I knew with a minimum of conjecture. He smiled when I'd done, patted my arm and told me the playground would be closed for the rest of the day.

He knew I would hover. He knew I would dance around the fringe of the investigators, making a nuisance of myself, pretending it was twenty years ago and nothing had changed. He knew it, and he didn't tell me to get lost. Only that the playground would be closed for the rest of the day.

For that I was grateful. More so when I stood on the sidewalk and my skin suddenly grew cold, my stomach lurched, perspiration soaked through my shirt. I should have gone straight home to bed and a brandy, or straight to a bar and a beer, or straight to Marve's office. Instead I went hunting for Catherine and, finding her, dragged her from the office and into the Inn. I told her what had happened, and after she had gone through the motions of calming me, comforting my soul, she ordered us stiff drinks and a meal I knew I couldn't eat.

But I drank, and I ate, and an hour or so later we were outside and walking.

"Those poor kids," I said, for what must have been the fifth or sixth time. "Damn, this is going to tear them up."

"I know what you mean," she said, her hand tucked around my elbow and squeezing when I couldn't contain a shudder. "Once is bad enough, but twice . . . they'll be having nightmares for a year. Especially that little one. What's his name . . . Steve?"

"No," I said, "not them. I mean El's friends, Davey and the others." I told her about the talk with Davey the afternoon before. "They're really scared, Cath, they really are. Now they're going to think that place is jinxed or something, and they're not going to be able to stand it, you know. It's a blow to their manhood, whatever they think that is. They're going to get worse, I know it. They're going to bother those children until someone gets hurt, and then they'll be in real trouble. Cop trouble."

"Kit, I think you're exaggerating."

"Yeah, well, you should have seen Davey. He hates those little kids, Cath, he hates them so much . . . well, what can I say? Marve was right. I'm going to have to carry something around with me from now on."

She stopped and pulled me up short. "What do you mean? A gun?"

"No," I said, moving us on again, not liking her expression. "I still have my nightstick stowed away someplace."

"That's barbaric, Kit! You can't mean that."

"I don't know if I do or not. Yes. Yes, I do. I don't want any of them, big kids or little, getting hurt. I don't want another El Daniels in my playground."

She stopped again, this time letting go of my arm and standing back a pace. "*Your* playground? Kit, what's the matter with you? It's not your playground, and it's not your beat. That's over, Kit, over. You're not a cop anymore, and those kids . . . if you try something, they could hurt you badly."

"No, they won't."

"Damnit, Kit, you're stupidly stubborn. Stop playing the role, will you, please? Will you grow up? Now! Before it's too late."

She left me then, standing in the middle of the block with my hands clenched in my pockets. I watched her go and I didn't try to follow. I was trembling, not because of what I had seen, but because if my hands had been free I would have struck her.

I walked on aimlessly, staring at but not seeing the old and well-kept houses, the lawns still green, the trees only hinting at the colors to come. I stopped at a drugstore and bought a pack of cigarettes. I sat for a while on a bus-stop bench and watched the traffic waver in the dusk, then vanish behind headlights. I walked again, where the sidewalks were alternately black and grey, where the September warmth was lost in October's chill.

I considered going to Marve to drown my sorrows. But if Catherine hadn't understood, he certainly wouldn't. He was a grandfather and didn't believe that people could be surrogates. Either you were or you weren't was his belief; and if I was playing any kind of a role at all, it was being a cop.

But I wasn't.

I'm not quite that stupid. Sentimental, perhaps, over the years I'd spent working my beat, but I hope I'm intelligent enough to realize when it's over and the door's closed behind me.

No. What I was trying to do, what I had done in my playground, was make myself available to the children for comfort. There were the mothers, of course, and the babysitters and the occasional father—but then there's the old man not quite so old who always has a place on his knee, an ear cocked, a joke, a stick of gum, the small things forgotten and so delightfully needed.

When I looked to see where I was going, I found myself predictably at the playground gates. It was dark inside, and the nearest street light had been out for days. I reached out to brush at the cold damp fence, and heard voices. Distant. Almost like the afterthought of a wind.

I squinted and tried to see through the dark to the other side. A muffled laugh, a stifled giggle, and I was into the woods and making away along the fence as quietly as I could. Twigs and thorns stabbed at my ankles, sliced my hands, but when I reached the mats I could make out a small group of children standing around the slide.

I couldn't believe it. I would have sworn it was Davey and his friends preparing some kind of destructive revenge; but it was Darlene and Tim and a half-dozen others. They were staring up at Stevie, who sat on the slide's platform, waved once, and pushed himself down. I tensed, waiting for the thud of his body, and frowning when I heard and felt nothing. I peered closer, and Tim was readying himself for the earthward trip. Steve was gone. I decided then that the best thing I could do was sneak back through the woods and find a telephone to call their parents. I don't know why I didn't call out myself, why I didn't scold them, scare them, send them running for whatever hidden exit they had. I don't know why, but I didn't.

And Tim swooped down the slide, reached the end, slipped off . . . and vanished.

Not into the shadows. Not into the darkness. He vanished. Into something not there.

So did Darlene. And Miffy. And each of the others.

Down the slide, off the slide, and . . . somewhere.

I was alone. And it was silent. A breeze caught one of the canvas-seat swings and twisted it. A ghost-thing that sent me careening out of the woods, down the street, and into my home, where I stood in front of the living-room fireplace and stared at the flames. Of course, I thought, I hadn't seen what my eyes were looking at; and I began to wonder if playing the part of a playground father included playing the part of a senile old man.

There was a table by the front window, and I turned around to reach for the decanter of brandy I kept in its center. As I did, I looked through the pane and out to the picket fence that bordered my lawn. Darlene was standing there, her hand on the gate latch. She was staring at the house. I ran quickly to the door, but by the time I had reached the lawn she was gone, her footsteps faint and fading under the nightblack trees.

Now I've done it, I thought. Now I've unwittingly intruded on one of their secret games. I'm done for. No more jokes, no more comforts. They'd have nothing to do with me now, nothing more ever.

I slept badly, then, and awoke only when Marve called me to tell me I was late and was I planning to quit. I grumbled an excuse—something to do with my drinking—and forced myself through a cloud of depression to the bench under the trees, where I took out my book, prepared for a day of loneliness.

Five minutes later I looked up to see myself surrounded by a gaggle of children. Grinning. Miffy giggling.

I opened my mouth to speak to them, to find some way to apologize and excuse my actions of the night before. I was ready, but suddenly they stiffened and backed away. A motion on my left, and I saw Davey walking toward me, two boys waiting by the gates and trying to look inconspicuous. I sighed loudly and leaned back to wait.

"Afternoon, Davey," I said cooly.

"Mr. Craig," he said, almost comic in his formality. Then, before I could stop him, his face reddened and he shouted something unintelligible at the children. They didn't move. He snatched at Stevie's arm, yanked him close and turned to me. "Ask them," he demanded. "Ask them what they did with Chuck!"

"Chuck? Davey, let that boy go immediately!" I rose and slapped his hand loose. Stevie didn't run away; he only sauntered back to his friends, and they moved in a pack toward the swings. "Now, what's this all about, damnit?"

Davey shoved his hands in his windbreaker pockets and wasted a few seconds scanning the overcast sky. I saw with a start, then, that anger and something else had combined to produce tears he didn't want falling. He swallowed several times, then ducked his head to gaze at the ground. "Chuck," he said. "He's run away from home. Just like El."

"Davey—"

"I was there!" he insisted. "I was sleeping over, right? I thought I heard this noise outside, so I got up and went to the window. That one," and he pointed to Darlene, "was standing in the backyard. Chuck was there too, talking to her. I ran downstairs, but they were gone before I got there. I must have run around that block a hundred times, Mr. Craig, and I couldn't find them. I woke his folks, but they only called the police. They didn't believe nothing about the kid. They wouldn't listen." He looked up, and the tears fell. "They done something, Mr. Craig, and if somebody doesn't help Chuck soon . . . there's only three of us left, Mr. Craig. It don't make no difference now what we do. God, you got to do something."

Before I could say anything, he raced to the gates and away, the other two following closer than shadows.

I must be getting old, I thought; I don't understand a damned thing that's going on around here. But Davey, for all his fool faults, had frightened himself into something bordering on hysteria. He probably knew Chuck had been in some kind of trouble—a girl, drugs, something like that—and when he ran away, Davey used a dream as his excuse. But I couldn't help thinking of my own dream that night; the kids and the slide and Darlene on the lawn. I knew it was weariness and a drink or two that made me see what I thought I saw, but it disturbed me nevertheless, made me walk slowly over to where the children were playing.

"Darlene," I said, "Davey tells me you were at his friend's house last night."

She only smiled and pulled at her braids. "Not me, Mr. Craig," she said when I repeated my not-quite-question. "I have to be in bed right after supper."

"Me, too," Stevie said, clinging to my leg, then sliding down to sit on my foot. "Me sleep, too."

"Good for you, Stevie," I said.

"Mr. Craig?"

"What is it, Darlene?"

They were all around me now, and I couldn't help a glance at the slide, the mats, the hole that wasn't there.

"We . . ." And she looked to the others, who were smiling broadly and trying not to laugh. I've seen that look before, when the children want to be solemn, want you to know that what they're going to say is important and yet they're embarrassed. Usually, they run away shrieking, immediately twisting the compliment into a game.

"We like you, Mr. Craig."

I was startled. Though I didn't know what to expect, that was definitely not it. Miffy took my right hand and rested it briefly against her cheek. And so did the others, one by one, until I found it hard to swallow and the light blurred at the edges of my vision.

"We really like you, Mr. Craig."

The years I had weighted my shoulders. I knelt, then, and Stevie scrambled silently onto my lap.

"Would you please visit us sometime? Sometime soon?"

I would have been pleased to see their homes, but I knew from what Marve had once told me that their parents were beginning to resent the influence I had over their offspring.

"Will you let them get us?" Tim said, pointing vaguely toward the gates.

"No," I managed to say through Stevie's insistent hugging. "Don't worry, kids. I won't let them hurt you."

They broke, quietly, and after a moment I realized I had been dismissed. And glad I was, because one more word would have had me bawling like a baby. It was a good feeling, a needed feeling, and it should have had me cloud-walking for the rest of the day, but I couldn't help thinking about Davey and his friends; they were so terrified now they'd be moved to do anything, and I was tempted to call their parents to warn them. Tempted, but I did nothing. It would only be meddling again, or so they would think. And if they complained loudly enough, Marve would be forced to take my playground from me.

I didn't want that.

But the following morning, Chuck was at the foot of the slide. Staring.

And people began to talk.

The disintegration was slow. A child here, a family there, but within a week or so after Chuck's death the playground was practically deserted, and even the comfort of my little friends couldn't stop me from seeing that proverbial handwriting.

Catherine told me, finally, while we were at dinner. Told me about the whispers, and the letters. "You should hear them, Kit, and read those things. It's disgraceful the way they're behaving."

"What can it hurt as long as they don't come out to lynch me?"

She puffed on her cigarette angrily, her face momentarily obscured by the smoke. When she waved it away impatiently, her bracelets jangled, the only harsh sound in the dim quiet of the Inn. Then she reached across the table and took both my hands in hers. "Kit, it's getting dangerous for you. I hear things in the office, I really do, and there's talk that you did it. All of it. Can you believe it?"

"Ah," I said. "Just because Gary was killed just around the time I came back, huh? I must have learned some foul, dark sins while tramping across foreign soil."

"I know it's coincidence, Kit—"

"Well, of course it is, damnit!"

"—but they don't know it. Marve called me today and asked me how you were feeling."

That hurt, more than if she had accused me directly. "What's his damned problem, huh? Can't he call me? He has to go through you, is that it? Hasn't got the damned guts to face—"

"I said you were a little tired is all. I said there was nothing seriously wrong with you." The "is there," however, was as clear as if she had said it.

I bridled, immediately paid the check, and took Catherine home. In silence. In anger. Wondering what the hell I had done that would make my own town turn against me like that. But all it took, obviously, was one frightened mother, one angry father . . .

I ran to the playground, ducked into the woods, and climbed the fence back by the mats. When I was over, I had to sit on one of the swings to calm my lungs, to wipe the perspiration from my face and palms. And when I was sure I could stand without my legs trembling, I went to the slide and walked slowly around it, touching it, pressing against it, standing at its foot and sighting along its length to the top, and to the mats not three feet from the end. They met in the corner, black slabs against the night, and I blinked slowly when I imagined I saw a hazed shimmering, a distortion of vision not quite circular. I rubbed a knuckle into my eyes and knelt on the ground in front of it. Reached out my hand.

And it vanished.

Into cold/warmth, a feeling of winter/summer, sunlight and clouds.

I yanked my hand back, scrubbed it against my side, and ran. Clambered over the gates. And ran.

Again I had had too much to drink. I know it.

But I can't help thinking:

About coming up undetected on a child in a room, listening to him talk seemingly to himself. There might be a doll, or a shadow on the wall, or a favorite stuffed animal, toy truck, tin soldier. There would be a scowl when he was interrupted.

About watching a child chasing himself in the yard, shrieking with delight—and that instant frown when an adult comes by.

About children sitting on the ground, solemnly and intently staring at a tuft of grass, an anthill, a sliver of bark.

Kid stuff.

But my hand vanished.

Suppose, then, there's a world—no, not a world, *the* world, where reality lies uncovered, to which children unaffected yet by us and our deceptions can escape. To remember, to know what it's like and return with resentment for what they are becoming.

Suppose, just suppose, they really get angry. With a kid named Gary, or Eliot, or Chuck. Suppose they invite Gary, Eliot, Chuck, to visit their world. Suppose they drop them down the slide and watch them vanish, rush in after them and haul out their bodies.

Why bodies?

Because despite their youth, Gary and the rest are already blinded; and the light they are exposed to frightened them to death.

We like you, Mr. Craig.

I don't believe this for a minute, of course. Not a word. Not a thought.

We really like you, Mr. Craig.

But I don't think I'm going to look out my window anymore.

Would you please visit us sometime? Sometime soon?

That way I won't see Darlene at the gate, the others beside her. Miffy with a bouquet of flowers in her hand; Stevie sucking his thumb; Tim with his baseball cap pulled down over his eyes. I'm their friend, I know, but what they don't know is that friendships can hurt more than enmity can.

And if I don't see them, maybe I won't hear them. Maybe I won't hear Darlene when she calls me out to play.

NEEDLE SONG

In a living room, sparse and battered furniture had been formed into a square so that, in her darkness, the old woman could find them, avoid them without the tap of her probing white-tipped cane. There were neither rugs on the floors nor pictures on the walls, and only a single shadeless lamp. No matter the day or the weather, she always wore the same dress, an oddly shapeless garment whose colors seemed dead for centuries. Her hair was decades long, braided and coiled into a silver basket round the top of her head, and her face and arms and thin-strong legs were shadowed with ancient wrinkles.

But as she sat at her piano, her hands glided out from long, laced sleeves, and they were beautiful.

Eric sat quietly on the family-room floor, his short legs pulled up tight in awkward Indian fashion, his back resting stiffly against the dark oak paneling that covered the walls to the ceiling. His hands, as pinkly puffed as the rest of him, were folded in his lap, and for a moment he smiled, thinking of how his teacher would approve. Caren lay on the overstuffed couch, her white-blonde hair sifting down over her face. One hand dangled almost to the floor, and when, in her sleep, she whimpered once it jerked up to her cheek, touched, and fell again. He was tempted to wake her but didn't want to move, didn't want to whisper. The slightest sound might spoil the battle, might make him miss the music, and then it would be too late.

He stared instead at the walls and the pictures there of his father's favorite game birds. Then he tried to count the floor's black-and-white tiles, but his eyes blurred and he had to shake his head to clear his vision. A fly, perhaps the last of the year, darted across the room, swerved toward him, and made him duck. Automatically, his hands unclenched, remembered, and settled again. His knees ached where he had scraped them the day before. Caren sighed.

Through the two windows above the couch he could see the brown-edged leaves of a ribbon of flowers his mother had planted along the front of the house. They had been green once, like all the others in the neighborhood; watered, dusted with aerosol sprays, and caressed with eyes that loved and appreciated them. By stretching very slightly he could see beyond the single row of faded bricks that separated the garden from the lawn. The grass was hidden, but he knew it was dying anyway, a perfect camouflage for the leaves that sailed from the elms and willows.

I wish I knew what I was doing, he thought as he lowered his gaze to Caren again. I never killed no one before. But I guess it's got to be done or she'll kill us all first. I know it. I know she will.

Visions of his parents, of Caren's, of all the others, lying in the street like so much discarded trash.

Visions of television shows, of movies, of twisted evil women burning at the stake and laughing, having their heads cut off and their mouths stuffed with garlic, fading to corpse-grey dust at the first touch of daylight.

Visions, and it was all supposed to be make-believe, and the witch/vampire/werewolf wounds just makeup that washed off with soap.

A strong gust of wind drummed twigs against the windows, and Caren moaned softly in her sleep. As she rolled over onto her back, Eric wondered if he should have talked to some of the others. But he knew most of them would have been too frightened to do anything but call for their mothers. In fact, Caren was the only one who believed all that he said, and was the only one who was willing to join in the fight.

Maybe, he thought, we're both a little nuts. Even in the stories, vampires only drink blood.

But his father, he recalled, had been complaining about something called deterioration, depreciation, and plummeting values just before he had been hospitalized, and perhaps if Eric understood it more he might be convinced that this was what was killing the street, and all the other streets in all the other towns. He frowned, scratched at his chin, and rhythmically, lightly, thumped his head back against the wall. Maybe. And maybe his father was so involved in just being an adult that he couldn't see what was real anymore. That's what Caren had said after her spaniel puppy had been killed by a driver who hadn't even bothered to stop to say he was sorry.

Murder.

The word popped into his mind unbidden.

"Eric," Caren had said that afternoon, "we can't just break into the house and kill her. How can you kill her?"

"I don't know. Maybe we can find a gun somewhere, knock her out, and I don't know, cut off her head or something."

"You're being silly."

"Kids kill people all the time. I see it on the news at night."

"Big kids," she said, pulling nervously at her hair. "We'll have to think of something else."

"Like what?"

"I don't know, but we'll think of something."

He shifted to ease the discomfort creeping up his back, then rubbed his palms against his thighs. The sun went down unwatched, and the windows went briefly black before reflecting the single light from the floor lamp near the steps. He stretched his legs straight out ahead of him, and his heels squeaked on the tiles. Caren jumped, swung her legs to the floor, and sat up.

"It's okay," he said, grateful for the chance to get to his feet. "Nothing's happened yet. Do you want to sleep some more?"

"No," and her voice was younger, smaller than the size of her dozen years. "Do you think she'll do it tonight? It hasn't been regular for a long time."

Eric shrugged, stretched up to his toes so he could see the house across the street. "Her light is still on."

"It always is. Even in the day."

"You want something to drink? I think Mom left some soda in the kitchen for us."

"No," she said. "I don't want to leave her, not yet. Maybe we should call Jackie and see if she can come over, too."

"She's always crying, Caren. She can't help. Besides, she's too young to understand. We have to do it alone." He placed his hands on his hips, a gesture his father used to indicate finality. "Do you think you can remember enough good things?"

Caren nodded, rubbing at her eyes, then began swinging her legs. The room seemed large with shadows in the corners, but neither of them made a move to turn on the lights embedded in the white ceiling. Instead, they stared at the backless clock on the far wall, and willed the hands to sweep to nine.

Caren marked the seconds by tapping a nail against her palm.

Eric wondered why no one else knew.

The fingers that rested on the keys were like ten wings of five sleeping humming birds, and they were slender and long. They hesitated, as if undecided about waking up and what to do when they did. The ivory was yellowed in blotches and stains, but the velvet-coated hammers were young and deep blue. The old woman breathed deeply to draw in what she felt, assimilated it and translated it to the language of the wings that fluttered now, darted and glided, a polka and waltz, and from the depths of the piano the music came back.

Hawthorne Street was a community unto itself, and no one who lived there would have had it any other way. Along its entire length, all families were neighbors and all children friends. The seasons were shared with garden-hose batons, snow-blower basso; pets roamed free, and every yard but one had a hole in its hedge for the passing of gossip. Tree houses sprouted, sidewalks were chalked, but the unofficial leader was Eric because his home faced the unlucky Number 136. Of all the houses on the street, only this one could not keep a family; three in less than two years, not because it was haunted, but because the people were not able to penetrate the tightly meshed lives of everyone else.

Then, Eric remembered, came last September and the smallest moving van he had ever seen pulled into the ragged blacktop driveway and unloaded: one odd-angled piano a disturbingly deep black, one polished cedar hope chest that took three men to carry, one greying wicker chair slightly unstrung, and a bench of burnished copper. He and Caren had loitered on the curb waiting for signs of children or pets, but there was nothing else in the van, and after one of the men had relocked the front door, it pulled away and did not return.

A week passed, and suddenly Caren had pounded on the front door, dragged Eric into the street. In Number 136, in the dirt-streaked picture window, were wine-red curtains. A light glowed behind them, and no one ever saw it go off. Four days more to a Saturday waiting for autumn, and an old, very old woman appeared on the front lawn. She sat like a weathered totem in the wicker chair, her head covered by a sun hat whose brim dropped to her shoulders. She did nothing but sit. Watch. And sit until dark. Repeated every day until November's cold drove her inside.

One by one, or in reassuring groups, the children passed by, waving, and receiving no response. Eric had been the only one with nerve enough to call her a greeting, but only a breeze moved.

"I think she's blind," he said to Caren on the way to school just before the Thanksgiving holiday.

"Deaf, too," she said, grinning, receiving a grin in return.

And though they pestered their parents daily, they could get no satisfactory answers about the odd woman's origins, her designs, why she never invited anyone in for tea or cookies and soda.

She became, simply, the Old Lady, and a superstition instantly born prevented any of the younger children from passing her house on her side of the street.

And then, one cold and snow-ready night, when Hawthorne Street stayed home and huddled, richly, in front of fieldstone fireplaces and gleaming Franklin stoves, the music began. Precisely at nine o'clock the November chill was warmed by glittering sparks that sifted through the windows and doors and startled the people who heard.

Hey, a circus, Eric thought, running to the living room to look up and down the street.

Hey, Mom, Caren had called, there's one of those guys with the monkey and the thing that you turn.

There was a lullaby, a love song, memories of dance bands, carnivals, and boardwalk calliopes on a hot August night.

For thirty minutes to the second before it stopped, and the notes fell like powdered snow to vanish into the ground.

"Eric?"

He spun around, blinking, then glaring at Caren's silent laugh.

"What's the matter, did I scare you?"

"Not me," he said. "You kind of just snuck up on me, that's all. What's the matter? You need something, or something?"

"I was thinking about the time she came," and she shivered an exaggerated chill, making him laugh. "Remember the time we tried to sneak a look through the back window and Jackie started sneezing because of her hay fever and we didn't stop running until we must have got all the way to the park?"

"I wasn't scared then, either."

"I didn't say you were, silly."

"Then why'd you have to say all that? Don't we have enough troubles?"

"I was just trying to remember, Eric, that's all."

"Okay, I'm sorry, but you'd better save it. I think I can feel it coming."

Remember, he thought in disgust. Just like a girl to waste her time remembering when we got things to do more important. And what good would it do asking for things to be the way they were anyway?

Throughout that winter, it seemed as if what rainbows there were had all spilled into a vast shimmering pot called Hawthorne Street, and all on the heels of the music.

Caren's brother was accepted into a European university with full scholarship honors; Eric discovered he had a natural talent for musical instruments, and horns in particular, and his teacher told him in all honesty that he would someday be famous; Jackie Potter's family won a state lottery and planned a trip across the country during Easter vacation; and there seemed nothing at all wrong in standing by the front window and listening to the piano drawing them closer, stirring their emotions while it accompanied snow onto the lawns, ice into puddles, and guided the wind to cradle dead leaves softly into the gutters. The snowmen were bigger, the snow forts more elaborate, and Eric's father came home twice with promotions and once with a car big enough to hold thousands.

Eric scrubbed his cheeks dryly. It was no good remembering things like that because it wasn't that way anymore, and it was all because of a vampire witch who sucked them dry with her music.

It was April when the weekly concerts stopped, and while most of the people worried for a while, no one thought to visit the old woman to see if there was anything wrong. It was as if the children's superstition had been universally accepted, and when Eric suggested they try again to sneak a look into the Old Lady's house, Caren became angry and told him to leave the poor thing alone.

In May a fire destroyed the oldest house on the street, Caren's brother was arrested for possession of drugs and assault with a deadly weapon, and Eric's grandfather died in the guest room, in his sleep. New grass was planted, was washed away during three consecutive storms that knocked out power for three days, flooded every waterproof cellar, and uprooted a maple that was reputed to have been planted by the town's original settlers.

Caren's puppy died.

Eric's father was forced out of work and into a hospital bed by a series of massive heart attacks.

The elms rotted from the inside, and the willows crawled with worms that soon stopped their weeping.

The music came again, at odd hours for nearly a week, stopped just as abruptly, and what grass was left began dying in the middle of a shower.

All the houses needed painting, gardens weeding, and red brick shaded to brown.

Something had been taken away, something was missing, but few people cared, fewer still knew.

"Hey, listen, if you're going to sleep, I'm going home."

Eric grinned stupidly. He was sitting against the wall again, and his head felt stuffed with cotton like a baby's toy.

"I thought we weren't supposed to be thinking yet."

"Okay, I'm sorry again," he said, crossing the room to sit with her on the couch. "I just can't help it."

"I know what you mean. Do you . . . do you think we can fight her?"

He looked at her carefully before nodding.

"What if we're wrong?"

"We're not, I told you."

"Then let's get going."

The music. It came at them through the dead leaves and grass and age-bent trees. The melody varied, wavered, changed.

"Maybe we should put cotton in our ears or something."

"Eric, I'm frightened."

There was a sliver of a tear in the corner of her eye, and he looked away to avoid seeing it slither down her satin cheek. "Don't be," he said. "Just remember that time we put the snake in Mrs. Green's desk."

"That was dumb."

"It was funny, remember?" He turned back, insistent, a hand reaching to grab her shoulder before it pulled away. "It was funny," he repeated slowly, and took a breath to laugh.

"Sort of," she said, hinting a smile, "but not as much as the picnic we went on with the Potters. Remember how you kept falling on your fat face in that sack race thing? I thought you were going to start digging holes with your nose."

The music, searching for crevices in their conversation, cracks in their memories.

Eric giggled, clamped a hand over his mouth, then leaned back and filled the room with high-pitched laughter.

"You—" he said, gulping for air, "you on that stupid pony. You should have seen your face when the saddle fell off."

Caren winced. "Well, it hurt, dope. Hey, remember the Christmas your father made me that doll? And your mother made all her clothes? I still have it, you know. Of course, I'm too old to play with it, but I like to look at it now and then."

"Good," Eric said, jumping onto the couch to look out the window. "Hey," he shouted, "what about the time we found the bird in the yard."

"Robin."

"Right. Remember how we used the eyedropper to feed it until it learned to fly?"

"A cat could have eaten it," Caren said, shuddering.

"Yeah, but we saved it!"

Eric clambered to the floor and improvised an impatient dance while he slapped at his sides to jog loose more memories, anything at all he could throw at the music.

"Wait a minute," Caren said. "What about the time we went to the beach that summer? You won me an elephant at the stand."

He stopped, almost choking in his desperation to find more words. "Nothing to it," he said finally. "Them bottles is easy to knock down."

Her hands stopped and she pushed herself away from the keyboard. Carefully, with the measured steps of the practiced blind, she crossed the bare floor to the old chest and opened it. With deliberate care she pulled out what was once a large black square of satin. It was covered, now, except for one small corner, with colors that danced, sang in harmony, and laughed; never blending, capturing light, repelling a tear.

"Eric—"

"Hey, remember—"

"Eric, it's finished!"

He blinked, listened, heard nothing, and let his small chest sag in relief.

"Hey," he said proudly, "we ain't so little, are we?"

She sat on the bench facing the red curtains. Methodically she arranged the satin across her knees, touching each thread line that led to the corner. A needle sharp with use glinted in her right hand, and a single web of many lights dropped from its eye into a plain brown sack at her feet. Then her eyes seemed to clear and she waited, poised, humming arcane tunes to herself and the chest that was filled to the brim with bright on dark.

"You probably think you're pretty smart," Caren said.

"Sure am. It was my idea, wasn't it? I put it all together and figured out that the Old Lady was taking away all our happiness with that music we was hearing, didn't I? And that's what was making all the bad things happen, right?"

"Well—"

"—and didn't I say that we had to show her that we were still doing all right anyway? And now that we did, she'll move away and never come back because we were too much for her. We beat the music."

"Well, it's done now," she said, and grinned.

"Sure is," he said, grinning, wiping his forehead with his sleeve.

The needle shimmered, dipped, ready to extend the rainbow.

"When's your mother coming home from the hospital?"

"I don't know. She said she was going to look in on someone, I don't know who, on her way back."

They stared at each other across the room, then gathered in air and screeched it out in a victory yell that shattered all their doubts. Eric fetched two cans of soda, opening one and immediately pouring it over Caren's head.

"I told you I was right, and I was, right?"

Caren grabbed for the other can, but he ducked away. "So what?" she said, laughing. "Nobody's going to believe us. They don't know she was some kind of a witch thing."

"What do you care?" he shouted, leaping onto the couch to avoid her grasp. "We're still heroes. And everything will be all right, you'll see."

The needle darted.

"One of these days," he said, "I'm going to be the world's best trumpet player, and you can come to my opening and tell everyone you know me."

"No thanks," she said. "You look like an elephant with that horn in your mouth."

He laughed, leaped over the arm. But he wasn't fast enough to escape Caren's hand, and in a minute the second container of soda was emptied over his head, and Caren, for good measure, rubbed it in like shampoo.

"I don't care," he shouted. "I don't care."

The corner was nearly finished. She hummed, knowing her fingers would stop in just a minute. Then tie. Bite. And she gathered the cloth to her chest and breathed deeply the musty mausoleum odor of the house. Then she dropped the spectrumed satin into the chest with the others. One day, she thought, she would sew herself a new dress of a thousand colors and be young again. But there was one more town . . .

She locked the chest with a pass of her hand.

And the light went out.

"Hey, we'd better clean this up before your mother gets home."

Eric looked at the still bubbling soda spilled all over the tiles, and he nodded. His arms felt leaden, his legs began to stiffen, and the stuffing in his head wouldn't go away. Caren prodded him again, and he ran toward the stairs, didn't hear her warning yell until it was too late. His foot slid in one of the puddles and, in trying to wave his arms to keep his balance, pitched face forward into the corner with the lamp.

Caren paled when he finally turned around, groaning, and she screamed when he dropped his hands from his face and smeared the blood that ran from his lips.

SOMETHING THERE IS

A mockingbird hidden in a broad-crested elm sang to banish the red eye of the sun. A woman called anxiously from a narrow back porch, a boy answered with a shout and ran laughing up Hawthorne Street, forgetting as he did not to step on the cracks. A dog rooting in the gutter snarled uncertainly at the not-quite-shadows of a hazy dusk. A speeding car backfired. A cat prowled

The wind keened and gathered black clouds. The trees hissed and showed faint white. And the moon had no chance to bring a peace to the night.

Martin White was tired. Tired of the failures, the hints, the bitterly long hours of fruitless searching. So tired, he was near enough to despair to be tempted to give it all up before he drove himself weeping to the edge of screaming. He rubbed a heavy hand over his face, trying futilely to dismiss an insistent drowsiness that stung his dark eyes faintly and blurred his vision at the burning edges. He ignored the coarse two-day stubble on his prominent jaw, and did not seem to feel the perspiration that welded his shirt to his back in spite of the tiny black fan that spun weakly on the sill behind him. Beyond the screen, July shimmered over the front yard, weighted and humid, threatening to dissolve the nightblue walls. After a moment of helplessness, then, he decided to finish one more chapter before giving it up, but when every sentence on every page read the same and meant nothing, he sighed an impotent curse, closed the book and rose to his feet, leaning against the chipped and battered desk for support. He stared dumbly at the dust jacket and shook his head.

"Sorry, Stoker," he said to the time-worn cover, "but I don't think I can make it tonight." He closed his eyes, waiting, opened them and grinned wryly. "Nope, I'm afraid not."

He yawned, shook himself, shuffled down the short hall to his bedroom, stiffly exaggerating his walk to loosen his muscles before he slept. Without turning on the light, ignoring the faint yellow glow of the still-burning desk lamp, he stripped and let himself collapse onto the unmade bed.

Where he waited patiently for the dream, and the promises it made him.

The first time it had come was two months ago. He found himself standing in a level of absolute darkness he couldn't believe was possible, was real. When he'd awakened he wanted to scream, but he was too excited; and the second time, the third, the fourth and the fifth, he had been in the same unimaginable someplace, yet increasingly aware that he was expecting something to happen and terrified because he hadn't yet discovered what it would be.

He wanted to believe it was at last what he'd been groping for, but didn't until the darkness came while he was awake.

He was in his classroom, aimlessly shuffling papers after dismissing his last class and wondering what the high schools would ship him next term. His eyes closed in weary relief . . . and he was in darkness again. Only the darkness. But now he was convinced this was the way to find her.

He shifted, kicked at the sheets until they fell to the floor, and slept. While a light behind his eyes drifted and ran, merged from red to yellow to gold to black. He was in a room without dimension or boundary, and he floated/sat on a nebulous ebony with cool air to breathe though he choked for the lack of it while his neck tightened into cords, his head trembled in the effort to relax, and his throat burned with words that crushed against his teeth and drew blood from unbroken lips. He drew his knees to his chest and locked his hands around his shins. He was walking, but there was neither heat nor cold, movement nor quiet; but he knew she was there, had to be there, and called her plaintively to hurry, to give to him what she had given to the others. Suddenly there was a crash, a booming, resounding explosion that thundered into a roar, and when he snapped open his eyes . . .

. . . he found himself at his desk, his pen lying at his feet. A slight predawn breeze pushed mud-brown curtains against his naked back, and he jumped at their touch. Blinked. Breathed deeply as he stared at the blank sheet of paper on the desk's cracked glass top. Two others were lying crumpled on the floor.

"Damn," he said with a tentative grin. "Damn." She had brought him here; he knew it. Finally, after reading all the books on the shelves several times over, she had heard his silent calling and had come to him, to guide him.

But she was still at a distance, and he glared at the books.

"Give her up," he said softly, intensely, "give her up. You can't keep her from me forever. I'm joining the club, and you can't stop me."

Mary Shelley, Guy Endore, Bram Stoker, leather-bound and silent while Martin laughed and strutted into the bathroom to take a quick shower.

Beaumont and Bloch, Lovecraft and Leiber, tattered and yellowed while he sang a tuneless melody of a woman beautiful beyond description and the light she would bring to his starving eyes, and the words she would conjure for his inkless pen.

While Saki and Dunsany stared blindly at the red rising sun.

It was well past noon when he awoke again, too refreshed and excited to be disappointed when an hour passed at his desk without producing a word. Soon enough she would contact him, this muse of the others; and meanwhile he bustled about the tiny six-room ranch cleaning and waiting. A quick canned supper, another hour of staring, and he was ready to throw in the towel when a telephone call reminded him of a party invitation he had unthinkingly accepted some days before. He hovered by the cradled receiver, unsure, apprehensive, with guilty glances toward his study door. At last, however, he decided that the relaxation would do him good, a chance to unlimber his mental processes and flex his imagination without the self-inflicted pressure that pilfered his sleep.

He dressed for the part. Turtleneck shirt, brown corduroy jacket, black slacks, and barely shined loafers. It was a stereotyped image, but one he enjoyed. The only thing missing was a well-used pipe.

By ten o'clock he was at the Bensons' home, ringing the doorbell and already wiping moist hands on his sides. Linda was his cheerleader, his patron, constantly stroking his ego and damning those who thought his talent was missing. "This is Martin T. White, the author," was her standard introduction to strangers, but it wasn't those he didn't know that he worried about; it was his friends and their well-meaning comments he had come to fear. If it wasn't for Linda, he would have stayed locked in his home.

And once inside, with a frosted glass in his hand, the ordeal began.

"Hey, Marty, how's it going? Still beating down those editors?"

"Well, Martin, still drumming up business for the old muse? Just remember, old boy, the formula for success: perspiration to inspiration, nine to one."

"Hey, White, when you make that first sale, you going to have a party? I won't hold my breath, but give me a call."

Martin grinned. Nodded. Refilled his glass.

There were faces, not people. Surefire plots with sly pleas for acknowledgment. Two ghost stories he had heard from the same mouths at the last party. Hints and suggestions from tired writing manuals and tired writing teachers. Gossip about Linda and her husband, Ted. Gossip about Linda. About Ted. About him. Someone dropped an ice cube down a woman's cleavage, and instantly he was besieged to include the incident in his next, his first, his whatever book.

He was ready to surrender, to drink himself into a stupor that would blot out the noise, when he recalled someone's mentioning his search for the muse. Instantly he was heartened. Their muse was an obscenity, distilled in alcohol and spoken in small type; but his, the real flesh-and-ink guide to his genius, was pure, beautiful, and shouted in capitals across a universe-wide marquee.

He was standing in the kitchen rinsing out his glass and smiling at his superiority over the plebian hypocrites when suddenly, without warning, the room went dark.

"No," he whispered harshly. "Damn, no, not here. Please, not here!"

He raced out the back door, realized he was still carrying his glass and threw it away, not hearing it smash on the side of the house.

Down Hawthorne Street.

A part of him noticing there was no moon.

Into his study, flinging himself into the chair and grabbing at his pen and the ream of paper. He took a deep shuddering breath . . . and a hot-cold wind wailed through his long hair, ripped at the skin around his throat, making no sound as he gazed unblinking into the nothing that buried him weightlessly while he crouched, naked, on swollen hands and blistered knees listening for her voice and hearing only a volley of thunder cascade through his chest. A bubble of spittle quivered at the corner of his mouth while mute echoes, deafening in their dumbness, competed with the rasp of his lungs to fill the void. A flash, then, of blue-white fire colder than ice, and he was thrown back onto his haunches . . .

. . . and heard the storm breaking over the house. Automatically, he reached behind him and pulled down the sash, switched on the fan, and turned to the top sheet of paper. It was blank, but he grinned. Blank, but he knew he was ready. She was coming. To him. To his pen.

He lit a cigarette and swaggered over to the bookcase, deciding to give himself some last-minute insurance with a booster reading. Just in case. With elaborate concern he scanned the collection of anthologies and novels, seeing each table of contents without opening a cover, searching with a sudden, disquieting apprehension for the bait he needed.

"Come on, my lovelies," he crooned to the spines, "which one of you is going to guide me tonight? Who's going to tell me what she's like? I don't have to know what she looks like, you know; but it would be nice to be able to picture her before she comes." His fingers darted, plucked, replaced, tapped his brow. "Come on, folks, don't be bashful. And for crying out loud, don't be so modest! After all, it was your combined geniuses that brought me this far, wasn't it? Come on, tell me what she looks like. Tell me how beautiful she really is."

The shelves were silent. He punched at the floor.

"Damnit, who the hell do you think you are? Do you really think you idiots can keep her from me?"

He snatched at a book, tossed it over his shoulder, and grabbed for another.

"Mrs. Radcliffe, you of all people should be glad that Gothics are all the rage. Too bad, though, because they're mutants, you know, hideous, monstrous travesties of every honest fear man ever had."

Another book, another toss.

"Mr. Machen, did you know that you and your kind have been called old-fashioned? Out-of-date and worn in a worn, cynical world. Poe, an ass; Hawthorne a pansy."

He glowered and swept a hand over the shelves, emptying them to his feet. "All of you. Dead. You need me, damnit, to make fear work again. You need me! Tell me! What does she look like? How do I find her?"

A sudden spate of bullet rain against the pane startled him into dropping his forgotten cigarette. He froze, looked stupidly at his trembling hands and was horrified. Immediately he crushed the smoldering butt under his heel and scuttled back to his desk, afraid to touch the books scattered on the floor, fearful they would desert him when he needed their help the most. And after what seemed like hours, he pulled open the center drawer and stared mournfully at the pile of rejection slips lying bleakly inside.

Nine years, he thought, nine years of nothing.

Hey, Marty, you old dog, how's the Pulitzer Prize looking this year? You got your speech all made up?

With a practiced hand he scooped up the papers and dumped them without ceremony into the left-hand drawer, noting dully as he did so that he would soon have to switch to the other.

You're a writer, huh? No kidding. That's nice, you know? But what else do you do, Mr. White? For a living, I mean.

"Perspiration, inspiration," he muttered angrily. "A decade is damned long enough for a man to sweat. God knows there's enough foul horror in the world. Why the hell—" and he slammed the drawers shut. "Why the hell can't I write about them?"

There was a correspondence course he failed to complete; a trip to the castles on the Rhine, Rhone, and Danube that took six years of his savings. Weekend flights to New England in desperate search of spectral Arkham, spring vacations in Haiti, Christmas in rural England, and a cold white dawn at Stonehenge. Midnights walking the streets in storms. And a year ago, the beginning of the collection that walled his study, reading and examining, hunting for a clue to the authors' ability to write eloquently about the unspeakable, darkly about the commonplace; over and over and over again until he had memorized nearly every florid, majestic, purple, and bitter bitten paragraph. Nightmares. Sweat. The sounds of blood dripping whenever he turned a page.

An aunt died, a raise in salary, and he redecorated every room in the house in every color of darkness he could find or create. The doors sprung heavy locks. The windows grew thick drapes that prevented the sunlight from fading black carpets, from admitting the day and keeping the air still.

But the words he had done did the worst to him. Worst by staying just out of reach, like the tip of a breeze, taunting him like so many harlots berating an impotent, cursing him from thick and thin brown envelopes efficiently and swiftly returned with his name and address neatly centered, neatly printed. They laughed, jeered, rearranged themselves to obscure the content from everyone but himself; and he cried out for understanding, vowed revenge on those who deliberately misunderstood, reveled in showers of self-pity, and haunted the summer/autumn/winter/spring parties for the Woman, and the Key.

Martin choked on a sob when the blood-weight of nine years threatened to crush him.

Hey, Mr. White, I'm told you're a . . . a writer? Well, listen, have you heard the one about the chubby vampire who managed a blood bank? No? Well, it seems that this girl came in one day . . .

The light bulb flickered. There was no wind, but the air moved. Martin reached for his pen. Waiting.

Really, Martin, don't you think you should try to write things that have . . . well, a moral? I mean, honestly! You should know that people just aren't scared anymore. Really!

Thunder and lightning born together, and the wet rush of the storm carried a faint ghost of laughter from across the street. Martin sat motionless, his eyes wide as if in shock. The pen moved without conscious direction, and he looked fearfully, gratefully at the bookcase, at the volumes he had thrown to the floor. But Matheson and Sloane made no move to comfort him.

Doesn't it interfere with your teaching, Mr. White?

Did you say horror stories, Mr. White? How . . . how quaint.

This course I was telling you about, Marty, the prof said you got to have a hook. You got a hook, White?

He yanked page after page from beneath the flow of black ink until his hand began to cramp and forced him to slow down. Slow down, and stop. Perspiration ran down his cheeks and soaked his collar. The fan had stopped. He took a breath, held it, blew it slowly out, and wrote again, ignoring the stinging smoke from the cigarette dangling from his mouth. He neared the climax. Laughed. Tears brimmed. Nearer.

No fooling, you really a writer? Never heard of you.

Suddenly, as if a hand had punched at his chest, he slumped back and the pen fell to the desk. Panic strangled him. His fingers tried to grasp but failed to hold the pen now rolling away, to the floor.

"No," he said quietly. Then, louder: "No, damnit, you can't stop me now!"

The room, house, street, were silent.

His voice rose to a wail, a moan, while rain dripped from the eaves and vanished into mud.

He hesitated, then dropped to the floor, scrabbling through the books randomly, opening and reading, forcing disjointed passages to jolt into his mind. Feverishly he grabbed, tore, read, wept, until the last page lay shredded at his feet.

He closed his eyes tightly, and clenched his fists against his thighs.

I need you, he pleaded silently. I . . . I can't finish, not without you.

And he was in a place not a time, nor a color.

A cat, owl, woman-girl screeched. Blood ran, water ran, white greyed, red glowed, and a thousand-towered castle rose and fell in stagnant green waters that loomed above scarlet mountains coated with wolves that flew like bats on broomsticks of lightning. An axe fell, guillotine hummed, knife whistled, stake thudded, and Martin smiled, holding out his arms as a road came and went beneath his naked feet. Suns came up, clouds, caves, homes of gingerbread, streets, paths, trails of thorns. There marched dolls with pink pins, men on jackals, and an out-of-step parade passed, parted over him, through him . . . and he was alone.

With a white-robed man who held worlds of choirs and hells of crowds in each massive hand, with golden dirty hair and his smile blinded.

"You're not the one!" Martin shouted angrily.

"You're right," the man said, sang, laughed, lamented.

Another man, short, ugly, fiercesome, a black halo and violet cloak his only dress.

"No, damnit, neither are you," Martin sneered.

"Right," the man said softly, almost sadly.

Martin whirled.

A woman, at last the woman, whose beauty crippled and gave him strength, with roses and ivy and hemlock at her breasts, and deer and hyenas cavorting at her feet. Symphonies and chantings, ditties and solemnities.

"Yes," Martin gasped. "I've been waiting for you."

"No," the woman wept. "No, not me."

Martin spun around, his arms wide to clasp, but he was alone again; and a sudden snap of thunder brought him back to the study. He was sprawled on the floor, his head toward the door, and the torn pages of his books had fallen snowlike over his chest.

"Oh, my God, please," he said in a monotonic moan. "Don't leave me now. Please, where are you?"

In spite of the thunder, there was fog.

In spite of the lightning, there was darkness.

And when Martin rolled to his stomach, there was a shadow in the corner.

"Here," It said. "We've been waiting."

TALES FROM THE NIGHTSIDE

COME DANCE WITH ME ON MY PONY'S GRAVE

In November, and an aged slate sky; a wind snapping across the fields like a bullwhip and cracking around a golden brown house that squatted warmly on the grey landscape.

Aaron, huddled in a winter-worn and crimson jacket, was slumped, seemingly relaxed, against the jamb of the open front door, his hands flat in his pockets. His eyes were narrowed against the wind, and they shifted quickly along the partially wooded horizon, blurring the Dakota spruce and pine to a green-and-grey smear of almost preternatural fear. Behind him the house was empty, and silent. There was only the wind and an occasional wooden creak.

He shivered.

Suddenly an explosive gust caught him unprepared and shoved him off-balance; a magazine was blown to the floor in the living room, and a shade snapped against glass. Reluctantly he closed the door and cut off the warmth from his back. His lips twisted into a half-smile. A good thing Miriam's not here, he thought as his mind mimicked her laughing scold: Aaron Jackoson, what do you think we are—Eskimos? Just look at my curtains blown all over, and the cold, Aaron, the cold . . . He grinned, shook his head, and closed his eyes briefly to allow her face to flash before him reassuringly. The wind gusted again, and his smile faded. Come home, Miriam, he thought (nearly prayed), come home soon—the boy frightens me yet.

Then he resettled himself to wait, arms folded and pressed tightly against his chest. He squinted into the cold, his eyes moving, moving as they had once been trained to do, watching and waiting . . .

. . . under a multigreen canopy of broad leaves, twisted vines, and knee-high, waist-high brush beside the paths he and his men rarely used as they climbed for hours through the bugs/sweat/heat/dirt world. A ragged clearing ahead where the village so often visited was hidden, and the smoke-skinned, half-naked Montagnards who gave them the news that the enemy had long since fled—all save one who, this time, belonged to them, not the soldiers. Water, then, with iodine tablets to kill the bacteria, and orange flavoring to kill the taste. While he watched the jungle and his men relaxed, finally. And the boy—eight, perhaps nine—stood by a black patch of earth where several men were racing the sun, digging what looked to be a grave. A shout . . .

. . . and Aaron blinked and watched a slight figure break from the trees and zigzag swiftly across the field, arms waving wildly in greeting. He grinned and, pushing himself away from the house, limped heavily toward the fence as grass crackled sharply beneath his feet. He shivered and wondered how the boy had managed to adapt so rapidly to the four seasons so radically different from the hot and not-so-hot of the mountain jungles.

At last the boy reached the yard and with a melodramatic gasp draped himself over the faded white rail, his face darker, but not red, from exertion.

"Hey, Dad."

"Hey, yourself."

"Boy, am I . . . bushed?"

Aaron nodded. "Bushed, pooped, beat, tired . . . in fact, you look like all of them rolled into one." He was tempted to ask where his adopted son had been, and thought better of it. "Come on inside, David, and get yourself warm. Your mother'll kill me if she finds I let you catch cold the minute she decides to go visiting."

The boy was thirteen and still quite short (would never be much taller), and as he dashed back to the house ahead of his father, his long straight black hair whipped his shoulders and the air, while Aaron watched carefully for hints of the past until he realized what he was doing and scolded himself silently for behaving like a damned fool. The boy, he insisted to his shadow, was an American now. But he could not help the growing feeling that, without Miriam, David thought of him only as the lieutenant who took him away. He glanced back at the trees and shut the door.

"Sit down, Dad," David called from the kitchen. "I'll make you some hot tea. Did mother call today?"

"Yes, I'm afraid she already has," he answered. "About ten, ten-thirty. You were out with Pinto, I think."

"Nuts."

Aaron laughed and, after shucking his coat, stretched out on the sofa, letting the room draw the cold from his skin to die in the dark glow of the beams and paneled walls. And everywhere, the scent of Miriam.

Then he heard a cup shatter, and he sighed when David, none too quietly, began muttering to himself. "Hey, in there," he shouted. "We speak English in this house, remember?"

The boy poked his head out of the kitchen and grinned broadly. "Sorry, Dad, but that's all I remember anymore."

"The swearing?"

"But, Dad, they're the best kind, don't you know? I heard the GIs use them all the time."

There was a sharp silence before David finally giggled and thrust out an open hand. "Look, Dad, I was only counting. I don't remember any more than that, honest." He waited a moment, staring, then frowned and disappeared.

Now that's got to be a crime, Aaron thought, recalling all the tedious, impatient hours he had spent scraping together enough of the tribe's language to make himself, and his mission, understood; there were still a few isolated words and phrases that returned to him when he pressed, yet the boy had forgotten a lifetime. So he said. Once, when Aaron had been feeling particularly moody over his crippled leg, he had asked David if he minded being away from his old home, toppled through a sargasso of red tape and interviews into a country and life-style as alien to the boy as the jungle was to

Aaron. David had smiled, a little softly, and shook his head. But the black eyes were expressionless; they always had been since the death of his father.

"Hey, Dad! Quit daydreaming, please? This stuff is hot."

Aaron smiled and took the steaming cup from the offered tray. David sat cross-legged on the rug, watching intently as Aaron tasted the tea and nodded his approval. "Your mother," he said, "will be jealous."

David finally returned the smile, then turned his head toward the bay window as if he were plotting the darkening sky, listening for the invisible wind. He squirmed. Coughed. Aaron amused himself with the boy's impatience as long as he could; then, softly, "Pinto must be starving. Is he on a diet or something?"

And the boy was gone. To a pony named Pinto, horse enough for a youngster who would never be tall, not even average. They had both arrived on the same day, and five years later they were inseparable. Wild, Aaron thought. Both of them.

The telephone shrilled. Aaron grunted away a cramp that knifed his mine-shattered leg as he headed into the hallway and picked up the receiver.

"Jackoson, that you?"

Aaron winced. "Yes, Mr. Sorrentino, it's me."

"Damned good thing. Want to tell you those wolves are back again. Went after two of my rams this morning. Saw them. Big as horses they were. Chased them into the woods, I did." Right to my place, Aaron thought bitterly, thanks a lot. "I got a shot at them."

"You what?"

"Said I got a shot at them."

"Damnit, Sorrentino, my boy was playing there today. You know he always—"

"Did I hit him?" The voice was singularly unconcerned.

"Christ, no! If you had, do you think I'd be—"

"Then don't worry about it, Jackoson. I'm a perfect shot. I hit what I aim at. That kid—"

"My son."

"—won't get hurt, don't you worry about that. But one thing, Jackoson . . . I, uh, don't want to make any trouble, you understand, but I wish you would straighten out your kid about where your property ends. Him and that damn pony scare hell out of my sheep."

"If I didn't know you better, Mr. Sorrentino, I'd be tempted to think that you were somehow trying to threaten me."

A raucous laugh and a harsh gasping for breath. Aaron wanted to spit at the phone. "Just wanted you to know, Jackoson, don't get so worked up. You soldier boys get excited too easy."

"I just don't like the tone of your voice, Sorrentino."

"So sue me," Sorrentino said, and hung up.

Aaron breathed deeply and grabbed the edge of the hall table. "I could kill you so easily, Mr. Franklin Sorrentino," he said to the wall. "So goddamned easily."

"Dad?"

Aaron spun around to face the boy standing in the hall . . .

. . . standing by the gash of a grave while the jungle severed the sun's scattered light and a pit fire substituted shadows for trees. Lieutenant Jackoson shifted uneasily on the ground and lighted a cigarette as the boy stared at him. There was no recognition in the black bullet eyes though the man and the boy had often played together whenever the squad came to stay and use the friendly village as a base. Now Jackoson saw only a new, weary emptiness, and deeper: a purpose. The grave was for the boy's father, the shaman of the tribe . . .

. . . the boy's voice was quiet. "I don't like him, Dad." The words spun high, and Aaron shivered a remembrance while he stood in the tunnel-dark hall. David moved as silently as he spoke. Even on the Shetland he was noiseless—in the early days, when the boy was still learning, Miriam had said: he's like a ghost, Aaron, and he frightens me. In the early days. There were still remnants of the mountain in him, but Miriam no longer saw them. "He's greedy, Dad, and doesn't . . . feel for things."

Aaron nodded, just barely stopping himself from patting the boy on the head. He had learned early that "sin" was too weak a word for such a gesture. Instead, he grabbed his shoulders. "Go watch some TV, son. Forget it. It's not worth worrying yourself."

They walked, the boy just behind, into the living room and

dimmed the lights. Before Aaron switched on the set, David curled into a corner chair where the age in his voice belied his thin body. "Why doesn't he like me, Dad?"

Aaron knew this was not a time to smile away a question. Five years before, his greatest fear had been what the other youngsters would think of his adopted son, but the smoke-grey skin and the hint of Polynesia in his features had given him instant acceptance, especially with the girls; David, however, was only always superficially friendly. "I don't know, son. Perhaps he's lonely with no children of his own, and that wife of his is enough for any man."

"He thinks I'm different." The tone said: he knows I'm different, and you're afraid that maybe he's right.

"Perhaps."

"I don't like him."

"David, he's not going to be the only one in your life to think you're . . . well, not the same as others. You're quite a unique young man."

"He hates Pinto. He say, last week when he run me away, it was a silly name for a horse. Pinto doesn't like him either. He try to kick his stomach once."

"Oh." Aaron, forgetting to correct the boy's English, thought he was beginning to understand Sorrentino's surliness.

"He missed."

In spite of himself, Aaron said, "Too bad."

The boy laughed quietly.

"Listen, David, Mr. Sorrentino doesn't really understand how you can . . . can *be* with animals. Most boys . . . do you know what rapport means?"

"No, Dad, but I think I can make guesses."

"Well, good. Rapport, you see, isn't always explainable. Sometimes it's something that just happens or belongs to a way of life that people just can't grasp. Like . . ." and he stopped, thought, and decided not to mention the shaman. "And, if you don't mind me asking," he said instead, falsely lighter, "why did you name him Pinto?"

David laughed again. "It suits him."

"How? He's all brown?"

"It feels right, Dad. It suits him. He runs and leaps and . . . he's like me in many ways. His name is right."

"Well, Sorrentino can't understand that, son."

"I know. He doesn't . . . feel. I don't like him."

Aaron frowned in concentration, seeking the speeches that would stifle the hatred he knew that boy was feeling. It was wrong to allow this to fester, wrong not to show the boy that some men must be tolerated, that, as the saying goes, it takes all kinds. He tried, but he took too long.

"I'm going to bed, Dad. Good night." David uncurled from the chair, stayed out of the light until his bedroom door closed behind him. Always closed. Sanctum.

Aaron hesitated in following, then sat again. For the first time since they had been together, David had lied to him. So blatantly, in fact, that its very obviousness pained more than the deceit itself. The language. He knew David had not forgotten all but the numbers. Once in a while, from behind the door, a muttering filtered through the house and filled him with dreams. Songs chanted on horseback across the fields and through the half-light in the pines; the whisperings to the animals. Black hair and black eyes and a strength in slender arms that contradicted their frailty. Montagnard. Mountain dweller. Outcast.

Christ! he thought and chided himself for allowing his mind to become so morbid. The weather, his leg, and Miriam's absence were getting to be too much. He decided to call her first thing in the morning and ask her to cut her visit short. Her mother wasn't that lonely, and he needed her laughter.

He dozed fitfully until the telephone twisted him stiffly from the couch. His watch had stopped. He stood, scratching his head vigorously, then stretched his arms over his head. "All right," he mumbled. "All right, all right, for God's sake." *Daylight,* he thought in amazement. That little dope didn't even wake me so I could sleep in a bed; how the hell did I oversleep? Glancing at the front window, he noticed streaks on the glass and the shimmer of ice on the walk. Rain, freezing rain, was the last thing he needed with David pouting and his wife gone. For a moment he was ready to let the phone ring and crawl into bed to hide. The house and that damned phone were making him nervous.

Still rubbing the sleep from his face, he leaned awkwardly against the wall and snatched up the receiver. "Yeah, yeah, Jackoson here."

"Aaron, this here is Will."

He stiffened. "Yes, Sheriff, what can I do for you?" There were excited noises in the background; a man was bellowing angrily.

"I'm over at the Sorrentino place. You'd better get over here."

"David?"

"No, nothing's happened to the boy. But Sorrentino accidently shot the pony. He's dead."

"I'll be right there." No thought, then, only an endless stream of cursing accusations: half in relief for his son's safety, half in anger at the rancher's murder of the boy's pet. His coat, first jamming on its hanger, refused to slide on easily. The pickup stalled twice. He shook uncontrollably, and his leg throbbed.

The truck skidded on the icy road, but Aaron, barely aware that he was driving at all, ignored the warning. Twice in two days he had wanted to kill, and twice he was unashamed for it.

There were two town patrol cars parked on the shoulder of the road when he arrived, and he nearly ran up the back of one as he slid to a halt and scrambled out. There was a small crowd hunched coldly in the vast well-tended yard: police, several neighbors looking ill at ease, Sorrentino himself pounding his arms against the air by the sheriff, and David standing quietly to one side . . .

. . . while the oldest men carefully lowered the body of the shaman into the oversized grave. They scuttled away, then, and the boy stepped up to drop in the trappings of his father's profession, a lock of his own hair, a brown seed, a young branch freshly cut. They buried the war-murdered man beneath black earth and passed the remainder of the night mourning. Lieutenant Jackoson continued to watch the boy—a onetime, now distant friend. He watched the boy sitting calmly on the grave, staring at the prisoner, a scarred man in a tattered blue uniform. Jackoson had warned his men to mind their own business this time, and they did, gratefully; but few slept and all were uneasy. And still the little boy stared . . .

. . . at the ground until Aaron placed an arm lightly around his shoulders and he looked up. No greeting. A look was all. Sheriff Jenkins, a scowl and sympathy fighting in his face, walked hurriedly over with Sorrentino directly behind him. Aaron glared at them, barely able to contain the rage he felt for his son. "How?"

he demanded without preliminaries. Sorrentino tried to bull forward, but Jenkins held up a hand to stop him.

"Frank here called me about forty-five minutes ago, Aaron. Said he was afraid he'd shot your son."

"I was just inside the wood, Jackoson," Sorrentino said, his voice oddly harsh. "I was chasing them wolves. I heard this noise right where I spotted them last, so I let go—"

"Without being sure?" Momentarily, Aaron was too appalled at the big man's stupidity to be angry. "You know kids are playing in there all the time. My God, Frank, you're a good enough shot to have waited a . . ." He stopped, seeing the retreat in the other man's eyes. "You . . ." He shook his head to clear it. "You . . . no, you couldn't have. Not even you."

"Now wait a damn minute, Jackoson."

"Shut up a minute, Frank."

"But, Sheriff, that man just accused me of deliberately killing that kid's animal!"

"He didn't say that, did he?"

Sorrentino sputtered, then wheeled and stalked away, muttering. Jenkins didn't watch him leave; Aaron did. "Listen, Aaron, I couldn't find any evidence that it happened any other way than he said. I know how you two feel about each other, but as far as I'm concerned, his story holds up. I'm sorry, Aaron, but it was an accident."

Aaron nodded, though he was just as sure the sheriff was wrong.

"Look, if you want, the boys and I will take the—"

"No," David said.

Aaron saw the look on Jenkins's face and knew it was the first thing David had said that morning. Against his better judgment he agreed. "We'll take him, Will. But thanks anyway. I'd appreciate it if some of your men would help me put him in the truck."

The sheriff started to say something, but the boy walked between them, past the neighbors to the truck where he let down the gate and stood by, waiting.

"The boy wasn't on the pony," Will said. "It must have wandered off while Davie was playing."

Aaron nodded. And what, he thought, was David playing?

Pinto's head had been hastily wrapped in a blanket now matted with blood. David sat stroking the animal's rigid flank. Through the rearview mirror, Aaron could see the hand moving smoothly over the cooling flesh. In his own eyes were the stirrings of tears. For once he thought he knew how the boy felt, to lose a friend much more than a pet. He drove slowly, turning off the road just before his own land began. There was a rutted path leading into the wood to a clearing where the boys of the surrounding farms had erected forts and castles, trenches and spaceships. At its western end was a slight rise, and it was there that they sweated in the cold noon of the grey day and buried Pinto. The wind was listless, the rain stopped. When the grave was filled, Aaron walked painfully back to the truck to wait for David, and an hour passed before they were headed for home, and all the way Aaron tried vainly to joke the boy back into a fair humor, even promising him a new pet as soon as they could get into town. David, however, only stared at the road, one hand unconsciously working at his throat.

Immediately they arrived at the house, the telephone rang and Aaron grabbed for it, hoping it was Miriam. It was Sorrentino, apologizing and sounding unsettlingly desperate; and Aaron, eager to talk, eager to turn from his son's depression, profusely acknowledged the other's story, and damned himself as he spoke. Sorrentino kept on. And on. He was babbling, Aaron realized, very often incoherent, and in his puzzlement at the rancher's behavior, he responded in kind, knowing he sounded like an idiot, trying not to admit that he was somehow, inexplicably, afraid of his own son.

When Sorrentino at last rang off, Aaron felt rather than saw the boy's bedroom door open. He would not turn. He was not going to watch grief harden the young face. "It'll be all right, son," he said weakly. "In time. In time. You . . . you have to give it time."

The boy was a shadow. "He could see, Dad."

"We can't prove that, son."

"He could see everything. The brush isn't that high."

"David, we cannot prove it. Things are different here, you know that. We have to prove things first."

And still he did not turn.

"He did it on purpose. You know that, and you won't do anything. You know it and . . ."

Turn around, you old fool. He's only a boy. He's only a boy, for God's sake . . .

. . . for God's sake, the lieutenant thought as he watched the boy sitting on the grave, how long is he going to stay there? His eyes, burning from the darkness and the fire's acrid smoke, shifted to the prisoner. The man was staring at the shaman's son, entranced, it seemed, and unmoving. He was unbound, but none of the tribesmen seemed to care. They were confident with knowledge that Jackoson didn't have, and Jackoson didn't like it. He tried instead to think of home and a place where people behaved the way they were supposed to . . .

. . . behave yourself, stupid, he thought, and send the boy to bed. He'll feel better in the morning.

"You'd better lie down, now, Dad," the shadow said. "Your leg must be hurting after all that digging."

Aaron closed his eyes and nodded, feeling for the first time since leaving the house eons ago the painful strain that nearly buckled him. A moment later he felt the boy's arm around his waist, guiding him firmly to the bedroom. In the dim curtained light, he watched David prepare the bed, then stand aside while he eased himself between the cold sheets. David smiled at him.

"We'll . . . we'll see the sheriff again in a few days, son. We'll talk to him."

"Sure, Dad."

"And David, don't . . . I mean, you know, don't try to do anything on your own, you know what I mean? I mean, don't go off chasing his sheep into the next county or smashing windows. Okay?"

The boy paused in the doorway. "Sure, Dad. You want your medicine?"

"No, thanks. I'll be all right in a little while. Just call me for dinner."

"Okay. I'm going to read or something. You need anything, please call."

Aaron smiled. "Go on, son." And after the door closed, he

wondered, not for the first time, if he had been right in taking the boy away. Neither, in half a decade, seemed closer to understanding the other than when they had started out on the plane from Saigon. They spoke the same language, shared the same house, but the rapport David had with the animals, with Pinto, was missing between father and son. The war was no longer a threat, its use as a bond had dissolved.

I don't know my own son, he thought.

A part of his mind told him to stop feeling sorry for himself; the problem wasn't a new one.

I'm not feeling sorry for myself.

You sound like one of Miriam's soap operas.

I don't.

He's an ordinary boy who needs time. He's seen war.

He's had five years, and so, by the way, have I.

And when he slept, he dreamed of a slight mound in a path supposedly cleared and the sound he felt and heard before waking screaming in a hospital in Japan with a leg raw and twisted. He had refused amputation. He needed the leg.

When he opened his eyes, it was dark. He tried to fall asleep again, but a rising wind nudged him back to wakefulness. Finally he swung out of bed and dressed quietly. He was hungry and thirsty. Cautiously, he crept into the kitchen to fix a snack and unaccountably remembered a rancher he knew in passing who had a string of Shetlands he rented to pony rides during the summer fairs. Maybe, he thought, he could persuade this man to part with one of his animals on credit. It would be easy enough to explain what had happened to Pinto. The man would have to help him. Slowly the idea grew, hurrying his actions, making him grin at himself. Without stopping to drink the coffee he had poured, he hastened down the hall to David's room.

It was empty. His boots were gone, and his jacket. There was a hint of panic before Aaron realized that David, still mourning, had probably gone out to the barn to Pinto's stall. Snatching his coat from the closet, he rushed outside, gasping once at the cold air and the strong wind that slid across the now-frozen ground. A digging pain in his thigh caused him to slow up, but long before he'd fling open the barn door, he knew the building would be empty. He stood in the barnyard, aimlessly turning, seeking a direction to travel until he saw the faint orange glow over the trees. He stared, hands limp at his sides, squinting, thinking, denying all the fears that founded his nightmares. He knew his century and still refused to believe what he had seen on the jungled mountain, dreaded what he might see if he followed the light.

It was just before dawn . . .

. . . and Lieutenant Jackoson was the only squad member still awake, the others sleeping in luxurious safety for the first time in days. Night noises. Night wind. He was drowsy and rubbed the blur from his eyes. Curiosity prodded him; he rubbed his eyes again. The fire burned sullenly at the side of the grave. The boy was naked, now, and standing . . .

. . . running over the ice-crusted ground, Aaron was pushed from behind by the wind. He ignored his leg as long as he could, concentrating on the wavering line of trees ahead. Then, just inside the tiny wood, his foot pushed through a hidden burrow and he slammed to the ground. Palms, knees, forehead stung. When he tried to stand, his leg wrenched out from under him, and he cried out. Before him, trunks and branches, brush and grass, twisted slowly in the light of the fire, weaving darkness within darkness. Aaron pushed himself to one leg, his teeth clamped to his lips and, using the trees for support, hobbled toward the clearing. His left leg went numb, the pain felt only from the hip, and finally he collapsed.

Not now, he begged, not now!

He crawled, forearms and one foot, seeing his breath puff in front of his face, seeing his hands turn a dry red from the cold. Then there was a break in the pine, and he saw the boy . . .

. . . on his father's grave, shuffling slowly from side to side, humming to himself as he stared at the mound beneath his feet. The tribe had reassembled, squatting in the shadows, silent. The pit fire cracked . . .

. . . on the rise, and the smell of burning pine pierced the brittle air. And between himself and his son, Aaron saw . . .

. . . the prisoner seemingly rooted in place, turned so his face was hidden. The boy, not looking up, not acknowledging the world's existence, muttered something and the man shuddered . . .

. . . beneath his heavy fur-trimmed hunting jacket. There was a rifle, useless now, dangling from one hand. Aaron tried to push himself up, to stand, but the agony was too great, and at the moment all he wanted was the heat from the fire that silhouetted the boy . . .

. . . shuffling faster, mumbling in rapid bursts while the prisoner swayed, slipped back, then lurched forward. Slowly, toward the grave, in the light of the fire. Jackoson thought he was dreaming . . .

. . . but the cold was too real, and he wondered how the boy, so lately his son, could stand the wind that whipped the flames from side to side and drew . . .

. . . the prisoner toward them, stiff-jointed like a grotesque marionette. The jungle . . .

. . . the clearing was quiet, and Aaron could hear the boy, chanting now, urging, taunting the big man forward. Aaron tried shouting, but his throat was too dry, his mind unable to break loose his tongue. All he could see was the rifle glinting. Sorrentino moved. Lumbered. Silent.

Prisoner/rancher reached the grave.

The boy, still chanting, reached out, palms up, waiting until the other grasped them (the rifle dropping soundlessly). A pair now, circling in slow motion. Dirt shifted beneath their feet. Aaron watched . . .

. . . more drowsy still from the fire's heat and the boy's monotonic voice, still undecided whether or not he was dreaming . . .

. . . numb from the cold and drawing blood from his lips as he fought the pain enshrouding his thoughts. He lay flat on the ground, his head barely raised, his eyes glazed.

The boy abruptly dropped his hands and stepped down from the grave.

The prisoner waited, standing, and made no attempt to resist when the shaman's hand/pony's teeth reached through the earth and took hold.

Jackoson slept, thought he was dreaming.

Aaron fainted, thought he was screaming.

David, smiling, picked up a shovel.

SMITH

THE THREE OF TENS

It was no more than a week past midsummer when I came home from playing, and my mother said to me, Jaimie, how'd you like to go to the fair tonight? Well, I looked at her, wondering if something had gone wrong, but she seemed no worse or no better than she always did since dad died. Her hair, not yet gone grey, was pushing into a knob at the back of her head, and there was always little bits like feathers flying about in the breeze she made rushing from one place to another. She seemed no more tired than usual, though her hand was shaking a little when she lifted the kettle from the burner. So I looked around the kitchen thinking maybe she'd been down to the King's Arms and carried home a pint or two. But there was nothing there, either.

"Jaimie," she said again, "don't you hear me, son? I said, do you want to go to the fair tonight?"

"Why, Mum," I said, "do you have a caller coming?"

I grinned, taking away the bite of what I was saying, and she waved me a quick no while she poured the tea and laid out the scones.

"I just want you to get out of the house for a while. You've been staying in every night past supper, and it's not like you."

I shrugged and sat at the table. "I don't want to go," I said.

"And why not, if you don't mind me asking?"

I shrugged again and fiddled with my spoon. "I don't know. I just don't want to go, that's all."

"Michael down the road is going," she said. "You could stay by him if you're afraid, you know."

"I'm not afraid," I said, a bit angrier than I wanted. "And I am so big enough to cross the road, you know." Then I saw the tease in her eyes. "Ain't I been taking care of you this past year, then?"

She sat down opposite me and took my hand, patted it once when she saw I didn't go for that, and leaned back. She tucked at her hair, brown like mine only longer, and fluffed the dress around her front as if it was too tight. "You have indeed been doing that, Jaimie," she said, "and to look at you now, nobody'd think you haven't even seen a dozen winters."

"Well, what do you mean by that?"

"I mean, Jaimie, that your friends aren't your friends anymore. I never see your old chums coming round, and you're getting a hard look a child shouldn't have your age. You go to school, you come right back and change and go to Mr. Harrow's for the errands he has for you, then back to eat and straight on to bed." She shook her head and let it drop forward slowly like it was too heavy for her to hold up anymore. "It isn't like we need the money, what with your dad's pension, and it isn't what I want for you, Jaimie. And I know he wouldn't want it, either." She jerked her head in the direction of the picture on the wall next to the Queen's, and then she pushed a pound note to me, and when I didn't take it up straightaway, she laid it in my palm and closed my fingers around it.

"Go," she said. "Stay until after dark and see the lights. Then come on back and tell me what they look like. Michael'll be by about half-past eight."

It was ended then, and whether I wanted to go or not, she had already made the decision and there was nothing I could do about it. She's funny that way, she is. And when I come to think about it, I decided I wouldn't mind spending a few pennies at that.

So, when Michael came around practically dragging that girl of his, I was dressed and scrubbed and ready. The girl—Charley, they called her because her stupid name was Charlene—takes my hand right off, and before I knew it, was hustling me between them to the fair.

In case you don't know the place, there's a roundabout directly past the town's center, and two roads coming off it have between them this big field of grass that stretches toward Windsor and climbs up a hill into a lot of trees. Off the road on the left is Egham, where I live, and off the road on the right that goes to Windsor is the Thames. Well, dead in the middle of this field was a large circle of caravans with their inside walls open for games of chance and things like that. There was a Big Wheel, some rides for kids littler even than me, and on the side of the circle with its back to the river was a wagon that was supposed to have a scary Fun House. Only it wasn't scary. I went through twice, and I know. There was a lot of people, it being Saturday night and all, and as soon as Michael and Charley walk me into the place where all the colored lights were, they patted me on the head, said ta, and made me promise to look for them once an hour to see that I was all right.

This didn't bother me, though, because they know I can pretty much take care of myself, and I didn't always care for the way Charley liked to mother me.

So I changed my quid for pennies in the gambling arcade and played a few of the machines and lost a bit, then did a ride on the bumper cars, which wasn't much fun because there was no one there I knew good enough to really bump into. I tried throwing some hoops around these blocks of wood to win a goldfish for my mother, threw a couple of darts at some balloons, and just was mucking about when, during my wandering, I saw this small wagon tucked in sort of by the side of the Wheel. There was this sort of old man sitting on a chair under a sign that said he could make me a ten if I wanted to pay.

"Hey, mister," I said to him. He looked up and smiled. He hadn't shaved in a while, and his eyes kind of looked like my dad's when he'd had one pint too many, but I didn't smell nothing in the air. So I took a step closer and asked him what a ten was and how much did it cost.

"Well, lad," he said, reaching into his hip pocket and pulling out a pipe what looked like it'd been dropped a hundred times from the top of Windsor Castle. "I'll tell you something you don't know," he said; "a ten is whatever you want it to be. You want it to be a special wee gift for your mum, then that's what it'll be. You want it to be something not so fine for the chappie what steals your lunch, then that's what it'd be, too."

He laughed, then, and I backed away a bit. I wasn't scared or nothing, you see, but when you get to be the man of the house at my age, you got to learn pretty quick who wants to do you out of a fiver and whose hand you'd better shake quick before he slips it into your pocket.

"That don't make sense what you said," I told him. "That's silly."

"No, it don't make sense," the old man admitted, sucking on that pipe and staring at the blue smoke coming out of the bowl. "And that's the gem of it, you see. It don't make sense, and that makes it better than some flippin' doll or a bag with a goldfish in it, don't it?"

I didn't really know what he was saying, but there was something about him that wouldn't let me get away. It was then he waved me closer, and I realized we'd been near shouting all the time to be heard over the people laughing and shouting, and the music and the noise. So I moved right beside him, and he reaches into a sack by his feet and pulls out a big handful of little boxes no bigger than my thumb.

"Tens," he said. "They cost tenpence each," and he laughed, and I could see his yellow teeth and smell the dead leaf smell of his tobacco. I kind of gave a shudder, and he stares at me before holding up the boxes. "They're numbered, you see," he said, "one through twenty. The odd ones are for your enemies, the others for your friends."

I tried to look close, but he pulled them back just enough so I couldn't touch. For tenpence maybe I could get something nice for mum, I thought, and I was going to pick out number twelve when I looked into his face. He was still smiling, the old man was, but there was nothing behind it, and when I saw those eyes the color of the river at night, everything kind of went away and I just stood there. Then I got awfully hot, and I started to feel dizzy and sickly like I'd had too many sweets. I felt myself holding out a hand and saw him picking out the pennies before he grabbed my other hand and dropped a box into it.

"What do I do with it," I said, sounding like I was far away at the top of the hill.

"You'll think of something," he said, "and mind you be careful with it, brat." Suddenly the smile went away, and he pushed at me with the end of his pipe. "Now go away, boy, and let someone else have a go."

"But—"

"Go on," he said, "before I have to call the manager."

I got mad and wanted to ask for my pennies back, but he kept staring at me all the time, and so I quick turned away and went to look for Michael and Charley. I didn't feel so big anymore, and I wanted Charley to take my hand for a bit. The lights, the noise of the rides, the people's faces all twisted and funny—the fair wasn't much fun anymore. When I finally found them at the shooting gallery, I asked Charley to take me across the road to the river, and she did it without asking why because that's the way she is. We walked along the grass for people to sit and watch the pleasure boats go by, and then I stepped into the weeds a little ways and threw the box into the water.

It wasn't heavy at all, but it sank right away.

"Now why'd you go and do that?" she said as we walked back to the fair.

I shrugged. "It weren't worth nothing," I said.

"Where'd you get it, Jaimie?"

"Over there," I said, pointing when we reached the Wheel. But when she asked again and I looked, the old man was gone and the sign was away, too. Even his small wagon.

"I think you've been taken, Jaimie m'boy," she laughed, and I felt bad at that for a minute, but then she grabbed me under the arms and lifted me over her head. "You'll not get down until you give me a kiss," she said, and when I stuck out my tongue at her, she laughed again.

"Hey," Michael said, coming up behind us while I was pretending to hit Charley after she let me down, "do you mind if I hit her a few myself, or is this a private party?"

"Jaimie got taken," said Charley, dodging around him to get away from me.

"Who?" Michael said, suddenly very mad and kneeling down to look at me straight on.

"I don't want no trouble," I said. "I shouldn't have done it, but he looked at me funny, and it was only tenpence—"

"I don't care if it was a hundred pounds, Jaimie," he said. "You got taken and that wasn't right."

I looked at him, saw his black eyes frowning, and grinned; I think that if I had any friends left in the world, Charley and Michael would be all of them.

"He was over by the Wheel," I said, "sitting by a wagon. There was a sign, too, but they're all gone now."

He put a hand on my shoulder, and we moved over and could find nothing but the smoking leftovers of the pipe tobacco in the grass. "He was right here," I said, looking around. "He was—"

Suddenly there was a scream, louder than the ones from the dumb girls on the Wheel, one that made the ones close to it turn around and look.

It was getting dark outside the caravans' circle, and the lights in the middle made it so bright that nobody could give a good account later of what they saw. But there was this man, this . . . something standing just in the shadow of the Fun House wagon, getting up from a bundle lying on the ground. Charley told me not to look and pushed me behind her, but I had already seen that the bundle was a lady and her face was all red and shining, and you couldn't see her eyes or her mouth for all the red.

Then the man-thing ran away across the field toward the hill, and it was a long time before anyone got enough nerve to follow him or call the police.

Of course, Charley took me home straightaway and dragged my mother into the kitchen, but she was so excited and crying and looking at the back door that mum calls me in, knowing I was hiding in the hall listening.

"Tell me, Jaimie," she said.

So I told her.

She gave us a kind of funny look and said, "What did he look like?"

"Big," I said, "tall as a house he was. He had a black thing on, like a greatcoat, but it was all wet. And, and his face was all . . . bones . . . and . . ."

And before I could help it, I was crying worse than Charley with shivers that wouldn't quit even when mum held on to me.

I didn't sleep well that night.

I kept seeing that face.

It had no eyes.

Well, the next day my aunt and uncle took us to Windsor Great Park to see the polo matches, and everyone there was talking about the excitement at the fair, and when we got home we saw in the papers all the stories about the murder. The police finally came after we'd left, and they chased after the guy, but they never caught him. They lost him, it said, in the forest park at the top of the hill. The funny thing was, a lot of people must have seen him, like me, but in all them papers there weren't no pictures at all. Not the camera kind, but the kind like they have them artists draw. All they said was: a man of unusual description.

Two days later, over in Englefield Green, a pharmacy was broken into and two people living upstairs were killed. The papers said their faces were smashed.

The fair was still on, but hardly anyone went. Even my mother decided she didn't want to go, even when I told her I had a good time.

Since we was into the summer holiday, I didn't have to go to school. So when I wasn't running errands for Mr. Harrow's shop, I spent a lot of time in the small front yard helping my mother with our roses, which were the largest ones on the whole street. The neighbors were always coming over and asking me how I do them so well. Then, all they talked about was the killer. My nights hadn't been all that good since that day. So when they started into talking like that, I always left. But one day Michael came around and told us that the killer had murdered a whole family, parents and two kids, on the other side of town. Egham being the size it is, that wasn't too far away. He said they weren't going to put it in the papers anymore because of the terrible things done to the people, and the police didn't want to scare anyone. But he knew a chum in the station who told him everything that was happening.

I started to ask Michael some questions about it, but my mother all of a sudden got mad and sent me inside to put on the kettle. She always did that when she didn't want me to hear anything bad.

It rained that night, and I could hear the police sirens just a couple of blocks away, down by the train station.

I kept having those dreams about the box.

That face.

One night I told mum I had to go out for a quick errand for Mr. Harrow, but instead I ran over to the fair. There was maybe ten people there, not counting the hawkers, but when I asked a couple of the workers where the man with the wagon was, they only shoved me away and told me I was too little to be out so late. I could see they was getting ready to pack it in, but then one man said I was too young to drink, that there wasn't any old man like I said, and there never had been.

"Then what about the box I bought," I said, grabbing at his coat before he could walk away like all the rest.

"What box?"

"The one I bought from him," I said. "For tenpence."

"Oh? Well," he said with his face telling me he thought it was all a joke, "well, where is it?"

"I threw it in the river," I said.

"Oh, well, then," he said, patting me on the head like I was a little boy. "It'll come back to you, then. Anything you drop in there always comes back. Didn't you know that?"

I ran all the way home.

When I finally got to my block, I started to walk, trying to keep my face from getting all red, otherwise mum would think I'd been up to doing wrong. All the houses were close together, you know, with two families in a house side by side, and unless you knew the numbers or the colors of the shutters or something, you really couldn't tell one place from another.

But when I turned into our gate, I saw the box.

It was sitting in the middle of the walk. There was a puddle of water around it. I looked at the roses, but they were dry. So was the little bit of grass we had.

I looked up at the house, then across the hedge to Mrs. Daniels's yard. Then I kind of snuck up on it, feeling my heart getting ready to break through my shirt and my fingertips getting all tingly. It wasn't hot that night—there were clouds and all—but a drop of sweat stung my eye, and I jerked my head to clear it away. I moved another inch and stuck out my foot to tip the box over. The number three was still on one side, but the bottom had been ripped off. I kneeled down so I could look inside, but it was just at sunset and I couldn't see anything very well.

And when something tapped my shoulder, I let out a horrid yell and fell over the box, felt it under me and rolled away, trying to crawl to the front door before that man-thing could get at me. But these hands grabbed me and pulled me to my feet, and I started punching and screaming until I opened my eyes and saw Michael ducking away from my fists.

"Hey, come on, come on," he said. "Settle yourself, Jaimie, it's only me, it's only me."

I got mad at him then, just as mum came running outside to see what all the noise was about.

"Why'd you go and scare me like that," I said, puffing like I'd just run in from London. "I could have done you harm, Michael."

He looked at me dead serious and nodded before turning to my mother, who was demanding that someone please say something she could understand. "Sorry," he said. "I guess I spooked him a little."

"Well," she said, wiping her hands on her apron, "you come in for a cuppa. The state he's in, I'm not going to spend the rest of the night alone with this vicious devil. And bring Charley with you."

I poked my head around Michael's waist, and there she was, leaning against the front hedge trying not to laugh at me. I frowned and poked a fist at her. She poked one back and came through the gate.

"You're out to kill my man," she said, cuffing the side of my head.

"No such thing," I said, pushing her away.

"Inside, all of you," mum said, and we were pushed into the kitchen before she really got mad. And we attacked some scones until I remembered the box, and Michael said something about the fair closing down because no one was going. So I told mum what had happened outside, and Michael got up right away and went to the front, and I could hear him on the porch before he suddenly slammed the door and came back in. His face was more white even than mine, and he told mum real quietly to bolt the latch and check all the windows. Charley he sent upstairs to do the same, and he waved for me to follow him into the parlor where he picked up the telephone and dialed 999.

"Michael, what's happening?" I must have sounded scared because he put an arm around me and pulled me close while he told the policeman who answered the emergency number that there was a prowler around our house and would he hurry and send a man round to check it. There was a mumbling I couldn't hear, and Michael nodded and rang off.

"Jaimie," he said, "I want you to go into the kitchen and turn off all the lights. You don't stop for anything. You come right on back."

"Michael?"

"It's all right, son," he said, and for the first time I didn't mind him calling me that even though he'd just started going to university himself. I did what he said as fast as I could, grabbed a tin of biscuits from the cupboard, and ran back. Charley and my mother were sitting on the sofa when I came in. And even though it was still summer, someone had lit a small fire. I didn't say anything; I was cold, too. The curtains were drawn tight over the windows, and the only light other than the fire was the small lamp in the corner.

"We'll just have to wait now, for the police," Michael said, "and I'll show them that box." He was standing in the middle of the room, his hands behind his back, kind of rocking on his heels like he was a mate on a ship. On the mantel over the fireplace I could see the box. It still looked wet.

Suddenly there was a smashing of glass, and mum says, "That's Mrs. Daniels."

Michael ran to the window and pulled back the curtain a little, but he said he couldn't see anything. But we could hear enough. There was a thumping, and one long scream that made me drop to the floor. We could hear plates breaking against the wall, and then something heavy, and it sounded like that whole half of the building was going to come down on Mrs. Daniels's head. There was another scream that Charley made, quietly, and then there was nothing.

Michael licked his lips and pointed me to stand by the fireplace. Charley and mum were holding on to each other tight, and Charley looked like a little girl and mum like she was a hundred years gone. I could see there were tears on her face, too. I watched while Michael picked up the poker and held it like a bat, but I could see he was almighty scared, and that made me scared, too, because if Michael couldn't do anything to help us, who could?

"Who is that man," Charley said, stuttering so bad I couldn't understand all her words.

Michael shrugged, but I said that I knew and told them what the man at the fair had told me about the box, and the river. He gave it and me a look, and mum said that it was nonsense and only the Gaels believed in things like that, but I could see she was just talking because she couldn't take her eyes off the mantel.

Now, I know there's a real lot of things that can happen whether you believe them or not, and if that box had something in it that could make the river give up one of its dead, then I didn't see how we were going to get away from it. But I didn't say all that out loud because I was scared enough, and I didn't want to make mum feel worse.

Then we heard the window in the back door smash onto the floor.

"It's your box, Jaimie, your box!" Charley shouted and jumped to her feet and pressed herself against the wall.

"No!"

Another smash, and the door slammed back against the stove, and there was the rattle of the soup pot falling onto the floor.

And wet noises. Like someone walking in out of the rain.

Michael turned out the lamp and whispered to the women to get behind the sofa. All there was when I got used to it was the light from the fireplace; I was on one side, and Michael was on the other.

Wet noises, dragging. And it came around the corner.

Charley and mum whimpering behind the sofa.

The light was moving from the fire, shining off the thing's coat that was dripping water. I could hear it. Nothing else.

All I could see was its hands and its face. The hands had no skin, the fingers sharpened from years of scraping along the riverbed; they were huge and clung to with lots of little things like pointed scales. It held them up and took a step into the room.

Its face. Bones. Hanging green-black things. Grey, like the belly of a dead fish in the market. And nothing, nothing at all where the eyes should have been.

Michael made a noise, and the thing moved to him, quicker now. It reached out, and Michael swung with the poker, hitting it near the elbow and making it lean back. Then it came at him again, like I wasn't even there, and Michael aimed for its head, but he missed and it grabbed him like they were going to wrestle. Its hand came up and Michael started screaming, and the women started screaming, and there was a pounding on the front door, and all I could hear was Charley shouting how it was my box, my box. I started shaking all over, and Michael and the man-thing bumped into a table, knocking it over with a lamp and a candy dish. I started looking around for something to throw, anything at all, when I remembered the mantel; and I stretched up and grabbed around until I found the box.

The thing was making noises and Michael was still screaming. I didn't like the sound of a man screaming, and I crushed the box under my foot and threw it into the fire. Then I don't know what happened to me, but I started shouting terrible things and ran to try to jump on its back, and suddenly there was this awful smell and the fire went bright for a second, so bright I could see the blood splashed on the wall, all over the thing's coat.

Then everything stopped.

The river-thing let go of Michael, who dropped back a step and fell onto his back, and his face was cut so much I couldn't look. And then it turned around to me, and I ran into the hall just as the door broke in and policemen started pouring into the house. They stopped, though, when they saw the thing standing there, but before one of them could use his gun, the coat folds like it was over nothing but air. The next thing I knew there was a pile of coat at my feet running out water, and everyone talking all at once. I tried to get to Michael, but then all the lights went out, and the next thing I saw was myself in a hospital bed and a nurse bringing in mum and Charley, and they were carrying all kinds of sweets.

Charley leaned over me and kissed me hard and said, "My second hero."

"I didn't do anything," I said. "How's Michael?"

Her smile went away, but she said he was going to be all right except they would have to do a lot of work on his face before it could look good again. Not, she said, that it ever did. But it was a sad kind of laugh she gave me, then, and I could see the crying in back of her eyes.

"Hey, Mum," I said when she bent over to take my hands and kiss me. "What am I doing here? I'm all right, honest."

"You are that," she said. "The doctors say it's for observation."

"What's that mean?"

"It means they want to be sure you're all right. You've had yourself quite a shock for a little boy, Jaimie."

"Well, what about—"

"The police took what was left away."

"Will I get my picture in the papers?"

"No, Jaimie. They're saying they shot the man while he was escaping capture. No pictures. No one would believe it."

"It was the box, Mum," I said.

"I know, dear."

"Something in the box, Mum. It got into the water and—"

"I know, dear. Don't tax yourself."

"The ashes! Charley, you got to be sure she throws out the ashes. Bury them. Get metal, a tin or something, and bury it in the yard. You got to do it, Mum. Charley, you got to see she does it."

I guess I was getting kind of loud because mum put her hand on my lips gently and nodded.

"I'm way ahead of you, Jaimie. It's done, don't worry. Not exactly like you said, but done just the same."

"Mum, what did you do?"

"I shoveled it all in a sack and flushed it. Nothing to fear, Jaimie. All the ashes are down in the sewers, stretched from here to London, most likely."

She winked. Charley smiled. Then the nurse came and said they had to leave, and I was left alone in the ward. Thinking about what my mother had done.

So, if you come to visit, if you come to find my house, knock loud and call out your name. But don't be surprised if nobody's home.

Anywhere.

DIGGING

I think it rather safe to say that I dislike fog of any kind as much as any sea captain who ever lived. I suppose that means I'm not much of a romantic. I can see the beauty of the beast on occasion, but I can also feel its clammy breath on my face, and I hate the sparkling white wall that jumps up in front of me when I'm driving. It's not that fog is necessarily creepy, or ominous, or even remotely lethal; it's just . . . inconvenient.

But there was a fog on the night I first heard the digging.

I was standing on my front porch smoking a cigarette, and not enjoying it at all. My guests had left some ten minutes before, but I still had no inclination to head inside and clean up their mess. I had purchased the house on its full acre lot because it had been, at the time, somewhat prestigious to do so and, frankly, because it was a considerable asset when stalking a woman. It is far easier to be cozy, to be candlelight-and-soft-music suave, in a house like this than in an apartment with neighbors who keep close track of you and who make a mockery of your walls. It didn't always work, of course, since that's the nature of the game. But I never regretted those who made the trip from the city with me.

I drew deeply on the cigarette, and shivered.

The fog was a thick one this time, the kind London would boast of before the classy dowager got modern and cleaned up her act. Cars ghosted by, sound was eerily magnified, and porch lights farther up the block were either totally obscured or sat like shimmering blotches of turned mustard in the air. It was not at all beautiful, and it was chilling me to the bone. Finally, after punishing myself enough for one night, I flicked what remained of the cigarette over the railing and turned to open the door.

And heard the digging.

The scrape of the shovel slipping into dirt not quite soft enough for an easy job; the thud of a heel shoving it in farther; the scrape of withdrawal; the thud of soft earth falling to one side.

Crazy, I thought, and cocked my head until I had decided the noise was coming from behind the house on the right—a tidy little thing that belonged to Roger and Betty Dillan. I walked slowly to the end of the porch and leaned out, listening. No doubt about it. Someone was digging in Roger's backyard. I thought at first it might be some kids lusting after Bet's prize flowers—they used to do it often, to save themselves the price of a florist. Roger had caught them finally, and they had stopped immediately. There had been no threat of police action or complaining to parents. There had been no violence, actual or implied. It was, simply, Roger. He had a way about him.

And if it wasn't the kids, then it must have been Alger, and I felt suddenly sad.

Alger was a purebred bloodhound of indeterminate age, yet obviously older than he had a right to be. Much older, if you believed the stories Roger told about him. And he was dying. Of this and that and whatever else dogs get when they've outlived their time. Roger, however, could not bring himself to take the animal to the vet. He wanted Alger to die at home, where he was born, as long as he was in no discernible pain.

The beast, then, was dead, and poor Roger was burying him.

I hurried back to the steps, crossed the damp lawn, and made my way to the hedge that separated our properties. When we were kids there were well-worn prickly tunnels through that eternally green wall, and now those gaps had been widened to accommodate us as adults. It was, I had always believed, something akin to a miracle that I had been able to buy the place where, like Alger, I had been born, a greater one that the intervening owners had not torn down that infernal green wall.

I pushed my way through, arms close to my sides and face averted, and was halfway up the gentle slope toward the Dillans' backyard when I realized the noise had stopped, the only sound my tobacco-labored breathing.

I hesitated, doubting for a moment I had heard it at all.

No, I thought; my hair may be pretending it belongs to the tide, but my hearing is still perfect.

So I fought through the fog's unpleasantly cool hands and headed straight for the steps that led up to the kitchen door. There was a light on, diffused and dimmed by the fog, and I knocked twice, once, on the storm door before letting myself in.

Roger was sitting at the kitchen table, a massive butcher block affair that almost dwarfed the room. And Alger, lips fluttering in a snore, was asleep by the stove.

I was not only relieved, I felt incredibly stupid.

"Insomnia?" he asked. "Or are you hiding again?"

My grin was weak, though the question was a fair one. I tended, on occasion, to get myself too involved with women I didn't know how to handle; and when I had no idea how to end the relationship cleanly, without spilling anyone's blood, I used the tried-and-up-until-now-true method of not answering the telephone, vanishing for a while, and finally precipitating an argument that ended it all in a cleansing rage. Hardly sporting, I suppose, but nevertheless effective.

"Neither," I said. "I heard someone digging outside there and thought the kids were raiding you again."

Roger was a head taller than I, but several pounds lighter. His hair was streaked elegantly with grey, and his face was enviously unlined. He worked as a nuclear plant troubleshooter for various power companies and reactor manufacturers up and down the East Coast. These were miserable times for him now; too many accidents making the headlines, and not enough answers to keep the public from panicking when antigroups shrilled, factually or not. It was a pressure he had not encountered before, anywhere, and I don't think the poor guy understood how to deal with it without losing himself in nightmares.

"Yeah," he said. His hands were folded loosely around a dark bottle of Irish beer. I rose and got myself one, though I had the distinct impression I wasn't welcome tonight.

"So?" I said, leaning back in the ice-cream-parlor chair.

"So what?"

"So the digging."

"It was me," he said, with a glance toward the door.

I took a drink and licked my lips. "In November? Garbage," I suggested then, giving him an out in case it was none of my business. It wasn't.

"Yeah."

I drained the bottle and tossed it cleanly into the white receptacle by the refrigerator. There was a green plastic bag folded into it, and it was practically full. I got out of the chair with a somewhat confused smile. "Foggy," I said, standing by the door. "Thick as pea soup."

Roger belched. "I hate it."

I hadn't caught the tone. "Yeah. Me, too."

"No," he said sternly. "I mean, I really hate it, Andy."

"No kidding? I always thought you always thought it was kind of Byronic or something. You know, Heathcliff on the moors and all that crap."

He smiled when I looked at him, and there was no mirth behind it. "I used to."

I had had enough. I opened the door as noisily as I could. "Look, Rog, are you going to talk, or are you going to keep on auditioning for Gary Cooper?"

"Yep."

I slammed the door and cracked my heels hard on the steps going down. The kitchen light barely reached the ground, but as I headed for the hedge I saw where he had been digging. It was a short, narrow trench, the raw earth already gleaming wetly, and obscenely, into fog-born mud. I wondered, then—and wondered why I didn't think of it before—if he had hit something on the road, a cat maybe, and had buried it. He was like that, Roger Dillan was. Killing things of any persuasion brought out the supreme guilts in him. In fact, I've seen him close to tears just because he'd barely missed clipping a rabbit. Me, I've sometimes succumbed to the urge we all have and never admit to and have actually aimed my car at whatever had no business being on my road. Since I've never hit anything, however, I don't really know how I would react. But I sure as hell wouldn't cry.

Roger, I thought, sometimes you're a real dip.

With my mood thoroughly soured I didn't bother to clean up. And I was no better the following morning. Scowling at the world, I decided it was wiser to leave the car at home and take the bus into the city—there was always the chance I might do something stupid with it.

Thankfully, the fog was gone. It was beginning to give me the unreasonable creeps.

I was, by modest and contemporary definition, an advertising man. Which is to say, I somehow managed with fair regularity to come up with enough viable and banal slogans for enough bland products to keep those paychecks and bonuses coming in without pause. I was middle-level on the executive scale, and as safe as I would ever be in my position because I aimed no higher. My ambitions, such as they were, were simple: a fair cushion in the bank against disaster, enough cash floating loose to buy dumb things when I wanted them or to lure women when I needed them, and to reach old age healthy enough for a nice swift departure when I was good and ready. And so far I was doing all right. You might even say I was years ahead of the game.

I also had a secretary—Jackie Bowman. Short, dimpled, just this side of pudgy; the perfect cheerleader who had traded in her pompons for bonbons. We had had a go of it a couple of times over the past five years, but I wasn't stupid enough to keep it burning all the time. She has this husband . . . and I have no guts.

"Crayton's looking for you, Andy," she told me, leaning over my desk to drop the mail into my hands. I stared boldly down her admittedly fine cleavage, saw nothing I hadn't seen before, and shrugged. She scowled and walked out. A moment later I followed, nodded to Bob Parker as I stepped into the elevator, and rode to the floor above where I was ushered briskly and impersonally into Anthony Crayton's office—ebony, mahogany, pine, and walnut, with a dash of brass here and there for color and class. My immediate superior, David McInroe, was standing by the window that almost framed the Waldorf. Both of them were smiling, Crayton holding in his hands a portfolio I had done for our newest heavyweight client.

I smiled back and sat in the red leather chair nearest the desk.

Crayton, never one to be subtle or wield the velvet glove, dropped the smile. "Andrew," he said after taking his own seat, "I must say I've seen you do better work. Much better, I should add."

This, after I spent the whole month of October wondering what leaving the city on time was like.

McInroe said nothing; the set of his bloodless lips should have been enough to warn me the moment I had stepped through the door. I'd still been thinking about Roger, however, and never noticed a thing.

"I'm sorry," I said. And I was. No matter how much I bitched about these two, at least Crayton gave me points for doing my best . . . even when my best, as in this case, wasn't good enough.

"Disappointed," he said. "Very."

"Do you want me to try again?"

He shrugged and tented his manicures under his chin. "I don't honestly know if there's time, Andrew. We're pressing the deadline hard enough as it is. The filming, as you know, starts right after Thanksgiving, and we have to have some decent idea of the graphics by no later than this Friday if we want to keep the budget trim."

"So I'll work nights," I said agreeably. "You know I don't mind that."

McInroe gave me a rotten imitation of a smile.

Crayton pulled his fingers from under his chin and examined them.

"I'm off it, then," I said dully.

Crayton nodded.

McInroe did not once try to alleviate the pain.

I began trembling, first with humiliation, then with rage. My vision blurred momentarily, but I blinked the obstruction away and strode out of the office, told Jackie I thought she was a lousy lay and to stay the hell off my goddamned aching back, and hid out in my office until well after closing. Still trembling. Clenching and spreading my fingers until I thought they would cramp. Watching the room expand, contract, while my breathing echoed and my blood sought to burst through my veins.

I hadn't been fired, but it felt like it—for the first time in my career I had been shot down . . . from behind.

And for the first time in my career I was glad I didn't keep liquor in the office. Drinking now would only lead to mayhem, and it never once occurred to me to feel sorry for myself.

I did not stop shaking until I got off the empty bus four blocks from my home. And there it was again—that goddamned sweep of fog. Stalking me. Waiting until it knew I was down and then kicking me by taking away the one thing, sometimes the only thing, that managed to keep me from screaming at least until I'd cooled off—the long, almost pastoral view of my street with its split-trunk elms and oaks taller than the houses, the carefully tended lawns that even in November did not seem as though they were ready to die, the toys scattered and patient in the driveways, the women working or walking or waiting or . . .

The fog took it.

When I needed it most, the fog took it from me.

Damnit, I thought as I jammed my key into the lock, why the hell don't you bother someone else for a change?

I kicked the door open, slammed it, and dared the house to complain.

That night there was more digging.

I had made a run down to the liquor store to get myself some Tanqueray for a nice evening's stupor, and I was leaving the garage when I heard it.

Scrape. Thud! Scrape. Thud.

This time I didn't bother to think about it; I set the bag on the car's trunk and headed right over. But he had beaten me again, was already back at the table as I went inside.

"Are you going to dig up every damned blade of your stupid grass?" I demanded, heading straight for the refrigerator and ignoring the beer for a slim bottle of Guinness. "Christ, a man can't have any peace in this neighborhood anymore."

"You," he said, "are in a lousy mood."

I dropped the bottle cap into the garbage and took the chair opposite him. "Marvelous deduction, Dillan," I said. Then I told him what had happened at the office, and his face rearranged itself into an excellent semblance of genuine concern. We were close, Roger and I—he was the only man I could call friend who took my troubles to heart, no matter how stupid some of them were.

When I'd run down, fighting against the renewal of my trembling, he shook his head slowly. "You're not getting fired, are you?"

"No, I don't think so. I've been there too long for one screw-up to put me in the gutter. But I'm sure as hell going to miss that bonus this year. I was counting on it."

"For what? Your old age?"

I did not appreciate the bitter envy in his tone, and when I demanded again to know why he was digging out there in the fog I suppose my frustrations showed more than they should have. I knew it wasn't fair, taking things out on him, but without a wife who the hell did I have left?

He didn't answer for a long moment, and I gave him his measure of reproof, drinking while I waited and wondering if Bet were upstairs. She was a marvelous woman, an extraordinary one. Tropical black hair, and a slender figure that enticed rather than vamped. I wished I had just a little less conscience so I could take her to bed again.

"There are things," Roger said at last.

I blinked rapidly and brought myself back to the kitchen, which was growing warm, growing small. "Things," I repeated.

He nodded.

"All right. Things. Where?"

He jerked a thumb toward the door. I looked, as I knew I was expected to.

"They . . . these things, they come from the woods, you see."

"Oh," I said, not at all liking the way he looked at me. "That kind of thing."

Behind our homes—indeed, backing the entire large development in this part of town—was a rolling stretch of woodland that covered the low hills for several miles, and most of that huge parcel was state-preserved. It had once reached all the way to the Delaware River, but it was inevitable that civilization would discover it, and it was now slowly giving way to bulldozers and prefabs. For that reason, more than ever in the past few years we were discovering deer and other increasingly scarce wildlife sometimes literally in our own backyards. Most of the younger families, and Roger, delighted in it. I, perhaps predictably, did not. I saw nothing cute or cuddly about a voracious raccoon attacking my garbage can at three in the morning, or a russet deer making a twilight meal of whatever shrubs I had.

"No," Roger said, and the hollow fear in his voice made me push the Guinness to one side. His eyes, now that I looked at them closely, were pouched and lined; there were creases at the corners of his mouth I had never seen before. He was pale—no sleep. I considered immediately some sort of trouble between him and Bet, and discarded it. It must be the job; he couldn't be crazy enough to let so-called *things* worry him this much.

"What's the matter, Rog," I asked quietly. I was getting upset. I didn't want to lose him. Not now. Not when Bob Parker and the others in the office were beginning to eye me like hyenas.

"Things," he said again. I almost couldn't believe it—the man was actually afraid. "You hear stories, you know? And you think when you're a kid they're really great around the campfire. Remember? Remember when we used to go back there with your dad and my uncle and scare the shit out of each other? Remember them, Andy? Creatures that live deep in the woods, never walk there alone, boy, or they'll get you sure as hell? Tear you up, sonny. Eat you alive. Spit out the bones. Leave your heart on a limb. You know . . . stories."

"Yeah," I said, remembering, though I felt no nostalgia.

"You didn't believe them even then, did you."

I shook my head. "Great for campfires, like you said. Lousy for reality, adulthood, and the American flag."

He looked at me sorrowfully; I wanted to cry.

"Now," he said, "they've no place to go. I mean that, Andy, don't look at me that way. I'm a scientist, right, I know what I'm talking about. I'm not crazy. I'm definitely not crazy. I've . . . I've seen them. They're here. We've pushed them too hard, took away their homes and their privacy, and now they're here. I'm not crazy, Andy. I've—"

I nodded suddenly, then wiped a sheen of perspiration from the back of my neck. "I see now, yeah. You caught them—these *things* from the campfires you're talking about—you caught them in the woods or saw them on your lawn . . . and you killed them." I had to say it because Roger couldn't. Monsters or not, he had killed a living creature, and that right there was tearing him apart as much as the realization—to him—that all those dumb stories had a basis in fact.

Careful, I warned myself then; don't let him see how afraid you are.

"They're horrid, Andy," he said with a violent shudder. "Fangs like you wouldn't believe. Claws. They're small, like cats, and fast as hell. I used . . . both times I used the shovel."

He drained his beer, fetched himself another while I listened to him muttering to himself. It was—and there's no other word for it—eerie. The warm kitchen, the too-bright ceiling light, the fog outside—I've never been able to tell when he was drunk, so now I didn't know whether to laugh at him, with him, or just break down and cry. It isn't fair, I thought angrily; damnit, Rog, I've got troubles of my own!

He took his seat again and spun the can between his palms. "You don't believe me." It wasn't an accusation; it was a statement of resigned fact.

I gave him my best smile. "Monsters, Rog? Come on, pal, you've got to be kidding."

"I saw them, Andy." He was implacable.

Reason, I told myself; you've got to hit him with reason and bring him back where he belongs.

"Look," I said, trying to sound patient and not condescending, "I don't doubt you saw something, Rog. And from the looks of you, I sure don't doubt you killed it, too. But Jesus . . . Jesus, don't ask me to believe in fangs and claws."

His large fist hit the table so hard, so unexpectedly, that I jumped.

"There have been deaths," he said, almost hissing. "That widow four or five houses up who was torn apart in September. Those two campers out by the stream last month. Torn apart. Claws, Andy, claws."

"Dogs," I said as firmly as I could. "Dogs gone wild. I read the rest of the article, Roger. All the medical people and the police said it was dogs gone wild. And it wouldn't be the first time."

"Bullshit."

Now I *was* frightened, but not of campfire fancies. This man, this romantic bean pole who worked with powers that could wipe out the earth a million times over, this man I had grown up with and had shared women with, this man had retreated into a children's world where the worst things imaginable were only—

I jumped, and my heart actually froze for a split second, when a loud slam echoed through the room. I looked immediately to the door, ready to believe *any* damn thing, when I heard the mocking laughter. It was Bet. She had come into the room and had punched the wall. Grinning, I could have killed her.

"You," she said sternly to her husband, "are drunk again. Alger, take him to bed." Roger looked plaintively at me, then shrugged his defeat and followed the limping, half-blind bloodhound into the hallway. I was already at the door, my hand on the knob, when Bet whispered for me to stay. And we waited until Roger had reached the upstairs.

"Well?"

She was drawn, obviously as tired as her husband. It hurt me to see her this way, worse because there was nothing I could do about it.

"Has he . . . has he told you?"

When I nodded, she slumped into the nearest chair and covered her face with her hands. Shook her head as though it were weighted with stone. Finally took a deep breath and worried me with a wan smile. "It's getting worse, Andy," she said hoarsely. "It's all he talks about anymore. Fangs, claws, those—"

"Bobcats," I said suddenly, snapping my fingers.

"What?" I could see her praying I wasn't as crazy as Roger.

"Yeah, sure, bobcats," I said again, feeling immensely relieved and rather stupid at the same time. "Hell's bells."

"Andy," Bet said, her voice dangerously low, "would you please explain?"

I leaned back against the door, partly for the role, partly to cover my suddenly weak knees. "A couple, maybe three years ago, the state forestry people released a batch of bobcats into the woods just north of here, in the state forest up there. One year it was males—to establish the territory—and the next it was females. They're trying to rebuild the population. Damn, I'll bet that's what he saw! A stupid bobcat. Both times. And they were probably more scared of him than Roger was of them. He could have waved or something, and they would have taken off like a bat."

"No," she said weakly, though smiling gratitude for the effort. "No, I don't think so."

"Damnit, Bet, it has to be!"

"But what about all those killings he keeps talking about?"

Patiently, softly, I explained to her about the dog packs, domestic animals that had been left behind when vacationers didn't want to take them home to the city. It happened every year, and at least once a decade a pack was formed and had to be cleaned out by the local police.

"Are you sure?" Her hope almost had me weeping.

"Believe me, Bet, I'm as sure about this as I am about anything." I almost left then, changed my mind and turned to tell her that the next time we had a fog I would dig up one of those things and show him what his nightmares were really all about. She almost kissed me, and I almost let her. But I settled instead for a long hug that stirred some memories and left the house near to whistling. For the first time that day I felt really good, and wished my own troubles could be just as easily taken care of. A hug. One lousy hug. And within the next few days a raid on a damned bobcat's grave.

In fact, I was still whistling the next day. I had driven in to work, windows down to the bright and unseasonably warm air, found a parking space almost immediately, and decided it was an omen.

Almost.

When I reached my floor Jackie was not at her desk, and her coat was missing from the bentwood rack. I wandered down the hall, poking into cubicles and offices, but no one was there. There was then a brief moment of stomach-lurching panic—a meeting? Had I forgotten a meeting or something? Was I supposed to have come in early and Roger's troubles had driven it out of my head? Damn!

I rushed to the elevator as I shuffled through my patented list of excuses, was about to step in when Bob Parker popped out of his office at the hall's far end. He lifted a hand and I held the door for him, nodded cheerily, and saw him frown when I hit the button for the fourteenth floor.

"Any problems, Bob?" I said. He and I did not exactly get along like brothers. He was young, I not so, and his ambitions outreached mine by the proverbial country mile.

"Why bother," he said. "No one's there."

The doors slid open, and I couldn't help but gape—the receptionist's desk was deserted. But it never, ever was left unattended. The doors slid shut again, and Bob pressed for the lobby.

I tried not to sound completely ignorant when I said, "I think I've missed something, Bob."

His eyes widened. "You mean . . ." He tried a laugh, and he failed miserably. "My God, Andy, you mean no one's said anything to you yet? Didn't anyone call you this morning? The radio—"

"No one called me," I told him, wondering at the sudden pallor beneath his year-round tan. "And I sang my way into work for a change."

"Jesus." He stared at the backlighted ceiling, the paneled walls, the tips of his shoes. "Holy God, this is dreadful. This is terrible."

My patience died. My fists clenched. "What is terrible, Bob? What in . . . what are you talking about?"

"Well, they called this morning, see, and I came in anyway just for a minute because I had these papers and . . ." He slapped at the wall, reached vainly for my arm. "My God, Andy, they're dead!"

I know I looked foolish, but I couldn't help it. His babbling wasn't telling me a thing. "Who?"

"Crayton, Jackie, David. They're . . ."

It was like being bludgeoned on a bright day in the middle of the park while little children played joyfully around your legs. I fell back against the wall, holding up a quick hand when Parker took a step toward me. "No, it's all . . . dead?"

He nodded. "Sometime after midnight it was," he told me. Then he lowered his voice as we left the elevator and headed for the street. "The police aren't saying anything much in their bulletins, but my brother, John, he knows this cute little clerk who works on the night desk. He said—now get this, Andy—he said one of the patrols found them. They were in that big Mercedes that David has, parked on the side of the road. Windows rolled up, doors all locked from the inside. They had to bust through a window to get to them. John says—and he'll kill me if he knows I told you this—there was so much blood around the bodies had to be washed off before they could find the wounds that killed them."

There was more, but I didn't hear it. I shook hands, I think, and made my way to the parking lot where I sat behind the wheel and smoked three or four cigarettes, each from the butt of the other. I kept the windows down.

Jackie: little breasts, big hips, rode me like a bull and had the same kind of temper; Crayton: stiff, pompous, fair in his way and completely ruthless; McInroe: a shell that looked like a human being and was filled with a bile that infected everything he touched, including my ambitions.

Dead. Blooded. Three with one blow. Wasn't there a fairy-tale tailor who did something like that?

I don't remember the drive back home, nor letting myself in or ripping the tie from my neck. Everything was a blank until I stood at the dining room's bow window and saw the low mounds of fresh dirt in Roger's yard.

Jesus, I thought, and pulled down the shades.

The next few days were remarkably clear and unusually warm again for the time of year; and of course, I attended the funerals. I registered none of the services, however, or the faces of those who stood with me; I only knew there were caskets, and they were polished, and they were sullied with fresh dirt.

Roger.

Bet called me a couple of times, pleading, and I told her at each call that I had not forgotten, that all I was waiting for was the covering fog.

I waited until there was nothing for it but that I would have to do it anyway, take my chances one night and pray that my friend hadn't gone all the way around the bend. I had seen him only once after the killings—the newspapers said dogs, but the windows were rolled up—and all he did then was look at me and nod knowingly.

Bet was standing beside him—a shadow, nothing more. Bastard, I thought, in the hope he could hear me; it was one thing to go about ruining your own life, you sonofabitch, but to take that woman down with . . . I glared, nearly lifted my middle finger to him, and stalked away.

The firm collapsed, and I did not like the looks of the future.

No one else died; and it was the night before Thanksgiving.

The temperature fell, the rain fell, and by twilight there was such a fog that not even the dowager London dared claim it for her own. It was thick in layers, each twisting away briefly as a timorous breeze crept through, then folding back again as solid as before. I had been in the city with my résumés and hopes, and it took me over two hours to get home again, another to warm up sufficiently to remember my promise, remember this was the night I had been waiting for.

Roger nodding and Bet a shadow—God, I didn't think I could hate so much!

In the garage I located a shovel I hadn't used in months. I hefted it, slipped into a black windbreaker, and went outside.

Through the hedge.

There were no lights in the Dillans' kitchen; one upstairs where I knew the bathroom was.

I shook a fist at it and mouthed a silent obscenity.

It was hard to breathe. Every time I inhaled it was like an invitation to a drowning. I had a small flashlight, and it flared the fog back at me mockingly. Calm, I told myself, and with the flash pinned between arm and chest I began to dig. The light bobbed erratically, showing me dirt, fog, dirt, fog . . . the fog that seemed to have pulled back now as though to help me, roiling like smoke, sprouting man-o'-war tendrils that were waiting . . . waiting. I saw faces. Snarling faces. Claws. Fangs. I saw monsters culled from every damned Saturday matinee I had ever attended.

The fog was cold.

Scrape . . . thud.

My hands were slippery with perspiration; once, my grip slid down the smooth handle and I nearly impaled myself.

Faces.

Stop it, I ordered myself.

Digging.

The bathroom light went out, and I was alone in the dark.

I'm not exactly positive what happened next, what caused it. I don't know if it was my rage at what Roger was doing to himself and to the woman I could never have, or the exasperation of hunting for a job that no one wanted to give me in spite of my experience, or if it was somehow those idiot stories I remembered from around a warm campfire under trees that grasped and winds that whispered—but suddenly I dropped to my knees and pushed the shovel aside, using my hands to work at that foul grave, not caring if anyone heard me, only wanting to get the ugly thing done.

And a minute or so later my fingers struck something soft, giving, and I snatched them away with a silent cry of disgust. Awkwardly, I held the shovel near the blade and scraped at the dirt, the other hand holding the flash until I could see what I was uncovering.

I didn't have to exhume the whole thing; the head and shoulders were enough. Despite all the time in the ground, despite the workings of whatever lived beneath the surface, I knew what those tufted ears were, those eyes slanted even in death.

It was a bobcat.

A goddamned bobcat.

Relief, then, and a boiling surge of anger.

I spat, and wiped my hands hard against my thighs; I sniffed, and rubbed a forearm under my nose; and I began to laugh quietly, shaking my head, dropping the shovel at last and holding my hands in my lap.

A goddamned more-frightened-than-he-was bobcat.

The porch light, the kitchen light, both snapped on. The door opened, and I heard footsteps coming down the stairs and across the sodden grass. I did not resist when hands grabbed my shoulders roughly and yanked me to my feet.

"Bastard!" Roger said.

"Me?" My voice cracked high. "Me? It's . . . it's a bobcat, you stupid sonofabitch! A lousy bobcat cub you could have chased off with a feather. And for this I've been through hell? For this you've turned your wife into a—"

He slapped me. He rocked me back over the uncovered grave,

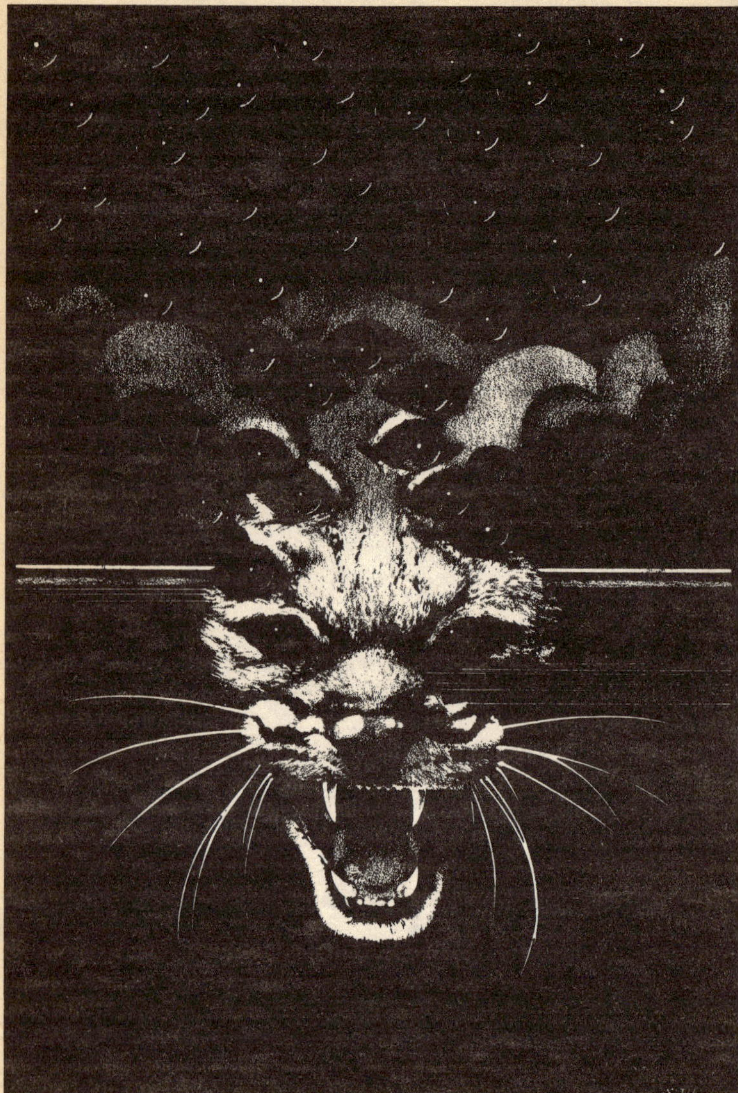

and I stumbled, fell flailing with the flashlight still gripped in my hand. I lay there for a long time, gulping for air and attempting to make sense of something, anything, that might prevent me from slamming the shovel across his thick skull. And he . . . *he,* the idiot, was standing there as though I had already done it. His lips worked, his eyes glazed, and I knew suddenly that I had done something to him, though I had no idea what. Killed a dream, perhaps, a child's dream that there were indeed things beyond a normal man's knowledge—and Roger had wanted it, he had wanted it desperately. So desperately that he had allowed his befuddled, pressure-ridden mind to create *things* for him out of bobcats and fogs and dark November nights.

I suppose I should have felt sorry for him. But he hadn't taken into consideration what he had done to Betty, and to me. Me, thinking all those people had been, might possibly have been, killed by some mythical fairy-tale beast. Me, praying each night for the fog that I loathed, the fog that I detested. He had made me make a fool out of myself, crawling around in the mud, digging up the body of a stupid—

I damned near screamed.

I do know I flung the flashlight behind me, heard it strike a rock, and saw its beam angle upward toward the trees. I know that I scrambled to my feet and took a step toward him. And I know that I saw Betty on the landing, the kitchen light clouding behind her as she held the collar of her bathrobe close about her throat.

And then I saw Roger smiling.

Crazy, I thought; the man's crazy.

But the smile was a curious one. There was . . . there was reason there, clear and present sanity, and such pure and joyous satisfaction that I stopped moving toward him and stared.

"Roger?"

His gaze touched me for a moment, then slid away.

Dear God, I couldn't help it—I turned around.

The lights from the house outlined it. The flashlight's beam caught the deep startling green of its myriad eyes. I admitted to the fangs; I acknowledged the claws; and I also knew it wasn't a bobcat. It was nightmares too large and deathshades too pale, and it danced too much like the fog that gave it form. It must have been this way when the stories were told, and it must have been this way when Jackie and the others had seen it, waiting for them out there on the dark deserted road. They had closed the windows, and maybe they screamed, but fog has a way of getting into places where nothing else can.

The only thing I didn't do then was try to decide if it was *my* anger that gave it direction, or Roger's. He was, after all, my dearest friend; his pains were mine, and my agonies his.

I took one last look at Bet, and I ran.

Roger whispered something to me, and I ran.

But there's one more thing about fog in the country—it's *there;* it's . . . *there.*

So when my jacket caught in the brambles of the hedge, I had no time to learn what made the fog . . . alive.

No time to move.

And Roger had whispered: "Andy, my friend, Betty told me all about you."

No time at all . . . in the swift-moving fog.

FROM ALL THE FIELDS OF HAIL AND FIRE

The Tanners' small living room was almost too comfortably warm to stay awake in, but Gary rubbed impatiently at the stinging under his eyelids, ignoring another invitation from his mother to sit beside her and watch one of his favorite television programs. It was Friday again, and if the fire was to come, he had to be alert. He knew no one would believe him if he fell asleep in the middle of his warning.

After a restless trip around the room, he perched on the broad inside ledge of the bay window and traced incomplete faces in the frosted mist that coated the brittle cold panes. Outside, the late January night seemed fragile without a moon, and he was sure that simply by stepping out onto the porch he could shatter the darkness as if it were a thin sheath of new ice. The fireplace burned a reflection without warmth, and he poked at it, then leaned his cheek against the glass and shifted so that he could see down the lightless country road toward the weak glow of Covington's business district. Behind him, the television muttered quietly, a cigarette lighter snapped, and his father slammed cabinet doors in the kitchen.

In spite of his determination and the chill against his face, Gary felt his eyes closing and shook his head sharply. He grinned, then, when he heard his father drop a glass, but before he could call out a teasing remark he blinked and pulled quickly away from the window as if he had been stung. One hand tugged nervously at his shirt, and he looked again.

"Hey, Dad?"

There was a deep-throated muttering in the hall, and "hush!" from his mother.

"Hey, Dad, I think there's . . ."

Suddenly, a screaming brace of patrol cars sped past the house, their circling warning lights turning the remains of the last snowfall an intermittent pink. The sirens barely had time to fade before the Emergency Squad alarm began hooting urgently across the valley. Immediately the room chilled as his father stumbled in, trying to slip into his bulky overcoat and lace his boots at the same time. Gary scrambled off the ledge and knelt to help with the laces.

"Hey, Dad, can I go with you?"

"No," his mother said. "Dave, he's been to too many already. They're not good for him. He doesn't sleep well as it is."

"Oh, please, Dad? I promise I'll stay by the car. I did all the other times, didn't I?"

"You heard your mother, Gary, and please hurry with those laces. One of these days I'm going to get a decent pair of—Pam, where are my gloves? And I can't find my helmet."

Despite his anxiousness, Gary couldn't help smiling as his mother rushed from the room to the hall closet. "Come on, Dad," he said when he'd finished and stood up. "Please?"

Tanner spun around and headed for the kitchen, Gary trailing, plucking at his father's sleeve.

"Please? I'll shovel the driveway for the next hundred years, I promise. Please? Come on, Dad, it's important."

"What's so important about another fire?" his mother said as she shoved the black-and-white CD helmet under Tanner's arm. Then she frowned at Gary's exasperation, scowled at his father's resigned and grinning acquiescence. "Dave, I wish you wouldn't."

Gary wasted no more time listening to the familiar argument. He raced to the closet and dragged out his own coat and boots. "For Pete's sake," he asked the voices in the kitchen, "what does being ten years old have to do with staying away from a lousy fire? I know better than that, Mom." Still buttoning his coat, he dashed past his father, kissed his mother quickly on the cheek, and was outside before anyone could stop him. Ten years old, he thought. It was practically the same thing she always said when scolding him for playing around the boulders in Savage's field.

A minute later, Tanner had backed quickly out of the driveway, skidding into a brief spin before racing toward town. A small blue light flashed from the front of the car, and Gary pounded a fist into his palm while he listened to the shortwave radio squawk frustrated instructions to the Squad's members. A mile from the house they passed an open field, the largest break in the valley's pine forest between the Tanner residence and the first of Covington's street lights. Gary immediately pulled himself up to kneel on the seat so he could see past his father to locate the configuration of boulders he knew lay beyond the low crumbling stone wall. But there was nothing but a black unmoving curtain, and he wasn't at all angry when he was ordered to turn around and sit properly.

"Dad, when are they going to catch the . . . guy that's doing all this?"

There was a shrug, and the car swerved to avoid a pothole. "Beats me, son. All I know is, if this keeps up there won't be much town left to burn."

"They keep getting closer to our house."

"So I've noticed."

"Is that why mom's so scared all the time?"

"Could be," he said softly. "And when you don't sleep, she doesn't either, you know. Her nerves aren't the best lately."

"All those kids . . ."

A gloved hand reached through the dashboard's green glow and tousled Gary's hair. He almost blurted the secret, then, because he knew his father thought Gary was drawn to the scenes of the fires to see if any more of his friends would turn up missing. He wanted to tell the truth, wanted to tell his father of the dreams and the boulders, but there was nothing believable in any of it until he could secure some tangible proof. And the only way he was going to accomplish that was by continuing to tag along until he either found something or was taken himself.

He patted his coat pocket and allowed himself to relax just a little; the camera he had been keeping there had not fallen out during his sprint from the house to the car. Tonight, he told himself. And he shivered.

"Cold, Gary?"

"No, Dad, I'm just thinking."

"Your mother was right. I shouldn't have let you come. I don't like to see you down so much."

"I'm okay, honest," Gary said quickly, suddenly afraid he would be taken back home. "I was just thinking, that's all."

The night parted reluctantly as the street lights became more frequent and the houses added their lamps, but all the imitation suns soon paled under the spreading orange-gold glow over the rooftops. Tanner swung off the highway and leaned on his horn, slowing to avoid the islands of people who were drifting into the street. The intersections became crowded, but he was able to get within a block of the fire before he was forced to pull over.

"Big, Dad," Gary said unnecessarily.

Tanner grabbed his helmet from the backseat and slapped it on his head. "Remember your promise," he cautioned as he slid out the door. "Damn, it's cold! You stay here by the car and don't let me catch you anywhere else. If you get tired, curl up on the backseat. There's a blanket there you can use."

Gary nodded, waiting until his father had rushed away to meet the pump engine before clambering outside and perching cross-legged on the hood. A quick glance around revealed nothing immediately unusual; except for the location, it was the same as all the others.

The first had been just a week before Christmas, an abandoned barn that had been used by local organizations' bands for practice and by church groups for fairs and dinners. And once in a while it was holiday-lighted to lure the high school crowd in for a dance. Its ownership was hazy, and the town generally assumed responsibility for its upkeep, but no one stepped forward to take the blame for the assumed deaths of the Markham twins.

The second and third were private homes near the grade school, and a mile closer to the town's center. The charred bodies of five adults were found huddled against the locked front door; three children were presumed burned beyond recovery.

The fourth was the store that belonged to Dawn Reiner's father. Gary had been there, had watched the blaze shatter the plate glass in front. The old man, Gary's uncle, his mother's brother, was found sprawled in an aisle. Dawn was missing.

A gust of wind blew furnace heat into his face, and he shook his head to clear it of the acrid stench of smoke, of the frantic shouts of the volunteer firemen and the futile curses of the handful of police who were trying to erect a sawhorse barricade to keep the curious safely away. Then he closed his eyes against the unrelenting bellowing of the fire, having seen that where the post office and Keagen's Stationery had been there was now a cloud-high torch. He filled his cheeks with air and blew slowly; his father and the others would be more concerned now with saving the adjoining buildings. There was nothing they could do to salvage what was already in flames.

Impatiently he switched his attention to the milling onlookers, searching for the lank and towheaded Kim Wilde and hoping his father had answered the fire call as quickly as did Tanner. Kim was the only person he had spoken to about his dreams, having done so in the belief that his friend would see their ridiculousness and kid him out of taking them seriously. But Kim had been having them, too.

There was a shift in the spectators then, as their numbers increased, and Gary's line of sight to the fire was erased. Quickly he slid down off the hood, ran to the back of the car, and climbed up onto the trunk. Kneeling, he leaned his forearms on the roof and chewed absently on his lower lip. If Kim hadn't been allowed out, then he would have to go to the field by himself. Not that I'm scared, he told his fingers as they drummed on the dark vinyl covering. But the Savages were aptly named, and they did not appreciate little kids running across their property in the dead of night. Especially when Tanner and most of the other men in town suspected the two eldest boys of being the arsonists.

It was almost a shame, Gary thought suddenly, that they would have to be let off the hook. But if they were not, if he and Kim could not unearth the proof they needed, then his father's prediction of the town's demise might not necessarily be gloomy speculation.

"Hey, Tanner! What are you doing way up there?"

Gary turned quickly, his eyes bright in the light of the fire, tensed when he saw the trotting Wilde in the center of the street. He waved and slid to the ground. Then, after the first few words of perfunctory greetings, the two boys said nothing. Their breaths burst whitely into the evening, mingling as they looked at each other, separating when they leaned against the car and watched, hands deeply into pockets, for the signs both had seen when Dawn had disappeared.

And in their dreams, *figures racing in maddeningly slow motion through a night blacker than a cellar shadow, carrying on their twisted backs limp figures dangling. Running, soundless, feet striking ground that heaved like heavy ocean swells. A freeze in a single glare of snakelike lightning, and the figure would be illuminated and* Gary would awaken, screaming silently because his throat was constricted and it was all he could do to breathe again.

"There!" and he grabbed Kim's arm and pointed to shadows cast against the walls of the store across the street. They seemed completely unaffected by wind or shimmering firelight, deeper silhouettes of black carved in the already existent shadows of the firemen and their audience. He blinked, turned away, and looked back again. The shadows were still there, but now they were moving, and on their backs were bundles that were kicking.

"My father—" he said after clearing his throat.

"No," Kim said. "By the time we can get him to look for them, they'll be gone."

Blue eyes into black, then, searching for excuses to label this night yet another dream. But there were no answers.

"Dawn," Kim said quietly.

"Right," said Gary, pushing away from the car. "We'll cut back down the road and go over the wall past your place."

Almost before he had finished speaking, they were dodging through knots of people who were huddled against the heat in front, the bitter cold that clung to their backs. Around the first corner the fire became a premature sunrise in the sky behind them. They said nothing, ignoring sidelong glances, and the sounds of their running, once submerged by the cacophony of the firefighting, slapped sharply against the walls of the houses, echoing until they were like an army of stampeding horses. Around another corner to the highway they raced, past Kim's unlighted house and into the tunnel of pines, the fingers of the great forest that covered the hills around Covington. And in the spaces between were small farms long ago deserted when their owners found riches in managing tourist camps farther back in the mountains.

Only one remained in partial operation. The Savage place.

At the time-battered fieldstone wall, Gary stopped and pressed his hands against his sides, the cold air slicing into his lungs and making his eyes water. Kim, just a few steps behind, draped himself over the chest-high barrier and panted loudly, shaking his head and covering his ears with his palms. The clouds that had greyed the daylight finally broke, and the moon—a bulging half—brightened that grey to a not-quite-silver. Ahead of them was the field covered with crusted snow, crystaled in spots to gleam like frozen sea-foam.

"Did we beat them?" Kim said, the words dropping like stones too heavy to lift.

Gary rubbed his eyes to clear them, saw nothing but the black wall of the forest, and the snow.

"Think so," he said.

"Then . . ."

But they did not move. From the beginning it had only been a talking for both of them, a whispering in the back of the classroom, a furtive plotting during recess. Neither wanted to believe in the creatures they had seen, neither wanted to know what they were doing with the missing children. But one afternoon following the last alarm, Gary had taken Kim into the field.

"There," he had said. "That's where they are."

He pointed to a quintet of ten-foot boulders squatting in the center of a field Savage had seldom bothered to plant. They were settled randomly on the ground as if they had been dumped by a giant's hand. Gary, despite the admonitions, used them as fortress and castle, ship's prow and battlefield, and no one else except Kim would join in risking the screaming wrath of old man Savage and his pack of sons. But they had never been caught, and it fast became the place where Gary's dreams took substance and his dark moods lightened; here his troubles were absorbed in the ridges and valleys, the rilles of the rocks of no particular color, no particular shape.

After the second fire, he thought someone was trying to drive him away; the largest boulder, his favorite, had shifted. Only a few inches, but he had been there so often a new pebble would not have gone unnoticed. After the third, the rock had been moved again, and he had spotted the shadows for the first time. And had had the dreams.

"Listen," he had said to Kim during one too-fast lunch break, "those rocks are getting spooky. Somebody's been moving them."

"Now you are nuts," Kim said. "I got a better story than that. Let me tell you about a dream I had last night. Scared me so much I slept with my mom and dad for the first time since I was a kid."

Their dreams *of figures running, of a lightning strike, and in that light there were twisted stumps given raven eyes, hawks' beaks, and hands clawed and broad. From their stubbed chins, charred backs, splayed feet, were drippings like blood, but brown and slow and stinking of ancient caves. And on their backs, wide-eyed, gaping, screaming mindlessly, were Gary and Kim.*

In a frightened silence then, the pact was made.

And later: "Listen, Gary, your pop's a scientist guy. He works with rocks and things. Let's tell him."

"Tell him what?"

"Well, look, we measured the rocks, right? And we know somebody's moving them. And it happens every time there's a fire. Then we tell him about the dreams and what we saw, the shadow things, and then he'll get some other men and they'll blow the place up with a bomb or something and then we can get some sleep. My mother thinks I'm getting sick."

"No. Listen, my dad's what they call a geologist, and he don't believe nothing that ain't in any of those books of his in the study. Nuts, we never even had a Santa Claus because he said it would rot my insides or something."

"Well, what are we going to do, Gary? We just can't let them take all of us away, can we?"

Suddenly a car raced past, briefly exposing them to its headlights, and they vaulted over the wall and crouched out of sight until they were sure they hadn't been seen. Then they began to run as best they could toward the boulders.

The crust broke several times beneath them and they floundered, the snow spilling like droplets of ice over the tops of their boots, down the backs of their gloves. They angled in from the left with no other plan than to observe. They would wait, listen, watch. And when they were sure they were not living a nightmare, they would run to the nearest house and get someone to help them before it was too late.

Just before the fourth fire, Dawn had called and told him about a dream she had had.

When Gary reached the outermost boulder, he slumped against it, his head sagging down toward his chest. There was a pounding in his ears, and the faint throbs of an impending headache struck across his forehead. Kim slumped to the ground in front of him, looked back and saw their moonshadows stretching darkly toward the road. Gary nodded at his silent question, and they crawled to the left before fingers and boots pulled them to the tableflat top of Gary's rock. Their scraping sounded like an avalanche, and he clamped a hand over his mouth to keep his breathing from giving them away.

And then, only the moon belted with strands of drifting cloud, the sough of the wind gathering speed on the hills to coast through the valley, an occasional car with bright eyes tunneling through the black, and the rush of blood like drums on a faraway continent.

And the clicking.

Gary stiffened and eased himself back until he could barely see over the edge. The game had ended, the fear begun.

They saw a pair of frighteningly familiar figures plowing through the snow, the details of their features invisible, their bulks outlined against the grey-white of the field. The clicking, closer, shifted into the tapping of dead branches rearing in a storm, and the creatures passed out of sight as they approached the far rock. Kim flattened his hands against the boulders as if to raise himself higher, and Gary tugged him down. His mouth was dry, his lips cracking in the cold as his tongue flicked over them. Another car sped out of the town and he wanted to cry out, dug his chin into the rock instead, and listened.

A rumbling came then, and he was sure the stone directly in front of them was moving. Kim placed his lips directly against Gary's ear: "Follow?" but Gary shook his head. Whatever they were, it would do the boys no good to try to keep up with them. They had no weapons and had no idea what they would be fighting. They had come to discover, and having discovered, it was time to let the others know.

When the rumbling ceased and was replaced by a rising wind, Gary pushed and slid to the ground. Without looking around, he began running, falling, spitting snow, and running again. He could hear Kim sobbing behind him, and when they reached the wall, a car pulled up beside them, and Gary hated himself for starting to cry.

"So," Tanner said half an hour later, "you really think that what you saw out there was real?" He urged with a wave, and Gary lifted the cup of hot chocolate to his chapped lips. The fireplace warmth was gentle, but he could not stop shaking and some of the brown liquid slopped over the edge onto his fingers.

"He's tired, Dave," his mother said, her arm refusing to leave the boy's shoulders. "Why don't you let him sleep? Hasn't he been punished enough?"

"Listen, son, you promised to stay by that car," Tanner said stubbornly. "Do you have any idea what went through my mind when I couldn't find you?"

"I told you why," Gary said sullenly.

"Son, what did I tell you about those rocks?"

"Dave," Pam said, her voice a quiet warning.

"Glaciers," the boy said. He sipped at his drink, and tasted nothing.

"Right. They are not magical, nor are they secret doors to some mysterious underground cave. This valley was formed too many years ago for you to understand by great hulking rivers of ice. Those boulders were left behind, and no one has since bothered to move them. They're too big, son. It would take a couple of sticks of my stump-moving dynamite just to budge them."

"Then what did I see?" Gary said angrily. "What happened to all those kids? Where are they? What about Dawn—"

"Gary, please!" Pam snapped, rocking him now, trying to soothe him.

"No, Mom, I'm sorry. I don't want to be bad, but I saw what I saw and you can ask Kim, too. Dad," he said, leaning forward suddenly, his discomfort momentarily forgotten. "Dad, were there more kids missing after the fire? The Keagens. Were they . . . there?"

Tanner looked away to the fire and scratched the back of his neck. "Don't know," he said finally. "They're still sifting through the ashes. It's too hot yet to do any real digging. Don't even know if they were home. Someone said they might have been visiting relatives over in Springfield."

"They'll be there," Gary said. "The folks, anyway."

Tanner glared down at him, his large hands closing into fists at his sides. "Son, I want you to go straight to bed right this minute."

"But Dad—"

"And you can stop your whining! Don't you think you've frightened your mother enough by going out there tonight? And with a camera yet. What were these creatures of yours going to do, pose for a group picture?"

Gary had leaned away from his father's anger, but when the words had been spoken and the silence had crept back in from the shadowed corners, he shrugged off his mother's arm, dropped his cup, and walked stiffly to the stairs.

"They won't be there," he said sadly. "And they won't be at their stupid relatives, either."

And he raced up to his room and slammed the door, leaned back against it until his chest stopped heaving. It isn't fair, he thought as he grabbed his pillow and punched at it until his arm ached. It just isn't fair. He threw the pillow back onto the bed and walked to the window, pressing his forehead lightly against the glass. The moon was disappearing slowly as a storm bunched its clouds overhead. He remembered the glaciers he had been told about and that day in school when it had all fallen together.

His teacher, after reading "Jack and the Beanstalk" and a story about Paul Bunyan, explained the difference between myths and legends, and the oral tradition of handing stories down from one generation to another. Superstitions, fairy tales; werewolves, vampires, the giants who roamed the earth before time was recorded.

"And what," Gary had said excitedly to Kim after school, "if those things weren't myths or fairy tales after all? Suppose they really were legends whose basic truths had been forgotten after thousands of years. And suppose they had lived during the Ice Ages, hibernated after and renewed themselves with periodic raids between."

Suppose . . .

Kim had laughed, but weakly.

Gary switched on the lamp by his bedside table and pulled from a drawer a sheath of clippings he had stolen from the school's library. This was, in conjunction with the pictures he'd been too frightened to take, part of the proof of his warning; they indicated the days when the temperature had dropped more than twelve degrees below freezing; they indicated the days just before and after each of the fires.

"Why aren't you in bed?" The voice was gentle, only hinting at scolding.

"I'm thinking, Dad," and he handed the man the clippings.

"You really do believe this, don't you?"

Gary hesitated before nodding, and Tanner sighed, carefully leading him to the bed, where he pushed until Gary was lying down. Then he sat on the edge of the mattress and combed at his hair with his fingers, rubbed at the dark stubble on his chin.

"If it will make you feel any easier about this, son, I don't think it's all your imagination. But—" and he held up a warning hand as Gary started to rise, "—I don't think monsters are the answer, either. I've been talking with your mother, just to get my thoughts out into the open as you and Kim tried to do. Well, you've heard the talk about the Savage clan?"

Gary nodded and rolled to his side, pulled his knees toward his chest and listened: the Savages, ingrown, some say a little mad, ornery enough to want the whole town to go away and leave them alone; arson, murder, and no clues left to warrant their arrest. A delegation, unofficial, was going to visit them tomorrow night to make it clear that the next time there's a fire, the Savages would not be left alone. Gary tried to shake his head at that, tried to deny the mistaken logic, but there was a weight in his head and a buzzing in his ears that pushed the droning words into the background, and when the dream came again, the figures were followed under the ground, and the threat felt more real, closer, and totally inescapable.

The lightning struck again, and when he sat up, it was already afternoon and he was hungry. His father had apparently undressed him while he had slept, and he wasted precious time trying to find the warmest clothes he owned before running downstairs and into the kitchen. His father was on the telephone talking about the Savages, and Gary closed his eyes briefly; it won't do them any good, he thought, not if they want to save Kim and me it won't.

"Well," his mother said cheerfully, "it's about time you got down here. You must have been a little tired, right?"

He smiled, nodded, and took his seat, trying not to gasp when he saw it was nearly time for supper.

"Do you feel better?"

He nodded again and watched her busying herself at the stove. Pretty, he thought, and wished he had noticed just how pretty she was sooner. He started to say something, and the light shimmered and he saw her blackened, her lovely long hair a flaming halo, her laughing mouth twisted into grotesque screaming. When his father returned to the kitchen, he was a walking charred corpse. Gary rubbed at his face and pushed away from the table.

"Mom, I have to go back to the shed for a minute."

She turned, staring. "In this weather? No, you're not, young man."

"Oh, Mom, please? I put the sled in there yesterday, and if we have lots more snow, I'll never be able to get it out."

"Well, why didn't you put it in the cellar like you were supposed to?"

"I forgot," he said, sliding toward the closet. "Please?" He allowed his voice to rise just enough, his eyes to open just enough, his mouth to quiver and turn downward.

"All right," she said, "but don't get lost."

"In the backyard? Come on, Mom!"

"Okay, Pam," Tanner said laughing, "stop teasing the boy. But," and he turned to Gary as he was slipping on his coat, "don't you try anything else, young man. Last night was the last straw for you, you understand?"

"Don't worry, Dad," he said at the door. "I'm going to take care of everything."

Once on the back stoop he yanked his red ski mask down over his face, jabbed with an impatient finger to align the three slits with his eyes and mouth. Then he pulled the fur-trimmed hood over his head and drew the ties snugly to his throat. This time he wanted nothing, not even the cold, to slow him down.

A few yards later and all he could see was the kitchen light's glow, a dozen yards more and he might have been alone on the top of a mountain. There was very little wind, but the snow was heavy enough to make walking difficult. The shed was at the far end of their property, hidden from the house even during the summer, and when he pulled out the padlock key and opened the door, he didn't bother to look behind him. Instead, he hurried directly to the far end and rummaged through his father's geological equipment, packages and boxes he was never allowed to touch on his own. Finally, on the floor in the corner he found what Tanner called his stump-moving dynamite. He had seen how it was done more than a dozen times, could still hear his father's stern words of caution, but when a draft iced across his lips he bent down quickly to grab sticks, caps, and fuse. He stuffed it all into one pocket and ran out without closing the door. If he was wrong, he thought, one spanking more wouldn't make any difference.

Carefully, he made his way to the road, and then began to run. It was almost too dark to see, but after a number of falls he came up against the stone wall and was able to pull himself along until he estimated he was opposite the boulders. Then he struck out across the field, pushing through the snow that rose up to cover his knees. He tripped once over a hidden log and, with arms flailing, fell forward; and when he had righted himself, he quickly checked his pocket to see that the explosives were still there.

Another thirty yards and he fell again, with the snow penetrating his sleeves, boots, the slits of his mask.

The wind began shoving at his back.

And there was thunder.

He sat up, forgetting the cold numbing his limbs. Only once before had he been in a snowstorm when it thundered, and the sound of it now echoing through the white made him jump to his feet. Again thunder, and the snow flared blue-white when lightning crackled over the hills. Something struck him on the head, the shoulders, and when he held out his hand he saw it was hail.

"Dad?" he said aloud. "Dad, where are you?"

Suddenly there was a hooting blare that froze him, drove spasms of panic through his arms and legs. He looked around wildly, and when a gust parted the snow before him he saw the faint yellow glow.

Kim, he thought.

"Kim!" he shouted.

On hands and knees he scrambled to the boulders, grabbing at the slippery rock as if it would protect him. Hail cracked around him, and his head began to ache despite its hooded protection. He was crying, and he curled up against himself and began to rock, humming tunelessly. The alarm continued to sound.

Wind, thunder, hail, and suddenly Gary straightened, crawled through the passages between the boulders until he found the opening in the ground. He wanted to go down, but not without Kim. Instead he scrambled to the top of the boulder, crying still, blinking rapidly to keep the flakes from freezing on his lids. His gloves were off, the hail striking like dulled needles; and his hands plunged into his pocket, out again, and he squinted to see through the tears. He had no idea if cap and fuse were affixed properly, but he refused to allow himself to think, watching only, as the lightning sunbrightened the storm, and the fire so distant it could have been a reflection raged.

Above him, the alarm; around him, the wind; in front then, and below, the clicking.

And out of the snow, neither magic nor dream, two black figures and on one, a silent slain. He wanted to shout to attract their attention, frighten them into dropping his friend, but he waited until they had ducked under the rock and the rumbling had begun before he leaped to the ground. He tugged open his coat and pulled out the lighter he had taken from his mother's purse, hunched and ignited the fuses. Then he leaned against the boulder, shouted to Kim, and dropped the dynamite into the closing hole.

Stumbling . . .

. . . down a passage steeply slanting . . .

. . . screaming . . .

. . . into a tree-tall cavern littered with decay and the dust of the dead . . .

. . . his mask torn from his face, his hood thrown back. He heard a muffled thunderclap, felt the earth beneath the snow tremble, spun around and saw a geyser of fire erupt from below . . .

. . . a man . . . a thing . . . propped against a wall, pale and emaciated and grasping with red-stained fingers toward the burden on the black thing's back; a giant of a man, a giant of a thing, waiting, feeding, the young and the cold . . .

. . . and in running backward, fell, his head striking rock, arms pulling him close to hide him from the storm.

And from all the fields of hail and fire, he saw his father's face, the tears, and the snow; and he gasped, wanting to ask about the other stones in other valleys, and all the nightmares soothed away with gentle words.

But when he opened his mouth he could only scream, and taste the sting of falling snow.

THE KEY TO ENGLISH

It was a May-and-mountain rain, falling less like drops than ribbons into grass and new leaves with a steady, unnerving hiss that wavered sporadically before a desultory wind. An all-day rain, neither stormy nor shower, not hard enough to obscure the campus nor driving enough to keep the students penned within their grey brick dorms. It fell, and dripped incessantly from gutters still clogged with autumn debris and disappeared into the several streams that patchworked the playing fields.

At a window on the third and topmost floor of Hamilton Hall a boy watched the day drag, and he frowned nervously. With classes ended and lacrosse practice postponed by the weather, he could only stare, uncaringly tracing the landscaped delta with the six-story Burr Memorial Class/Administration Building at its apex. He stared, saw and ignored the looming presence of the glass-and-blue-steel structure and the split tongues of walk that joined it with its sisters at the triangle's base. Four o'clock sessions had just ended, and windbreakered students hurried toward him, huddled like driven sheep, with not one stepping on the grass.

With his hands burrowed in his pockets he blinked at the rain and turned around, propping himself against the damp sill. He had just awakened from a restless nap and for a panic-dark moment believed he'd been caught. His underclothes had been drenched, his hands fisted, and tendrils of a dream trailed behind him to the shower.

There were Chandler and Murray and Simpson, smiling . . .

He thought about visiting the girls' dorm to see Barb or Irene; he thought about sitting, decided to stand. He knew the signs, smiling at himself, but cautioned his breathing that he would have to wait as he'd planned. Evening would be soon enough; it would have to be whether he liked it or not. In his pocket, fingers curled around the stolen key. The metal was cold, despite his grip, and only disquietingly comforting in its promise. He was beginning to wish his father had never heard of DelMer.

"Listen, son," the seldom-seen man had said this past August. "Public schools and you just aren't getting along. Now this DelMer doesn't seem to be a place for geniuses. It's where normal guys go to get a step ahead of the college game. I've been there, and the instructors seem as tireless and enthusiastic as any I've ever seen. I think you should try it. Maybe it can give you something I can't. What do you say?" Later, the boy had learned that he'd been already enrolled, and his answer had been a mere formality, as always.

But Dad, he wanted to say now that the fear had come, it's no fun here. Everything is too damned perfect, you know what I mean? Those instructors of yours know all the answers all the time, and you can't really kid with them. At least if I needed help in the city, I could stay after for a while. Here, if I don't grab somebody by last class, I'm out of luck. They disappear. Sometimes they hang around the lounges—remember those crummy pictures in the brochure?—but God Almighty, all they do is talk about the school and how great it is and how we're the look of the future and we should tell all our friends what a great education we're getting. They sound like public relations people, not teachers. I tell you, Dad, it scares me sometimes. It really does.

"And I think I know why," he said aloud. "And that scares me even more."

. . . Becketton, Ainstrom, and Tander, grasping; and faces that froze in smiles and frowns, and faded at sunset to rise at dawn . . .

A distant thud of thunder turned him back to watch the rain, then turn again after pulling down the red-grey shade against a chill that ignored the thick smoke-glass window. At the same moment the door slammed open, and a boy fully a head taller than he stalked angrily in, shaking water from his poncho.

"Randy!" he shouted, "that Becketton is a bald-headed evil-minded bastard." He yanked the slick green plastic over his red hair and threw it into a corner. "Do you know what he did? Do you have any idea?" Randy only smiled. "He waits until we're all there dripping and sneezing, and then tells us we deserve a break and we should all go back to our rooms and take a nice long nap! I don't think I'll be able to eat dinner I'm so mad. That guy just isn't human. He is just not for real."

Randy's smile broadened to a grin and he shook his head, saying nothing. Kartre's intolerance of the faculty's penchant for being human once in a while was legendary and fanatical, and no one took him seriously when he threatened to revive the long-dead school paper and expose them all.

"Life is hard, Kart," he said while his roommate disappeared into his bedroom and returned in dry jeans and a too-large sweater. "You should learn to take the good with the bad, the evil with the innocent. Remember what Shelley said about blithe spirits and birds."

"Assuming he said anything at all worth remembering, I could care less. It sounds like you had an English Lit session this morning. What did dear old 42C Chandler bull on about that's filled you with such epigrammatical wisdom?"

"I really couldn't tell you," Randy said. "I was thinking most of the time. About tonight." He glanced up at Kartre, but there was no reaction, and he frowned. "All I remember was that she wore a high-necked dress."

"Aha!" Kartre said from within the depths of a refrigerator they'd hidden in the room's only closet.

"Aha what?"

Kartre returned to the room empty-handed and immediately staked out his favorite chair, a rocker that never seemed able to tilt back far enough to suit him; as a result, he always appeared to be talking to the ceiling. "Aha, someone's been pinching our beer. But to return to our favorite girl: it sounds like Headmaster Ainstrom had a long talk with her about the birds and the bees after that no-front thing she wore last week. Shame on her! It certainly wouldn't do to have us wee boys see too much ripe sex. The chicks here are bad enough the way they flaunt themselves."

Thinking of the comparatively drab Philadelphia girls he'd been used to, Randy said, "You should have done three years in a public school, you wouldn't be complaining so much. I—" A pause then as a heavy knock interrupted him. He started to his feet, his hand automatically covering the key in his pocket. "Come on," he called. "Only God and Ainstrom need passes here."

Barbara Black and Irene Rosen were the only girls not intimidated or repulsed by the boys' rough manners and rougher play, and for that reason the four of them found themselves oddly united against the world, faculty, and freshmen until graduation blew them apart. This night, however, Randy noticed immediately a perceptible split in their front. Barb, with rounded face and hair as dark as her name, headed straight for the refrigerator without acknowledging either boy's greeting. Irene, who seemed to Randy to be the incarnation of Walter Scott's Rebecca, roughly shoved his legs aside and joined him on the sofa, her hair gleaming wet. She fluffed at it a minute, then pulled a comb from her purse and began pushing it back from her face. Silently. Her eyes nervous, her mouth tightly shut. Kartre began an atonal whistling, and Randy felt the room closing darkly around him.

"All right," he said resignedly. "What's up?"

"You know Evan Johnston?" Irene said. "He's the—"

"Junior, yeah," Kartre interrupted. "We know him, don't we, Randy? Soccer center, shortstop; he's in our chem class."

"Was," Irene corrected. "He's gone. Clothes, books, furniture, everything."

"Uh," Kartre grunted, almost as if he'd been punched. He paled suddenly, and one hand worked at his chin. "Oh, brother. He saw Ainstrom, I guess, huh?"

"He had an appointment first thing this morning," Barb said, gulping her words to keep from crying. "Karen was in the office when that night proctor of yours, Owens, brought him in. Old lady Tander chased her out when she tried to hang around, and she didn't hear a thing. After English she went up to his room, and the door was wide open, the place cleaned out. Like he'd never been there." She stared at the can of beer in her hand, then drained it and popped open another. "I don't think we should go on with it. I'd just as soon not get shipped out that way. It's happened—what, three times? I get the creeps, I don't mind telling you. The least Ainstrom could have done was let him say good-bye. I mean, he was a nice kid, really. Not like a jock at all."

"For crying out loud, Barb!" Randy snapped. "You sound like he was dead. You'll get to see him when his mother comes to fetch him. For crying out loud!" He stood abruptly and went to the window, staring at the shade a moment until he snapped it up into the glare of lightning. He was frustrated, becoming frantic because, despite his rising anger, he sympathized with his friends. Though DelMer had few regulations, their violation brought radical response, and none of the four had any doubts about the reaction to what Randy had planned for that evening: it was the same investigation that had just cost Evan his junior year, or more.

"We won't even get a letter," Irene said quietly.

And then there were the stories whispered from senior to senior that terrified and tempted. But tales they were, and he was only interested in what was so damned important about the storeroom on Burr Memorial's sixth floor. Closet skeletons intrigued him; school secrets mesmerized him.

"All right, come on," he said loudly, turning suddenly and clapping his hands so that Barb jumped and Irene scowled. "I ain't going to steal anything, so what's the worry? If I get caught and hustled out, my dad'll raise hell and I'll be back in a week. If not, damnit, I'll write."

"No one else has," Kartre said sullenly.

"Okay, okay," Randy said, sitting cross-legged on the floor. "I can take the hint. You want out, right? You're still scared, and you don't think one lousy room that cost a pal his education—and God only knows how many more there are—you don't think that's worth the risk of getting expelled."

Barb nodded quickly. "It's just too silly, Ran. Just because you've got a . . . a thing about this stupid room doesn't mean I have to risk my Vassar acceptance. It would kill me to lose it."

"She's right," said Irene. "You and your damned imagination have made a lovely little mystery about this, and it's really quite good. But adventures belong back in your precious Philadelphia, not out here in the middle of nowhere."

Randy began rocking on his buttocks to the tune of the urgency he felt growing with their retreat. "Do you really think this place is so hot? I mean, with teachers you can't talk to, computers that whistle and do tricks with books, TV screens all over the place like a damned spy movie? You call this education? My God, I thought this place was supposed to be experimental with the big sweet government pouring in the money to make us special. Well, where does it go? What's the goddamned experiment? DelMer, shit! Hell, we had computers and TV in Philadelphia too."

"Damnit," Kartre said, ceasing his nervous rocking and leaning forward on his forearms and knees. "I wish you guys would quit your fighting. I want to get this thing settled."

"What's to settle? We're not going," Barb said, looking to Irene for her nod of support. "We're scared. We don't want to get caught."

"But we won't get caught," Randy said, much louder than he'd intended. "All you guys have to do is stand and watch. I'm the one who's doing the breaking in. What's the big deal?"

"Risk," Kartre said levelly, and Randy twisted around to glare at his betrayal. "Irene's right. Barb's right. Maybe your dad doesn't care about you like you always say, but ours do. We're not going to blow this chance for college. We're not that smart, Randy, but this place gives us an in. I'm sorry, pal, but I'm not going either."

"Well, thanks a hell of a lot. You sure picked a great time to tell me."

Irene, her eyes deer-scared, slid from the couch to sit in front of him. "Randy, you've been on your own for so long, you just can't understand. We have to be safe. We can't afford the risk."

Randy brushed his hair back from his forehead and rubbed his eyes. He was tired, and he wanted to sleep, wanted to drown. "Listen . . . there are risks and there are risks. Ever since I was nailed for going up those stairs, I've wanted to see what it was they're hiding in that storeroom."

"They're not hiding anything!" Kartre interrupted. "It's only a goddamned place for supplies. What's so damned important about supplies?"

"We are not communicating," Randy said slowly. "It's just that . . . well, look, remember the day Chandler ran out of comp paper and I offered to go get it? Don't you remember how she looked? Like I'd asked permission to rape her! That's the only time she's ever lost her cool in front of the class. In fact, that's the first time I've seen any of them be anything else but reasonable, calm, and god-awful smiling. Now, doesn't something like that get on your nerves?"

"What?" Barb said. "Their smiling?"

"Oh, hell," Randy said in quiet desperation. "How dense can you get? Why would she get so excited about a lousy supply room? Why did I get in trouble for trying to get up there? Why was Johnston expelled? Have you ever seen the parking lot? It's practically empty all the time, every day, even when there're classes going on. Why? Why the hell is that proctor, Owens, so concerned about our room checks? I mean, where would we go?" He stopped, stared, seeking answers in their sympathetic expressions and finding only more sympathy. He scrambled to his feet and headed for the door. "If I'm not back by eleven-thirty, cover with Owens for me, will you, Kartre?"

"Hey, wait a minute! You're not going to try this by yourself!"

"Why not? It's the story of my life." And he slammed the door before they could respond, before he started crying. He hesitated on the landing, then took the stairs two at a time, the hand gliding on the bannister for balance burning by the time he skidded to the bottom. The lobby, green and gold, was empty; the proctor, he thought, was probably out hunting a cup of coffee. He leaned back to look up the stairwell, but he heard no pursuit, no calling him back. He trembled, then clenched his fists and ran across the polished floor and out into the wind.

The campus was still. The walks, dotted with light from dark-hooded globes, were deserted and gleaming wetly. The spotlights that flooded the front of Hamilton Hall blinded him until he sidestepped, hunching against the wall away from a rising wind. He wiped a sleeve under his nose, shoved a hand through his hair in a vain attempt to keep it from his eyes. A moment, then, as he watched juniper and holly twist away from him in the path of the wind. Indecision. A radio's blare.

. . . caught in a fog web while expert fingers, wristless, molded womb-warm plastic to his face, whispering equations in his ear, laughing . . .

A girl's laugh, a boy's reply.

. . . while his featureless father shrugged and shredded his picture his dead mother, formless, took when he was two . . .

Slowly he pushed himself away from the building and walked with eyes down until he found himself beyond the triangle on the edge of the soccer field. The clouds, regrouping, blackened the stars, and the vast treeless field ahead seemed less in shadow than drowned in black water.

"There be demons," he whispered, and turned away, keeping the triangle on his left as he headed toward Burr Memorial. A night watchman, preceded by a wavering pool of grey light, suddenly rounded a corner of the Student Union, and Randy ducked behind a tree, pressing his back to its winter roughness, the spring dampness. The watchman hurried by, muttering to himself, and Randy could not help but grin. Wiping a splatter of rain from his cheek, he waited until the man's footsteps were taken by the wind before he resumed his walking.

He moved slower now, reluctantly allowing his friends' timidity to clutter his thinking. They were as bad as the instructors, promising warmth and withholding it when it was needed. He had had enough of so-called experimental education, of seminars with a TV screen and discussions with soulless men who brooked no humanity outside the norm. He had thought his father had rescued him from cousins and aunts in the city, but realized now that the man could care less. In Philadelphia, at least, he had come to treasure a sense of being alive among living people. At DelMer he had begun to feel like a graveyard caretaker.

The key to English, Miss Chandler had said, is precision of language to facilitate communication.

"Damn, Miss Chandler," he said to the tips of his shoes. "Why don't you practice what you preach?"

And when he looked up, he had reached the rear of the Memorial, as dark as the front was lighted. Cautiously he stepped along the side of the walk, using the grass there to muffle his footsteps. There was a door on the side that the watchmen used to exit for their rounds. On four previous nights, he'd noticed they'd kept it from locking so they could return without trouble. He smiled at their innocent sense of security. DelMer students apparently did not have the nerve to explore. He broadened his smile. Having only been there since September, he had not been conditioned to think that way; and he waited a long and windy minute before dashing to the door, pulling it open, and sliding inside.

He immediately flattened against the wall, panting as if he'd just run a wind sprint. The rear stairwell was dimly lighted, and he moved upward without hesitation, on his toes, avoiding the stairs' metal edges. His right hand slid along the outside wall as he climbed in a half crouch, his ears trying to encompass the silence of the building and isolate potential danger. A noise; he froze: the sighing of the wind. On each of the first five landings he hurried past the glowing red fire-exit signs; on the sixth floor, no light, no sign. Only a door without a window.

Cupping one hand into a fist, Randy blew into it to dry his palm. His legs, strained from the awkward ascent, trembled slightly, but not enough to worry him should he have to run. It was like old times, then, creeping around school after basketball games, looking for open lockers or doors and the mischief they promised. Gingerly, he took the door's bar handle in his hand. The sudden thought that it might be wired jerked the hand away, but there was nothing but his counterpoint breathing to the keening wind. He regrasped the handle and pulled slowly until the door slid toward him. Closing his eyes momentarily, he expelled a breath he didn't realize he'd been holding and quickly eased through the opening.

The darkness was unrelieved, and he felt a surge of panic when the door shut silently behind him. Hastily he tested it to be positive he could leave, then shuffled down the hall. He knew the English Department storeroom was just around the far corner, and, in spite of himself, he hurried, gliding his hands along the tiled wall until a doorknob cracked against a knuckle. He took a lighter from his pocket and checked the tiny hand-printed card tacked to the frame.

"Bingo," he whispered to himself and pulled out the key, still cold, and heavier than he'd remembered. He snapped the lighter shut, and the renewed darkness immobilized him until his eyes adjusted to the more-than-faint glow that drifted from the front of the building. Using both hands, he felt for the lock and slid in the key, turning it as slowly as he could until it caught and the tumblers clattered over. He pushed with his shoulder and slipped in, shutting the door behind him. He leaned back against the wall and blew in relief when he felt the light switch pressing against his coat. Without turning around, he fumbled until the lights came on, and, in spite of his suspicions, it was all he could do to keep from screaming.

At Chandler, Murray, Simpson, Becketton, rigid and blank-eyed, in a neat ordered row against the far wall. At clothing racks, shoe racks, tie racks filled.

He knew that his mouth was open, and he felt silly. Then he shook off a billowing giddiness and inched forward to examine the androids more closely, unable to convince himself that they could not see him. He stumbled once and reached out a hand to steady himself. It came down in something soft, and when he looked down, it was a piece of cherry pie, quite fresh, Proctor Owens's favorite. As if it were blood, he wiped it hastily on his coat and extended a finger to trace Murray's stubbled chin, brush Chandler's gently molded cheek. On impulse, he tousled her hair, pinched her breasts and leered.

He was about to tug at Becketton's beard when suddenly he felt drained, felt nothing. He stared a moment longer, then slumped, backing away until he was somehow in the hall, on the stairs, on the wet grass in the wind, walking until the sun rose and created more shadows. There was the sound of a car speeding noisily away. Still walking. And the harsh sound of a faraway siren as he crossed the still-empty parking lot.

"Hey, Randy! Hey, Baptiste!" Kartre's voice did more than his words to convey his worry, but Randy continued to walk. "Hey, Randy!" and Kartre grabbed his arm and turned him around. "Damnit, man, where've you been? Didn't you hear that ambulance? Evan's mother came to pick him up, and when they hit the turn down by the bridge, they smacked into a tree and went into the river. Barb was out riding and said a cop told her they were both dead. Hey, Randy, can't you hear me or something?"

The rush of words dammed for a moment, but Randy only nodded and said, "I have to see the old man."

Kartre's eyes widened. "How'd you know that? I was just coming to get you. Old lady Tander just called the dorm. I covered for you like you said, but you'd better get over there. She sounds like she's ticked."

"I'm going," Randy said.

"Hey, wait a minute! Did you get into the room? What did you see? Was there anything there?"

"Nothing," Randy said flatly, pulling away from Kartre's grasp. "Nothing at all."

"Well, damnit, wait a minute, Randy. What kept you? Where were you all night?"

Randy walked away, and a moment later Kartre stopped talking. Watching his roommate walk. Across the grass, through the glass door that marked the front office, ignoring the glare Miss Tander gave him, into Ainstrom's office without knocking.

"You sent for me?" he said.

Ainstrom looked up from a file folder he was holding and nodded. "Sit," he said.

"You even sound like a robot. Does it take you all morning to warm up or something?"

Ainstrom, unimpressively vested and grey-haired, smiled. "If it'll make you any happier, Randolph, I'm real."

"Our proctor, Owens?"

"Sharp lad, indeed. Yes, he's real. You sound a bit bitter, Randolph."

"I thought I was getting an education, not getting experimented on."

"Poor attitude, Randolph."

"Randy."

Ainstrom nodded at the correction and gestured for Randy to sit. "I'm sorry you had to be so curious, Randy," he said when Randy only stiffened.

"So now what? Are you going to expel me like the others?"

The headmaster finally replaced the folder on his empty desk and leaned back. "Expel, Mr. Baptiste? You underestimate me. Surely you can imagine the reaction of parents if they knew their darling children were being taught by androids. They, unenlightened, would react with . . . horror? Perhaps only disgust, like yourself. It sounds unfortunately melodramatic, but there would undoubtedly be something like a witch hunt, and I'm afraid my, uh, supervisors couldn't allow for that risk until the first class—your class, sir—has graduated and proven itself."

Randy finally stopped screaming where nightmares are born and began to cast for a way out. But his options were narrow and thorned with fear. "You're going to kill me?" And he knew his voice was getting younger all the time.

"No—not quite."

The siren. He blinked. Kartre. "What about Evan? You probably rigged that one."

Ainstrom began to frown. "He was too close to his family, and his family was too large. You, on the other hand, are very much different." Randy backed away as Ainstrom stood, as tall as the rumors had made him. "Remember what Miss Chandler has taught you, young man. Precision of language is the thing: the key to English is communication. Expel is the wrong word."

Unbidden, Randy remembered his dream. "All right, then, what the hell is the right word?"

"Replaced, Mr. Baptiste. Replaced."

There was nothing Randy could say.

A few minutes later, Ainstrom poked his head out of his office and beckoned to Miss Tander. "You'd better get that Baptiste guy on the next plane back. His son is being expelled."

Miss Tander said nothing. There was, in fact, little she was programmed to do except glare and be threatening. And at that she was an expert.

WHITE WOLF CALLING

Snow: suspended white water humping over hidden rocks, slashed by a slick black road that edged around the stumped mountains and swept deserted between a pair of low, peaked houses that served as unassuming sentinels at the mouth of the valley; drifting, not diving to sheathe needled green arms that bent and held in multiples of thousands, spotting indifferently the tarmac walk that tongued from the half-moon porch of the house on the right. A snowman with stunted arms and holes for eyes squatted awkwardly beside a solitary spruce, watching nothing and making uneasy the brown-bundled man who stood by the mailbox. He leaned heavily against a broad-mouthed shovel, staring at the home opposite, turning his red-capped head to look beyond it to the forest that wavered through the sailing crystals up the slope to blend before the summit into the grey-white air.

No wind. Breathing only as he listened to the sunset, strained to hear the summons of the wolf.

"Mars?"

The shovel skittered from his stiff hand, banged against the walk, and angered him with its rifle-volley clatter.

"You think you have the power to move that house with just your eyes?"

Turning, he bent to retrieve the shovel, waving his free hand to indicate he had heard, and did not approve. Not so many decades before, he had begun calling his wife Venus because of her shortening of his own name to laughingly deify him; hers was Samantha, but his Venus she was. On the porch now, with crimson cheeks and her back reed-fragile, she folded her arms against the cold, waiting as he took a frustrated poke at the soiled snow the village plow had left to harass his cleaning. The mount was almost ice, and he glared at his gloves as if to blame them before hurrying to the house.

"Get inside, you dope, before you catch your death."

"I haven't seen the wolf, Venus. I'll probably live forever."

"Quit your smiling, Mars. That isn't funny at all. Get inside."

"You go on ahead. I'm almost done."

"I'm stubborn, Mars Tanner. I like to watch you killing yourself while that shiny new snowblower I gave you for Christmas lies rotting in the garage."

He pinched at her nose, tugged a lock of hair. "I may not be as young as I used to be, kid, but I can still handle anything that comes out of the sky."

She made a face and thumped him on the back as he went through the door, then rushed down the darkened hallway into the sweet-smelling kitchen before the warm stinging yanked at his parchment face and dried his lips.

"Tea?"

"No, thanks."

"Coffee?"

He cocked his head and raised an eyebrow. "Every time you ask, and every time I have to tell you, dummy, that coffee gives me gas. When are the boys coming back?"

"If they're sober, they'll be back in time for supper, as always," she said, taking his cap and stiffly new coat to hang by the wood-fed stove. "Some boys. They're almost forty, you know."

"In age, maybe, but their heads are at least two dozen years behind."

Venus tugged at the strings of her apron, letting the blue and yellow cloth tighten around her waist before she wriggled to settle it into place. Her hair was bunned grey, narrowing her face, sharpening her nose to a pale robin's beak. Only her chin remained youthfully rounded, even when she was mad.

"I don't like the way you make fun of them, Mars. They've come to hard times, in case you've forgotten the accident. It wasn't easy for them, losing both their wives as suddenly as that." She stared at him standing by the refrigerator. "Two daughters-in-law, and no grandchildren. It hasn't been easy for me, either."

"Those so-called women, and I'm sorry to say it, thought the boys had money, Venus. They took one look at our property here, didn't think anything at all about how land is cheap in this part of the state, and they talked themselves into believing we were rich. And neither Carter or Jonathan did anything to discourage them. Those women were too young and too damned impatient, and neither of my sons had brains enough to handle them."

Suddenly annoyed with himself for speaking when he should have been thinking, Mars poked aside the curtains on the back door and glared at the first staggered row of pine at the end of the yard he had cleared himself during their first summer in the valley. Seeing nothing, more angry because he thought he might, he sat at the table and dry-washed his hands. Venus moved behind him, rested her cheek against his still-thick hair, and sighed just loud enough for him to hear. Knowing she would soon begin to caution him about little Tommy across the road, he shifted uneasily and cleared his throat.

"Into town today, I heard Pierson talking at the barbershop."

"It's about time you got a haircut," she said, sitting, one boned hand snaking unconsciously across her face in remembrance of a time when her hair was black and hung in gleaming ripples in front of one eye. "You're beginning to look like a sheep dog. Doesn't look like a very good one, though. Even without my glasses I can see it doesn't look like a very good one."

"That's because I didn't get one. I was to the hardware store looking up a new hammer when Pierson called me in for a chat. He says, and you know how Pierson is when he says anything, he told me fat McKenzie saw the wolf last week, just before his car smacked into the telephone pole."

"He was drinking. The newspaper said so. And that mechanic had done something to the steering. You think they had a trial for nothing?"

"McKenzie was scared. He told me."

"Of what, for heaven's sake? That mechanic? Mac owed that man a fortune for gambling, and practically everyone in town heard them fighting one time or another. My God, Mars, Mac outweighed him by a hundred pounds. If he was scared of anything, it was of having to pay the man and have nothing left for his wine. You know he always drank. I knew him for thirty-five years and can't remember the day he was last sober. Even on his wedding night when he married that Cranford woman."

Mars grinned. "You were there, I suppose?"

"Mars!"

"I wouldn't be surprised. You do get around, you know."

She feigned a roundhouse slap, he mimed a ducking wince, and they laughed, forgetting for the moment what McKenzie had seen.

"I'm going to take Tommy out to the cabin tomorrow to help me with the wood."

Venus wiped at the smiling tears in her eyes and shook her head. "That boy's not good for you, Mars. He's not your son, you know, and I doubt that the Dovnys will approve of your trying to make him."

"Oh, for Pete's sake, Venus, his father's never home, and his mother's flat on her back because of that skiing accident that busted her back. He happens to like my company, and I happen to like his. And with no one else his age around close to play with, we get along just fine."

"Well . . ."

"We can take care of ourselves, dear, don't worry. If I see the wolf, I'll spit in its eye."

Venus tried to smile, rose instead and bustled meaninglessly at the stove where supper was already steaming in three huge black pots.

Neither of them admitted believing there was a snow wolf in the mountains, had never even heard of such a green-eyed creature until the Dovnys' purchase of the land opposite them where they had constructed the house Mars hated because it spoiled his rocking-chair view. He had met the Slavic father only once, at a Board of Education luncheon two years before at the village school. The man's English had been formal, as if memorized from a grammar book, but he charmed and was charming, and Mars had become friends with the blond-banged son when he had straightened a runner on the little boy's sled. The boy was the one who had told him and the village about the white wolf.

"Oh, I get it," Mars had said as he pulled boy and sled up a slope behind the house. "You're talking about one of those werewolf things. I've seen them a lot on television, on those horror show festivals."

The boy frowned bewilderment until Mars had explained, then shook his head and squinted to think harder. "No, the wolf only comes when someone is to die. It's not a person."

"Funny, but I never heard of that until you came around. How does it work? Is it kind of a family tradition? Maybe a Czech folk story, something like that?"

The boy had shrugged.

"Have a chocolate bar?"

The boy nodded and stuck it in his pocket.

Mars had completely forgotten that day until Samson O'Brien claimed he had shot at a wolf bigger than any he'd seen in his life. He was jeered when he failed to produce a pelt, or the tracks when he led a group of men to the site of the hunt. A week to the day later, his wife knifed him in the back when she learned he had been seeing the daughter of the mayor.

"Mars, are you trying to hypnotize yourself, or has my company gone stale after all these years?"

He blinked, tried a boyish grin before shaking his head. "Sorry," he said, leaning back in his chair. "I was thinking."

"Well, stop it. The boys are home. I heard them on the stairs."

"You want me to go up?"

"What for?"

He shrugged. "Talk to them. See what their plans are. God knows there isn't any paying work around here."

"We won't be around that long, Pop," and Mars grimaced when he turned so abruptly he twisted his side.

The sons were twins, dark-haired, taller than their parents and heavier about the chest and waist. Carter was the younger by three minutes, but his face was shadowed with lines and puffs; Jonathan was the same as he had been at thirty, except for the eyes that seemed perpetually half-closed.

"I wasn't trying to ease you out," Mars said, almost pouting, while they noisily took their places at the table.

"I know, Pop," Carter said.

"Of course he knows," Jonathan said, not bothering to disguise a slighting sneer. "He knows everything, don't you, Carter boy? Even took Pop's advice and knew enough to put the girls on that goddamned beat-up excuse for a train."

"That's enough!" Venus said, slapping plates down in front of them. "The past is past, and I won't have that kind of talk in my house. You two have got to get back on your feet again, and soon. Your father's too proud to admit it, and too good to say it, but we can't have you around here indefinitely. It's too much of a strain."

"I know," Carter said, rising to help ladle the soup. "Just need a little readjusting, that's all. Besides, my leave's up in a week and I'll have to be getting back to camp."

"My goodness," Jonathan said, "does even a captain have to run like a buck private? Something else I didn't know. When are you going to make major, by the way? Ever?"

"Go to hell," Carter said.

"Language, brother," Jonathan said, scooping chunks of butter onto steaming slices of homemade bread.

"That's enough from the both of you," Mars said. "Your mother's right as always. My pension can't handle everything. We love you both, but soon you've got to make a move. I'm talking especially to you, Jon. Your brother at least has a check coming in."

"Pop," Carter said before his twin could snap again, "why don't you sell the house? Maybe move to one of those retirement places. I know you love it here and all, but for crying out loud, the physical upkeep alone is going to do you in one of these days."

"I'll buy the place," Jonathan said, suddenly solicitous.

"Neither of you will," Venus said, taking her seat. "We've been here since you were born, and I'm not about to leave it now. Say grace, Mars, before I lose my appetite."

And dinner passed into evening as the snow greyed, crusted, and was littered with snapping fallen branches weakened by ice. Fireplace flames shadowed the living room in spite of the lamps, and Mars stood at a window, listening to his shattered family playing at cards, listening later, as he wandered the house looking for sleep, to whispers: the house itself, talking down to dawn through the mouth of the furnace, the pops of cooling wood in the fireplace, the creaks of boards searching for a comfortable place to shy away from the rising wind; the wind, riding the back of the snow, drifting powder over the road, pushing against thin glass, humming to itself in wires strung through the air, once to a crescendo covering hushed words; the words, snapping, biting, accusing, and prodding the weaknesses of the old man in vain attempts at deadly prophecy, husking laughter when one suggested the other do Mars the fatal blow.

Standing in the hallway, Mars shivered at the door of his sons' room, pleading for a prayer, sucking back the trembling that directed him to break down the barrier and cast them out.

He thought of Tommy, the surrogate son, and cursed his lack of wisdom that had made him a failure.

In his own bed again, wondering, he listened to the wind, heard faintly the cry of the dead calling for death.

And in the morning, after he had seen the brothers off to the village to notch another day at the tavern bar, after picking up after himself in bedroom and bath, he stood in the backyard and waited as Tommy ran awkwardly through the snow to him, dragging a sled still shining with varnish. Mars smiled, adjusted the peaked cap that covered the long blond hair, pinched the rounded cheek with his glove, and led the boy into the woods, up the slope to a narrow plateau where freshly cut stumps pockmarked the ground.

A makeshift shed euphemistically called a cabin stood bleakly at the far end of the clearing. It was missing a front wall, served as a storage area for the logs Mars cut twice each winter. Tommy scrambled from stump to stump, climbing, daring Mars to spill him into the snow. The old man smiled, encouraged the boy to play on his own while he pulled a tarpaulin from a handmade toboggan and began loading the split wood, strapping each layer from front to back, finished with the canvas strapped side to side.

It was noon, and he was sweating, gasping, but not yet ready to give in to the aching that stretched his muscles and pounded through his lungs. He pointed out to the boy the peak where three hunters had lain wounded when a local man had gone berserk one evening in the tavern, escaped from the sheriff, and had done some hunting of his own. They had endured the freezing night unprotected except for their clothes, only one surviving to testify at the trial, dying shortly after in the county hospital.

"They saw the wolf," Tommy said solemnly, and Mars laughed, cuffed him on the back of the head.

"You never did tell me how that works," he said, deliberately light.

Tommy rubbed a black mitten across his nose and sniffed. "I told you. The wolf comes when somebody's to die."

"But no one's been killed, much less even scratched, round here in a hundred years. By a wolf, that is."

Tommy looked up into the old man's face. "The wolf doesn't do it, silly. Father says the wolf . . . I don't know. It just comes. I don't know what it eats, but it causes, not does."

"You know, maybe I should get to know your father better," Mars said, taking hold of the unraveling grey rope that was tied to the ends of the sled's steering bar. He waved the boy on, and they moved up past the cabin. "I haven't seen him in nearly two years to talk to properly. I hope he doesn't think I'm unfriendly. I just never got around to it somehow."

"He works in the city," the boy said proudly. "He comes home on weekends and sleeps most of the time. He's very tired."

Mars nodded.

"Mommy's sick all the time."

"I know, son. I heard about it in the village."

"She can't sit up like us. Her back hurts all the time."

Tommy jumped off the sled, and Mars sighed gratitude as they trudged in tandem toward the run they had made the week before.

"You know something, Mr. Tanner, I think my father's trying to scare me with the wolf story. He said it comes all the way from our home in . . . in . . ." He stumbled silently, mouthing the name and trying to give it voice. Mars had learned early not to help him. Czechoslovakia was the boy's private problem. One of these days,

SMITH

Mars thought, he'll pronounce it right and we'll have a damn big party.

The snow crackled beneath them as they turned around, hissed like scraping glass when Mars lay on the sled, Tommy climbed onto his back, and they raced down to the clearing.

Grinning and shouting, Mars sideswiped a log and spilled them both into a wave of snow that seeped down their necks like traces of ice. Lying with his face up, Mars squinted at the impossibly bright clouds, widened his eyes as a shadow darkened them, and saw the laughing boy hugging his face.

"Mars, I think I need you."

"My God," Mars said and clasped the boy to him, closing his eyes to keep them from emptying, opening them to see the wolf.

It was white to its tail, with glittering beads of snow and ice clinging softly to its unmatted fur, swinging as it moved silently around the edge of the clearing. Breath in turbulent rivers of misted grey snorted from its nostrils while it turned around and faced them, its ears upright, its head slightly cocked. It stalked, slowly, and Mars rocked, still chuckling in his throat, keeping the boy's face pressed to his chest. The white wolf circled, and Mars twisted on his buttocks to keep the animal from getting behind him. Snow flecked from the sky, veiling but not hiding the green eyes that were deep close to black in the creature's magnificent head.

A ghost or a god? Mars thought as he pulled his legs from underneath him and struggled to stand without releasing Tommy.

"Hey," the boy said. "You're hurting me."

"Maybe," Mars whispered, "but you're tough. You can take it."

"Sure," Tommy said and squeezed harder, laughing.

The wolf backed away when Mars steadied himself, watched as man and boy sidled toward the toboggan. It bobbed its head once, whipped its tail, and trotted off without looking back.

Tommy began coughing.

"You got a cold?"

"Same one I had last week."

"Come on," Mars said, swallowing to keep his voice level, "I'll get some warm soup into your craw."

"What does that mean?"

"It's a foreign word, son. Foreign to you, that is."

"I know a lot of foreign words, too."

"Good. Maybe someday you can teach them to me."

"When, Mars?"

"I don't know. Someday. Soon, I guess."

With the runners freshly waxed and the slope working with him, Mars had little trouble hauling the load of lumber down to the house. Tommy pushed from behind, calling out every few feet to be sure Mars knew he was helping. And when they parted, Venus handing him a pot of stew to bring to his mother, Tommy waved, stepped into the road, and was nearly struck by the car that raced out of the village and into the driveway.

"Goddamnit, you idiot," Mars shouted at Carter. "Why the hell can't you watch where you're going?"

Carter heaved his bulk out of the car and stumbled past silently, muttering nothings and leaving a waft of mixed beer and liquor.

Mars grabbed him by the shoulder and yanked him around. "Where's Jonathan?"

Carter shrugged, shook the hand off, and staggered into the house, brushing past Venus without taking off his coat.

Cursing, then, his own thoughtlessness, Mars spun around, but Tommy was already on the first step of his own porch. He turned and waved, and Mars wanted to call out. He lifted a hand instead and sagged into the kitchen. Despite Venus's proddings, he remained silent throughout the evening meal, wondering what would have happened if Tommy had seen the green-eyed specter. It was a miracle he hadn't, and Mars was moved once to laugh at his suspicions of the divine. That he was frightened he wouldn't admit, not even to himself.

Jonathan was returned by two of Mars's friends just before midnight, and the three of them carried the unconscious son into the bedroom, making little attempt to keep their voices low since Carter was already asleep and would not awaken until his stomach decided it was time to empty.

The fireplace, then, and the aroma of burning pine while Venus went to work on some knitting of hers: a scarf she had started the winter before but hadn't the patience to finish when its perfection eluded her clumsy fingers.

"What is it, Mars?"

He looked away from the fire.

Thinking: *McKenzie.*

"I saw the white wolf today."

"You didn't." She set the yarn at her side and leaned forward with her arms resting trembling on her thighs.

A bubble of sap boiled.

"Bigger than life and twice as heavy. Damndest thing I ever saw in my life."

"Why didn't you say anything?"

"We didn't believe there was such a thing, remember?"

"You saw it," she said. "It must be so. You never did have much imagination, Mars."

Thinking: *three men bleeding.*

"I think it was trying to get the boy to look at it."

Venus hummed nervously, then left her armchair for the sofa and curled her legs beneath her as she rested against Mars's unmoving arm. "Now you are imagining."

"You just said I never did, but maybe you're right, I don't know. I was thinking, though, that this thing, whatever it is, was never around before the Dovny people came."

"You saying maybe they brought it with them? A pet of some kind?"

Mars didn't know. From the time he had returned to the house from the clearing, he had been seeing movement in the corners of his eyes that escaped when he turned his head, white movement speckled green.

"O'Brien," he said without realizing he had spoken aloud.

"Hush that talk," she said, gliding a hand against his mouth until he kissed it and carefully placed it between his own. "All those men were just bums, flops, failures, and I don't mourn their passing. And that wolf is just a wolf and had nothing to do with them."

Sleet began exploding like glass against the house.

"One of these days it'll move out to the city."

"Into the city?" She laughed, gasping, incredulous. "Come on, Mars Tanner, can you really see that beast walking the streets of a big town? With no one doing anything but staring or running scared? In a city, Mars?"

He thought: as he had left the clearing with Tommy, one

backward glance had been sufficient to note that the snow where the wolf had been pacing was clean. There were no depressions to indicate an animal of that size had walked a warning.

"Mars, you're frightened, aren't you?"

He watched the sparks like fire-rain rise up into the chimney. "Venus," he said, "we've done bad by our children. One we drove into the army, the other we just drove. I don't think we ever really knew how to be parents."

"We did the best we could."

It was a tired argument, one that usually left them not speaking for hours.

"I should have cared more, I guess, been more ambitious, but the store was good enough for me."

"They went to school, Mars. They learned things."

"Yeah," he said, scratching his stubbled jaw, "and blamed me for not doing the same."

A commotion on the steps forestalled her answer, caused her to straighten as if her sons would have been affronted by their parents' intimacy.

They came down into the foyer carrying suitcases and already wearing their overcoats. As Mars strode angrily toward them, Carter lifted a hand. "Don't say it, Pop, but we have to go. It's no good here, and you were right yesterday."

"The dear captain's going to get me something at the PX," Jonathan said.

"But why now?"

"Listen, Pop, there's no sense in our making it any harder on any of us. Some folks got the touch to do things right, and some don't. We don't."

"What's the matter with your eyes?"

"I been drinking a lot, in case you hadn't noticed. Just let us go quietly, and maybe one of us will write when things get settled. When we get the time."

Venus remained on the sofa, tilting her cheek to her sons' kisses, brief and without even momentary affection. And they were out the door before Mars could think of an appropriate farewell to forty years.

"Samantha," he said, his back to the room, "don't ever let anyone tell you that I didn't love you."

Suddenly there were shouts, and Carter came running back inside.

"Your rifle, Pop, where is it? Never mind," and he snatched at the weapon cradled in the wall rack in the hall. Mars hurried to the door, but Carter brushed past him, answering with a wordless shout the urgings of his brother.

"God," he said, stopping long enough to pull a box of cartridges from a breakfront and stuff the magazine. "You should see that animal, Pop. Biggest damn thing in the world."

"Oh, my Christ!" Mars said and ran into the kitchen, grabbed his coat, and slapped on his hat. Venus he pushed back into a chair as she tried to follow, and with a muttered "Samantha" rushed outside, nearly colliding with his sons who were standing on the edge of the porch. Jonathan had the rifle to his shoulder, sighting, waiting until Mars saw the white wolf trot unconcernedly from behind the spruce in the center of the yard. His son fired; the bright star flared from the barrel, and a puff shattered from the snowman's head. The three men descended to the walk when it was obvious Jonathan had missed.

"Never could shoot worth a damn," Carter said, grabbing for the stock, being pushed roughly aside.

"That will make a hell of a coat," Jonathan said, stalking now as the wolf padded from the yard to the slippery road. Immediately, lights in the Dovny house blinked on sporadically until the grounds were lighted with squares of pale sun. The front door opened and Tommy stepped out.

Mars watched the progress of the wolf, unable to speak, dizzy from the cold that lanced at his face in droplets of sleet. Tommy called out, waving, and began to climb down from his porch. Jonathan swung the rifle and fired again.

"The boy!" Mars shouted. "Goddamnit, Jon, watch the boy!"

"Shut up, Pop," one of them said.

Tommy had reached the bottom of the steps, was angling across the front of the house, when the wolf broke into a run toward the corner nearest him. Tommy sprinted after it, and Mars, unthinking, ran across the road toward him.

Someone shouted and the wolf halted, grey now beyond the light.

Tommy clapped his hands and shouted encouragement as Jonathan moved to the center of the road and took aim.

The wolf moved, placing the boy between it and the rifle.

Mars, arms spread and mouth open, flung himself into the air.

Jonathan fired.

And in the silence echoing from flake to flake as sleet turned to snow, Mars sprawled on the ground, twisting his head from side to side as if searching for a door into a room without pain. He gasped as Tommy roughly rolled him onto his back, heard the careless shriek of tires as a car skidded, straightened, and bulleted toward the village. They'll never make the turn at the railroad, he thought.

Distantly, he heard Venus screaming.

Into the snow he opened his eyes and saw Tommy kneeling beside him.

"You never ate the chocolate I gave you," he said through the sparks that wouldn't leave him be. "Probably threw away the stew, too." He arched his back and gasped. "Don't suppose I could get a second chance, could I? I could do better."

Tommy shook his head. His left arm nestled in the ruff around the neck of a white wolf. His right hand stroked the head of another. He bent his face closer to peer into Mars's face, and Mars saw the glimmering green in his eyes, feeding on his failure before he died.

"Daddy's home," the boy whispered. "You said you wanted to meet him."